'Thomas Enger is one of the finest writers in the Nordic Noir genre, and this is his very best book yet. Outstanding' Ragnar Jónasson

'A gripping narrative that begs comparison to Stieg Larsson' Bookpage

'Suspenseful, dark and gritty, this is a must-read' Booklist

'From the gritty tension of the plot, to its emotional depths, this is a powerfully compulsive page-turner' LoveReading

'Visceral and heartfelt – a gripping deep-dive into the secrets that hold families together and tear them apart' Crime by the Book

'The plot is satisfyingly challenging, and the tension is maintained throughout, with characters like Trine revealing their story in instalments, and the swift movement between characters in page-turningly short chapters ... there's also a clever, sleight-of-hand ending' Promoting Crime

'Thomas Enger is such a skilled writer that you can only marvel at the intricate plot' Books, Life and Everything

'It is cleverly and intricately written, and I am in awe of Enger's ability to make such complex relationships and background stories come together so seamlessly!' Portable Magic

'The author does a fantastic job of creating a dark, twisted story, one soaked in criminality and which left me breathless ... If you like a good crime series with a slice of dark menace – I would definitely recommend this!' Chillers, Killers and Thrillers

'Enger has weaved a magical plot to once again leave me breathless, the storylines coming together in such a sleek and intelligent way it's impossible to find a single fault' Emma the Little Bookworm

'Fast-paced and so very tense, I was gripped! Dark. Chilling. Emotive' Ronnie Turner

'A poignantly beautiful book ... There can't be many crime novels that I finish with the tears rolling down my face, but then there aren't many that are so sensitively and evocatively written. I cannot recommend it highly enough' Hair Past a Freckle

'A gritty crime thriller, for those readers who really like to get their teeth into a book, best read over a shorter period to keep on top of the plot, but highly recommended by me ... Now to get my hands on Thomas Enger's other books!' I Loved Reading This

'It had a fast-paced, compelling story line that kept me wanting to read on' What Cathy Read Next

'Enger combines emotional turmoil, grief and guilt with solid crime scenarios, then infuses his story with a healthy shot of Scandinavian *je ne sais quoi*' Cheryl M-M's Book Blog

'Brilliant Scandi Noir from an accomplished and exciting writer. What more could you ask for? Highly recommended' Reflections of a Reader

'Amazing. Gripping. Thrilling. Cleverly written. Blew me away. That prologue will have you hooked. The whole story had me hooked. Fast-paced, easy to read. You literally won't want to put this book down' Gemma's Book Reviews

'In Enger's searing fifth and final novel featuring Oslo investigative reporter Henning Juul, Henning ... obsessively pursues the criminals responsible for his son's death. Meanwhile, malignant figures relentlessly stalk him ... Enger seamlessly integrates ... individual stories into a larger tale of dirty business and politics. As Henning approaches the end of his painful journey, he longs for the certainty that he has touched someone's life. His excruciating ordeal will touch the heart of every reader' *Publishers Weekly*

Inborn

ABOUT THE AUTHOR

Thomas Enger is a former journalist. He made his debut with the crime novel *Burned* in 2010, which became an international sensation before publication and marked the first in the bestselling Henning Juul series. Rights to the series have been sold to 31 countries to date. In 2013 Enger published his first book for young adults, a dark fantasy thriller called *The Evil Legacy*, for which he won the U-prize (best book, Young Adult). *Killer Instinct*, upon which *Inborn* is based and which is another Young Adult suspense novel, was published in Norway in 2017 and won the same prestigious prize. Most recently, Thomas has cowritten a thriller with Jørn Lier Horst. Enger also composes music, and he lives in Oslo.

Follow him on Twitter *@EngerThomas* on Facebook: *www.facebook. com/thomas.enger.77* or visit: *www.thomasenger.com*

ABOUT THE TRANSLATOR

Kari Dickson grew up in Edinburgh, Scotland, but spent most of her summers in Norway with grandparents who couldn't speak English, so spoke Norwegian from an early age. She went on to read Scandinavian Studies at UCL. While working in theatre in London, she was asked to do literal translations of two Ibsen plays, which fuelled her interest in Norwegian literature and led to an MA in Translation at the University of Surrey. Having worked initially as a commercial translator, including some years at the central bank of Norway, she now concentrates solely on literature. Her portfolio includes literary fiction, crime, non-fiction and plays. Her translation of Roslund & Hellström's *Three Seconds* won the CWA International Dagger in 2011. Kari currently teaches Norwegian language, literature and translation in the Scandinavian Studies department at the University of Edinburgh.

Inborn

Thomas Enger

**ORENDA
BOOKS**

Orenda Books
16 Carson Road
West Dulwich
London SE21 8HU
www.orendabooks.co.uk

First published in Norwegian as *Killerinstinkt*, 2017
Copyright © Thomas Enger, 2019
English translation copyright © Kari Dickson, 2019

A catalogue record for this book is available from the British Library.

ISBN 978-1-912374-47-2
eISBN 978-1-912374-48-9

This book has been translated with financial support from NORLA

Typeset in Garamond by MacGuru Ltd
Printed and bound by CPI Group (UK) Ltd, Croydon CR0 4YY

For sales and distribution, please contact *info@orendabooks.co.uk*

Publisher's note:

Inborn is based on Thomas Enger's YA thriller, *Killerinstinkt,* translated from the Norwegian by Kari Dickson. The new book contains a complete update and rewrite by the author in English.

PROLOGUE
THE NIGHT OF

Before he made the mistake of opening the door, Johannes Eklund was thinking about the show. He thought about the cheers and the admiring looks the girls had given him, the beers he was going to drink once he caught up with everyone at the opening-night party. The sex, God willing, he was going to get.

In those minutes that passed before he stepped through the doorway and stared in disbelief at what he saw in front of him, Johannes' mind had been filled with dreams. High on the praise that the night's performance had received, his eyes had been firmly fixed on the future, on private jets and sold-out concerts, on a way of life he had yearned for every single day since his father introduced him to Stone Temple Pilots and the glamour of rock 'n' roll some four years ago.

Right before his throat made that anxious little noise, Johannes wasn't giving the slightest thought to the fact that he had school tomorrow, nor that he was due to hand in an essay on social economics later this week. School was no longer going to be important to him. Tonight's show had only made that even more evident.

But then his presence was noticed, and he stood there watching for a few seconds, trying to comprehend what was going on in front of him. Then the stench of urine, sweat and metal rose to his nostrils and made him forget all about the distant future and the very recent past. He couldn't even process what he was seeing. All he could think was that he wasn't supposed to be there. That he had to get out.

Now.

His shoes, still wet from the rain, slipped on the floor as Johannes started to run, but he managed to stay on his feet and pick up some speed. The sound of boots, hard against the floor behind him, made him force his legs to move even faster. Heart racing and lungs screaming, he reached the end of the corridor. As he was about to open the door that led to the staircase, he turned and caught a glimpse of the person speeding towards him, eyes so dark it made Johannes tremble and whimper.

He grabbed at the door and ran through. He was about to descend the staircase, when he felt a powerful hand on his shoulder. He turned and raised his hands as if to protect himself, whispering a plea that died on his lips as intense pain jolted through his jaw, paralysing the rest of the muscles in his face. His feet lost touch with the ground, and as the back of his skull made contact with the top of the staircase, it felt and sounded as if something in his head had smashed into a thousand pieces.

He didn't pass out, but part of him wished that he had. He tried to get up, but something connected with his upper body and pushed him forcefully further down the stairs. Unable to break his fall, he landed on his back and shoulder. Then he toppled down the stairs and came to rest at the bottom.

He couldn't move.

Couldn't think, at least not at first. He wanted to scream for help, and he managed to cover his face with his arm, but it was pulled sharply aside. He squinted up at the person above him. Only then did Johannes fully understand how much trouble he was in.

His thoughts turned towards his family and his friends, to the songs he had yet not written, songs that would never be loved, and the tears began to roll down his cheeks. As he felt blow after blow raining down on his face, feeling the numbness travel from his head to the rest of his body, Johannes' mind drifted away from what was happening to him. He thought about all the fun he had planned. The dreams that would never come true. And as the white lights above him started to fade, he thought of the taste of a girl's lips. The feel of her body. And when Johannes Eklund could no longer feel a single thing, he could not help but wonder what on earth he'd walked in on, and why the hell he had to die.

1

NOW

'Nervous?'

The court officer at Romerike District Court looks at me with a tentative smile. She's been sitting next to me for fifteen minutes, but this is the first time I have noticed that her teeth are yellow. I stop picking at my sweaty fingers, and nod.

'First trial?' she asks.

Her breath smells of stale coffee and old cigarettes. I nod again.

'Hell of a case,' she says with a sigh. It seems like she's talking to herself now.

I think about the hours ahead of me. Everything I need to relive and remember. Everything I will be asked, everything I need to talk about, in front of everybody. I remind myself to stick to my story. There are details the court and the judges – and the whole of Norway – don't need to hear.

The door in front of me opens. A man in uniform gestures for me to get up and follow him. I take a deep breath and stand up. I look at the male officer and wonder for a brief second what he thinks of the case, what he thinks of *me*. For months the newspapers and the TV stations have been reporting on what happened in Fredheim last October. But I can't tell one way or the other what he thinks. His look is just dead serious.

I straighten my trouser legs, button my jacket and pull down my slightly too-short shirt sleeves. I wonder whether anyone is going to believe me. They have to, I tell myself. They simply have to.

The uniformed man leads me through a wide door into a big room. Just like on TV, a sea of faces turns towards me. There's a sudden silence, then it gives way to whispering. I try to focus on the stand ahead of me, grateful that I still have about twenty feet to walk before I get there. The sound of my own footsteps gives me something to concentrate on.

My mother is here. I can see from her face that she's having a hard time. I wonder how much she's had to drink and if she's brought a flask with her.

When I reach the witness box, I turn and look at the crowd of people in front of me. I don't really see anyone in particular, just heads. Every seat in the room seems to be taken. People are even standing at the back. As I begin to focus, I see reporters, laptop screens. Familiar faces from Fredheim. Some of my friends, schoolmates – if I can even call them that anymore. Police Chief Inspector Yngve Mork is here, as is Mari's mother. I can't see her dad, though, nor any of Johannes' parents.

The lawyer for the prosecution is a slim, small lady. She looks slightly masculine in her tight dark-blue suit. I don't really know anything about her, except that her name is Håkonsen. She takes a sip of water from the glass in front of her and looks at me with inquisitive eyes. As if she's wondering whether she will be able to break me, or something.

She wishes me a good morning, before politely asking me to state my name and address – for the record.

'My name is Even Tollefsen,' I whisper.

'Please speak up', the judge says.

I move closer to the microphone and cough slightly before repeating myself. I try to give the two other judges an apologetic smile. I don't get one in return. I tell them our address – Granholtveien 4 – and that we live in Fredheim.

'It's about an hour's drive from Oslo.'

I don't know why I said that. They know where Fredheim is. After what happened in October, everybody does.

'How old are you, Even?' the prosecutor continues.

'I'm seventeen.'

I can't keep my voice steady, so I try to take a deep breath. My chest hurts.

Now the prosecutor wants me to talk about my family. I catch a glimpse of my mother again. She's slumped down in her seat. It looks as if she's trying to hide.

'My father died in a car crash when I was seven.' I say, my mouth feeling dry. 'So I was basically brought up by my uncle Imo.'

'Imo?'

'Sorry. Ivar Morten,' I say. 'Everyone in Fredheim calls him Imo.'

There is a slight chuckle in the room. It relaxes me a little.

'But you lived with your mother?'

'Yes.'

'And your brother Tobias.'

'Correct.'

'OK. Would you say that you had a happy childhood?'

I look at my mother again, before staring at the table in front of me for a few seconds. 'Like I told you, my father died when I was very young. So no, I wouldn't necessarily say that I was a happy kid. Depends on how you look at it, I guess.'

'Are there other ways to look at it?' the prosecutor wants to know. I move about in my chair.

'Obviously, I missed my father,' I say. 'And we moved a couple of times, back and forth, and my mother ... she wasn't doing very well, to be honest, but I managed to make a lot of friends. So I guess in some ways I was a happy kid. It helped that I played football.'

'Alright, Even,' Ms Håkonsen says. 'Do you mind if I call you Even?'

'Not at all.'

'OK. Thank you. Let's move on a little bit.'

She gets up and starts to walk up and down in front of me, as if she's thinking deeply about something. Suddenly she stops and says, 'Mari Lindgren.'

Ms Håkonsen stares at me for a few seconds. 'Could you please tell the court what kind of relationship you had with her?'

Just hearing her name makes my whole body ache. I take a deep breath again. 'Mari Lindgren was my girlfriend,' I say, my voice tiny and sad.

'For how long?'

'About five months.'

The courtroom is so silent even the slightest of movements can be heard.

'But she wasn't your girlfriend on Monday the 17th of October last year, was she?'

I don't answer straight away. I just wait a few seconds then shake my head.

Ms Håkonsen looks at me sternly. 'For the sake of court proceedings,' she says, 'you have to answer the question aloud.'

'Um, no,' I reply. 'She wasn't.'

'Why wasn't she?' Ms Håkonsen asks. 'What happened?'

'She ... broke up with me.'

'And *why* did she do that?' Ms Håkonsen sounds as if she is already getting tired of my answers.

'I don't know.'

'You don't know?'

'Well, I didn't. At the time.'

'You mean you didn't know on the night of 17th October?'

I lift my head slightly, searching for Mari's mother. My eyes lock on hers. She instantly looks away.

'Correct,' I reply.

'But you know now.'

'I do.'

Ms Håkonsen looks at me for a few moments.

'I understand why you don't want to talk about that, but I'm afraid we will have to go into the specifics or your break-up a little bit later. Just so you know.'

'OK,' I say and cough into my palm.

'Good. When did she break up with you?'

I can feel the sweat starting to form between my shoulder blades. I hope it won't show on my face as well.

'A couple of days before...' I stop for a few beats.

'A couple of days before the 17th of October?'

I nod, angry at myself for not being calmer and cooler about this. Ms Håkonsen is about to reprimand me again, but I quickly answer:

'Yes.'

'OK. Alright. Let's talk about the morning after. The morning of October the 18th. Tell us what happened.'

2
THEN

Yngve Mork had never spoken to God. He hadn't even thought that he could, or should; but the previous night, at a quarter past two, he had sat up in his bed, lifted his gaze towards the ceiling and addressed Him directly for the first time in all his sixty-three years.

He had asked if she was OK now, if she had found peace. He asked if she was still angry with him and if He might allow him to see her one more time – for real. But his words had been quietly absorbed by the faded yellow plaster of the ceiling. They hadn't even been spat back at him like a mocking echo.

Some mornings he woke up with the lingering remnants of a dream in his mind, and with the sudden, panicked thought that she might have come to see him during the night; that she had given him some sign he had missed or already forgotten – a wave or a kiss. He was always hoping that she really was trying to reach out to him, trying to tell him something – trying to say that she had found it in her heart to forgive him.

Today, though, Yngve's mobile phone alarm startled him just before seven. It had been yet another one of those almost-sleepless nights. He had turned over again towards the empty side of the bed, only to see that there weren't any fresh dents in the linen, no marks on the pillow from the pen she had used while trying to solve a newspaper crossword. He had sniffed, searching for a hint of her perfume, the smell that had been beside him for forty-one years; but all he could register was his own odour, a smell that seemed even older and more useless now that he no longer had anyone to share it with.

All the other women in Åse's family had grown old. It was the men who found death at an early age – and under the strangest circumstances. A clumsy bicycle accident or a tumble down a ladder when trying to clear leaves from a gutter. A piece of meat that got stuck in a throat during a celebratory dinner. The women could be sick for years, but somehow they seemed to recover.

So why couldn't Åse do the same?

Another question Yngve had asked The Ceiling.

He got up and went downstairs, and sat at his breakfast table with a buttered slice of bread and a generous helping of Danish liverpaste in front of him. He had coffee and a glass of orange juice as well, but there were no sounds to keep him company other than the ones he made himself: the flipping of a newspaper page, a knife quietly placed on the side of the plate. A quick sniff to get rid of an itch just underneath the tip of his nose. He didn't want the radio on in case he interrupted her hummings in the bathroom, her steps that might appear in the hallway, the drawers she would open and close whenever she got dressed. Even if she would never do that ever again.

Yngve's coffee needed some sugar, so he got up and opened the cupboard above the stove. There he stopped and stared at a yellow box of tea he had bought for her two and a half weeks before she died. It was still wrapped in plastic.

Could you put the kettle on, please, Yngve?

Her distant voice made him sob. But before he was sucked into yet another typhoon of grief, the phone rang. He looked at the number and saw that it was being redirected from the 113 service. He would have to take it – he was on call. But first he grabbed the kitchen sink with both hands and steadied himself for a moment. Then he answered, giving his full name and rank.

At first he didn't hear anything but breathing. Then came a rush of words. He had to ask the person on the other end to repeat them – twice. 'He's dead,' the voice finally managed to say. 'He's just lying there. He's ... there's blood everywhere.'

The voice, Yngve now realised, belonged to Tic-Tac, the janitor at Fredheim High School.

'OK,' Yngve said. 'Don't touch anything, just go to the main entrance and stay there. Don't let anyone in. I'm on my way.'

Yngve hung up and took a deep breath. Glanced over at the breakfast table. The one plate. The one glass.

He was on his way, he'd said.

On his way where?

That you have to figure out for yourself, Åse had said to him one night when they were talking about the future she would no longer be a part of. *But I want you to move on, Yngve. I don't want you to forget me, but I want you to continue with your life. Can you do that for me?*

He closed the cupboard without looking at the tea bags again and put on his leather uniform coat. He was about to step out into the rain, when she came in through the doorway, almost startling him.

'Oh, hey,' he muttered. He hadn't even heard her coming. Even now, when she looked sleepy, her skin pale and dry, he was struck by her incredible beauty. He always was, especially when she had no make-up on. Not a single raindrop seemed to have landed on her completely hairless head.

'I'm sorry,' he said. 'I have to go; I don't have time to clear the break-fast table.'

She said, with her eyes, that it was OK.

'I'm sorry,' he repeated, for a lot more than the fact that he had to leave. He looked out of the open door and said: 'God, it's really raining.'

He heard her ask where he was off to, what was going on.

'I don't know yet,' Yngve said. 'But it doesn't sound good.'

🗇

Yngve parked as close to the school entrance as possible. Two girls and a boy were standing outside the door as he approached, eager to get in. They stared at him, intrigued.

The janitor opened the door for him.

'I did as you told me to,' Tic-Tac said, his voice shaking, a spasm seeming to twist his face. 'I've been standing here the whole time.'

'Can we come in, too?' one of the girls behind Yngve asked. 'It's so cold.'

'No,' he said with a firm voice.

'What's going on?' the boy asked. 'What's happened?'

'We don't know yet,' Yngve answered and closed the door. He turned to Tic-Tac. 'Where is he?'

Tic-Tac pointed to the stairs. They moved along the hall, their wet shoes making squeaking noises on the floor. 'I didn't touch anything,' Tic-Tac stuttered.

From halfway along the passage Yngve could see a leg and a shoe. As they approached the stairs, more and more of the body became visible. Thin legs, blue jeans. Dark-red stripes that seemed to form a neat pattern on the young boy's skinny fingers. There was blood on his coat, too, and on his other hand, arm. On the stairs, the wall.

Tic-Tac was right, Yngve thought to himself. There really was blood everywhere.

Fredheim was a small place, but Yngve had seen a lot during his tenure as a police officer here. Body parts in ripped-apart cars, corpses that had been rotting away in the forest throughout the winter. He had seen what people looked like after they'd been hanging by a rope from the ceiling for a couple of weeks, images that sometimes haunted him on nights when sleep was hard to find.

But this...

The young boy's face looked like mince. Skin, blood, muscle. Teeth coloured red.

'It's Johannes Eklund,' Tic-Tac said.

'How can you tell?' Yngve asked without taking his eyes off the kid.

'His coat,' the janitor said. 'The logo on his chest.'

Yngve spotted it now, sewn onto a pocket: an old plane in the middle of a turn, an 'S' and a 'C' on each wing.

'He was the singer of *Sopwith Camel*,' Tic-Tac added. 'He had a stunning voice. You should have seen him last night. A genuine star.'

'There was a show here yesterday?'

'Yeah. In the auditorium. Opening night of the annual school theatre show.'

'When?'

'Between eight and ten, roughly.'

'And you were here? You watched the show?'

Yngve turned to look at the janitor, who was scratching his left palm.

'I watched a little bit of it, yes.'

'What time did you leave?'

He seemed to be thinking for a moment. 'I don't know, long before the show was over. I knew I had an early start today.'

'So you didn't lock the doors before you left?'

Tic-Tac shook his head violently. 'There was no need. The doors lock automatically at eleven. Everyone should have made their way out by then.'

'Evidently, not everyone did, though.'

The janitor didn't reply.

'What happens if someone does stay behind after eleven? Can they still get out?'

Tic-Tac hesitated for a moment, now scratching his left temple. 'They can, of course, but it triggers the alarm, and if the alarm goes off, the security company will be here in minutes. We have two surveillance cameras on the outside wall as well, pointing towards the entrance, so it's easy to find whoever's responsible. And they get the bill.'

'The alarm didn't go off last night, did it?'

'No.'

'So if people want to avoid triggering the alarm ... can they?'

Again, the janitor appeared to be thinking. 'I guess people will find a way out of here, if they need to. But it's never really been an issue. People know the rules. Plus, there's a reminder ten minutes before eleven, a ding-dong sound that's played for about thirty seconds over the school's PA system. That always makes people hurry out.'

Yngve considered this for a moment while turning back to look at Johannes Eklund. Not even the persistent banging on the entrance door could persuade him to wrench his gaze away from what used to be the face of a good-looking young man. Yngve had seen pictures of Johannes in the *Fredheim Chronicle*.

'Can you see who it is?' he asked Tic-Tac. He coughed to clear his voice. 'Let them in if they're police or from the ambulance service. No one else can enter.'

Tic-Tac moved quickly, his keys rattling on the chain that hung from his jeans. Yngve took a few more steps towards the staircase, being careful where he placed his feet. He squatted down beside the body and examined it more closely. Now he could clearly see lacerations on the left side of the boy's forehead. He quickly scanned the stairs and hall for a potential murder weapon. Nothing.

The sounds of footsteps at the entrance made Yngve stand up. It was his colleagues from Fredheim police station Vibeke Hanstveit and Therese Kyrkjebø. He had called them, on his way to the school. Normally Hanstveit, officially in charge of every investigation they conducted, would stay away from the crime scene, but the second he'd told her that a young boy might have been killed, she'd headed for her car. Kyrkjebø did the same.

Yngve met them with his arms raised, telling them to brace themselves. Then turned and led them over to the stairs.

Hanstveit put a hand in front of her mouth. Kyrkjebø made a gasping sound. None of them spoke for a few seconds.

Finally, Hanstveit cleared her throat and said: 'Have you called the forensic team yet?'

'No, I was just about to,' Yngve replied.

'Let me take care of that,' Hanstveit said. 'You have other things to tend to right now.'

Without waiting for his reply Hanstveit pulled her phone from her coat pocket and walked a few steps away. Kyrkjebø edged past Yngve to the foot of the staircase. Drips fell from her clothes onto the floor in front of her, so she moved back slightly. Then she just stood there. And looked. Only her eyelids moved. Her face seemed to lose more colour by the second.

She swallowed, then swallowed again. 'He must have been here all night', she said in a quiet voice. She wiped her wet face. Touched her neck. Then squeezed the tip of her nose between her thumb and index finger.

Yngve placed a hand on her shoulder. He could feel the muscles tighten under her uniform jacket.

'I'm sorry,' she said. 'It's just that...'

'I know,' Yngve said quietly.

Kyrkjebø blinked. A tear squeezed its way out. Yngve looked up to the ceiling and sent another thought to God. An angry one.

'Let's search the rest of the school,' he said. 'For all we know the killer could still be here.'

3

Yngve asked to borrow Tic-Tac's keys, then instructed him to go and guard the main entrance door. Once the janitor was in position, Vibeke Hanstveit agreed to stay where she was so she could both monitor the crime scene and keep an eye on potential movements by the door.

Yngve and Therese then began to search the ground floor, checking every schoolroom, washroom, closet or trash bin. But they didn't find anyone – or anything that might have been used to kill Johannes Eklund.

'We need to find out when they last cleaned this place,' Yngve said.

'I'll get right on it,' Therese said, her voice still only a whisper.

Yngve looked at her. Twenty-eight years old, one child at home, another one on the way – although this was hard to tell, except maybe in the slightly more rounded cheeks. He noticed how hard she was trying to steel herself, to think professionally and clearly, something she normally managed easily. Sights this brutal, though, especially with young kids involved, were impossible to prepare for. Pictures in books, however real, never came close to the real thing. Some things you just had to experience the hard way.

Vibeke Hanstveit was still on the phone when Yngve and Therese got back to the staircase. Just as they arrived, a tall, grey, bearded man emerged from the staffroom at the other end of the hallway. Yngve recognised him immediately. It was the school's principal, Tor-Olav Brakstad.

'How the hell did he get in?' Therese asked.

Yngve started to walk towards the principal, raising a hand in the air to get him to stop.

'There's been a crime here,' Yngve said to him. 'We have to shut down the whole school.'

'What?' Brakstad asked. He had a bewildered look on his face. 'What's happened?'

'I can't go into any details just yet,' Yngve replied. 'We only got here a few minutes ago. How did *you* get in?'

'The janitor's door,' Brakstad explained and nodded in its direction. 'On the other side of the school.'

'The janitor has his own entrance?' Yngve couldn't quite believe what he was hearing.

'It's right next to his parking space,' Brakstad said. 'For me it's a short cut. But what...?'

'I'm sorry, but you have to leave. No one but police or medical examiners can be here right now.'

'But...'

Brakstad tried to look past Yngve. The police officer made himself as big as he could in order to block the view. 'Have you seen or heard anyone else in the building – since you arrived, I mean?'

Brakstad shook his head. 'But...' he started.

'You can't be here now,' Yngve said firmly while glancing out of the windows. More pupils had arrived, and it was impossible for them all to fit under the canopy over the entrance. So they just stood there in the rain, alarms and questions written all over their faces.

'Can I get my coat first?' Brakstad asked. 'It's freezing out there.'

Yngve looked at the clouds of steam pouring from the students' mouths, then instantly evaporating. 'Be quick about it,' he said.

Brakstad hurried away and returned a minute later. Again he tried to see what was going on at the end of the staircase, but Yngve put a hand on his shoulder and led him towards the exit. Tic-Tac opened the door. The noise from the thunderous rain made Yngve raise his voice: 'I'll find you later.'

Brakstad turned and shot him another quizzical look. 'I'm going to need help,' Yngve continued. 'With information, first and foremost. We just have to get a grip on the situation first.'

He then turned to the students: 'Go home, please. There won't be any school today.'

'What's going on?' one of the boys nearest the entrance asked.

'Please, just go home,' Yngve pleaded. 'You're making it harder for us to do our job.'

But neither the boy nor any of the other children made any attempt to leave. Instead they began to throw questions at both Yngve and the principal.

Yngve didn't reply. He simply closed the door and addressed Tic-Tac: 'You didn't tell me about your door.'

'Hm?'

'The door on the other side of the school.'

'Oh. *That*.'

He laughed nervously. 'I didn't think to mention that.'

'Really. Is it connected to the alarm system?'

'Um, no.'

'So ... when I asked you about other exit possibilities, you didn't think to mention a door you probably use on a daily basis?'

'I'm the only one with a key,' he said in a quiet voice.

'Apparently the principal has one, too.'

'Oh yes, that's true. I forgot about that.'

'You forgot about that too,' Yngve said with a sigh. 'Is there anything else you've forgotten to tell me, Tic-Tac?'

He thought about that for a few seconds. 'I left my door open last night.'

'You did?'

'Yes, Imo asked me to.'

'Imo. You mean Ivar Morten Tollefsen?'

'That's right. He said there might be a lot to do after the show, and he didn't want to trigger the alarm when he left. You know, standing ovations, people to talk to afterwards. The local press, even. I said it was OK, as long as he didn't spread the word. Imo is a good man. I've known him for twenty-odd years. I trust him.'

'Why didn't you just give him your key?'

'Like I said, I knew I had an early start. I would be needing my own key to get in, as the doors don't open before seven-thirty a.m.'

One of the kids outside cupped his face and tried to look in. Steam from his breath hit the glass.

'Just ... stay here for now,' Yngve said. 'Guard the door. I'll get someone to take your place in a little while. We need to talk some more later.'

'OK.'

Back by the staircase Yngve stopped in front of Vibeke Hanstveit, just as she was finishing her phone call.

'Can you ask some of the nearby districts to spare us some hands?' he asked. 'We probably have to conduct hundreds of interviews over the next few days.'

'I'll see what I can do,' Hanstveit replied.

'Good. Thanks. As many as we can get.'

Hansveit was already dialling.

Yngve turned to Therese. 'We have to talk to whoever was responsible for ticket sales to the show here last night. We need to find out exactly how many people were present.'

Therese was squatting in front of Johannes Eklund's body, but didn't seem to be looking at anything specific. Yngve took a few steps closer.

'OK,' she finally said in a thin voice, without looking up at Yngve.

He waited a few seconds. Then said, 'Are you OK?'

Therese got up and nodded, carefully at first, then with more and more force, as if trying to convince herself. She mindlessly stroked her belly, avoiding his gaze.

'Let's have a look upstairs,' Yngve said. 'There might be traces on the staircase, and our shoes are still wet. So be careful where you put your feet.'

Therese nodded again.

They slowly ascended the staircase, staying as close to the bannister as they could. The steps and walls were spotted with drops of blood.

'Look.' Therese pointed to the door at the end of the staircase, the small, red drop right next to the door handle.

'He probably walked this way afterwards,' she whispered. Yngve removed his coat and slowly pushed the door inwards with his elbow, making sure he didn't touch the blood. He held the door open so Therese could enter, then found the light switch on the other side of the door. One by one the fluorescent lights in the corridor lit up.

It was empty.

They checked the classrooms and washrooms, all locked or empty. They reached the auditorium. The stage at the front was covered with a thick, dark-green carpet. In front of it, red plastic chairs were lined up in rows. Without saying anything, Yngve pointed to a door further in on the right.

It was open.

They approached it slowly and carefully, but their footsteps broadcast their every move. Yngve could now make out the sign on the door. It said *MUSIC*. He pointed to the handle and stopped in front of it. More blood. A congealed spot.

He walked through the doorway.

And stopped again.

'Oh dear God,' Therese said, as she came up beside him.

On the floor in front of them was another dead body.

4

I woke abruptly, not sure what time it was or even if it was day or night. My head was spinning, pounding. I tried to remember when I had gone to bed, but I had trouble recalling what I'd done the previous night.

Then it all came back to me.

I'd been thinking about *her*, about what I'd like to do to her when I saw her. Who the hell breaks up with anyone by text and then goes into hiding for two days?

Just the thought of Mari made my heart start to race, but not in a good way. Not excited. A strange sensation spread through my whole body, an uneasiness I really couldn't explain. I wasn't nauseous. I wasn't nervous, either. I just felt ... weird. Like my gut was doing somersaults or something.

I got out of bed and checked the time. It was still early. I had time for a shower before breakfast. Neither the hot water nor a couple of *knekkebrød* with butter and goat's cheese helped, though. It's just the lack of sleep, I said to myself. That, or the crap food you always stuff down your throat.

I went into the hall and started to get ready for school. I looked at myself in the mirror and wondered, yet again, what on earth I'd done to her. Had I said something? Done something? Was it something I *should* have done? Or did she simply not like me anymore?

I ran my fingers through my hair and rubbed in some wax. Stepped back and looked at myself. I thought I looked pretty good. Six feet tall now. Not much fat on my body. I was pretty smart, too. Wouldn't have any trouble finding another girl. Trouble was, I didn't want another girl. I wanted *her*.

In the mirror I saw movement behind me. My younger brother, Tobias, was padding down the stairs, hands in his pockets, joggers almost falling off. He'd changed so much over the past six months. He was almost as tall as me now, and I could tell that he had put on some muscle. He'd let his hair grow longer, too, and he sometimes put it in a man bun, like I did. Usually, though, he just stuffed it underneath a baseball cap, like he didn't care. He didn't care about much, to be honest, except maybe his online games.

Tobias was not an easy person to get close to. Never had been. More than once I'd wondered whether he ever talked to anyone outside school. He was a speak-when-spoken-to kind of kid. It didn't help that his face was always covered in acne, dark and red.

'You don't have much time if you're going to get to school,' I said, gesturing at the clock with my head.

Tobias stopped at the bottom of the stairs but said nothing.

I pulled on my waterproof trousers. It was pouring down outside – solid, hard rain.

'Well, get a move on then,' I said, trying not to sound like a nag. 'School starts in half an hour.'

Tobias didn't answer. Just shuffled off into the kitchen. 'There's no milk left, by the way,' I called after him. 'Don't think there's any cornflakes either. I can get some later.'

'Awesome,' he said, then closed the door behind him. For some stupid reason he had started to use that word a lot lately. Awesome. Like he meant the opposite. I wondered if he had any intention of going to school at all. Perhaps you should wait, I asked myself, just to make sure. Mum wouldn't be around to check, or care, even. She was at Knut's.

Then I thought about Mari again. I wanted to see if I could catch her before the bell, so I could finally get her to talk to me. I decided to let Tobias be.

⌐

It was a young girl, probably no more than sixteen years old. She was lying on her back, eyes wide open. The skin on her face was pale white, lips light blue. She had dark-brown eyes and a small crack in her upper lip. The pink winter coat she was wearing had been opened, as if someone had tried to undress her.

'I know who she is,' Therese said almost soundlessly. 'She came by the station the other day. Her name's Mari Lindgren.'

Yngve turned to Therese. 'Why did she come to see you?'

'Not me specifically. She just came by, asking questions about an old car accident. I think she was working on a story for the school newspaper.'

Yngve turned to face the dead girl again. Her hair was neatly spread out across the floor. As if she was posing for a picture.

'She has dark spots on her neck', Therese said. 'Perhaps someone strangled her.'

Yngve wasn't listening. For a brief moment it was Åse lying there, staring up at him. Just as she had one of the last times he had visited her at the hospital.

I can't do it, Åse.

You have to. For me. Please.

'This is going to get nasty.'

'Hm?'

Therese pointed at the dead girl.

'Two murders in a school in this tiny little town? People will go crazy with fear unless we catch the bastard quickly.'

Therese's lips continued to move, but Yngve couldn't make out the words they formed. He lifted his gaze from Therese's face; because that's where he saw her, standing against the wall. Åse was looking at him with those shiny, bright eyes that always made him feel like the most important person in the whole world. He blinked a few times. Then she was gone.

5

'Shall we check out the rest of the school?' Therese asked.

'Sorry?'

'There are a few more classrooms we haven't checked yet. On either side of the stage.' She made a nodding motion with her head.

'Oh,' Yngve said. 'Yes, of course.'

She looked at him for a few seconds. 'Are you alright?' she asked.

'I'm fine,' he said. 'Let's go.'

They went down the corridor that led back from the right-hand side of the stage. The floor was covered in footprints and smudges of dirt. They walked past an empty can of Coca-Cola, a box of *snus*. Therese grabbed the handle of the first door they came to. Locked. Yngve tried the next one. Same. Therese tried the handle of the door at the end of the corridor.

It was open.

She looked at Yngve but didn't open the door right away, as if afraid of what might be found on the other side. Yngve came up behind her, about to say 'Let me enter first', but Therese was already on her way inside.

She flicked on the light switch.

There was no one there, only four desks filled with office supplies, stationery, pens, coffee mugs. On a huge whiteboard were written the numbers 4/16, with a few keywords underneath: *EDITORIAL*; *SCHOOL PLAY*; *EVEN TOLLEFSEN*; *CHRISTMAS PARTY*; *FEATURE STORY: PRINCIPAL BRAKSTAD*.

'This must be where they make the school newspaper,' Therese said. 'I wonder if one of these desks is Mari Lindgren's.'

A tapping sound made Yngve look around. One of the windows was open; it was gently knocking against the window frame. Therese pointed her finger towards yet another dark spot on the wall in the corner.

More blood.

'This must be where the killer left the building,' she whispered and pointed through the window. 'He probably wouldn't dare leave through the main door downstairs.'

'Yeah, too big a risk,' Yngve said. 'Too many possible witnesses. Plus there are surveillance cameras down there as well.'

He pulled his dry shirt sleeve from under his coat sleeve and used it to open the window fully. The wind and cold hit him in the face. Checking there were no marks, he carefully placed his hands on the windowsill then stuck his head out and looked upwards. He had to blink fast as the raindrops were hitting him hard. Right next to the window he noticed a drainpipe that reached all the way up to the gutter.

He came back inside and said, 'We have to get up there and see. It's easier to get away unseen on the other side of the school. I think there's a fire escape ladder up there, too.'

'Maybe we'll be lucky,' Therese said. 'Maybe he got stuck on something or lost something that will make it easier to identify him.'

'Maybe,' Yngve said, and began to climb onto the windowsill.

Therese stopped him. 'What the hell are you doing?'

'I'm going up.'

'No, you're not.'

'Yes, I am. It will take ages before the forensic teams can do this. They aren't even here yet. And the school is huge – several thousand square metres at least. The teams have to comb through every inch of it. We don't have time to wait. It's pouring outside – we might lose vital evidence.'

He could tell that Therese was still unsure.

'I'll just take a quick look around and see if I can find anything before it gets flushed away,' he said.

She held back another protest as Yngve once more stuck his head out into the cold. The rain trickled down his neck and shoulders as he peered out. He looked down. A fifteen feet drop, at least. Below more and more students had arrived. The media was there too. Like cattle they had gathered around the perimeter tape.

'Be careful,' Therese pleaded behind him.

Yngve pushed himself up onto the sill then leaned out and grabbed the black drainpipe with his hand, making sure he had a firm grip. He carefully placed his boot on a small bracket that held the drainpipe in place and made sure it held his weight. Then he kicked himself out with his left foot and clung on to the drainpipe with both hands. The freezing rain made them cold in an instant.

Yngve pulled himself up a few inches and put his left boot on another bracket. As he was about to push himself up, the sole of his boot slipped, and for a split second Yngve thought he was going to fall to the ground. He managed to cling on, his knuckles going white. He could feel how heavy he had become, how little exercise he had been doing since Åse became ill.

Therese called to him from the inside. 'Come back in!' she shouted. 'Please.'

Yngve looked down and blinked. The rain made his hands slippery. But he still had a firm grip on the drainpipe, and there were only six or seven more feet to the edge of the roof. He placed his boot on the bracket again but this time pushed his toes into it as hard as he could. And slowly, inch by inch, he was able to pull himself upwards. Soon he was able to reach the gutter. He stretched out and got a good grip of it. Then he slung one leg onto the roof, and with a final effort made it up safely.

Vapour was pouring out of his mouth. *What the hell are you doing? You're sixty-three years old. Are you trying to give yourself a heart attack?*

'I'm breathing,' he said out loud. 'Trying to, at least.'

No one could hear him up here in the noisy rain. Wet and cold, Yngve glanced around. Below one of the ambulances still had its blue lights on. They danced on the school walls, on the trees around the building. Yngve knew that his uniform jacket had reflective strips that shone in the dark, that he probably looked like a skeleton silhouette up here. But then it occurred to him that not just anyone could do what he'd just done. Certainly, it wasn't a fine display of strength and agility, but you needed a bit of both to be able to get up on a roof like that.

The roof itself was almost flat, which made moving around easy. The surface was covered with gravel. In the dim morning light Yngve could see it was littered with pine needles and dead branches, brought here by the wind.

He paused for a moment, trying to think like the killer. He or she must have been preoccupied with getting away without being detected.

Taking small, careful steps, Yngve made it over to the other side of the roof. He couldn't see any houses nearby that had windows facing the school; there were only trees, an open field of grass, then another cluster of trees. Behind that was a kindergarten, which Yngve knew hadn't been open last night. The chances of anyone having seen anything, at least on this side of the school, were slim.

Yngve walked as close to the gutter as he dared, trying to wipe away some of the water that was streaming down his face. At the far end of the roof there was a fire-escape ladder. He walked over to it, knelt down, leaned over the edge and stared at the ground below. A white van was parked close to the wall. The janitor's vehicle, probably. There was only room for one car. Yngve tried to imagine which direction the perpetrator would have taken. There were several possible escape routes. But if the killer had had blood on him, Yngve thought, after the fight with Johannes Eklund, which was most likely, he would have tried to get rid of his clothes as quickly as possible. Outdoors, preferably. Underneath a cluster of trees, perhaps.

Yngve's eyes searched the area and stopped at a red object that seemed to be stuck to a nearby branch. A piece of fabric, maybe. He decided to climb down to get a closer look. The ladder was slippery and cold against his fingers. Finally on the ground, he made for the object he'd seen from the roof. On closer inspection it turned out to be a piece of rubber from a broken balloon. Yngve cursed under his breath. He couldn't see any footprints on the ground, either, no sign to show the killer had stood here to undress. Maybe he just removed his jacket, Yngve reasoned. Or maybe he had managed to sneak his way home, wearing his bloodied clothes, without being seen. It had been raining heavily the previous night. And it had been dark.

Yngve walked over to the white van, examining it more closely. It was, indeed, parked on a spot marked JANITOR. He peeked inside. It was filled with empty soda cans and rubbish. No traces of blood.

Yngve glanced at the windowless door right next to the parking space. He tried it, only to find it locked. He thought about Tic-Tac for a brief second, then returned to the other side of the building, where he was once again bombarded with questions from reporters, pupils and staff. Yngve 'no-commented' his way back inside.

At the main entrance Vibeke Hanstveit met him with a quizzical gaze. As Yngve explained what he had done, deep furrows scored her forehead.

'You could have fallen,' she said when he was finished. 'You could have hurt yourself badly.'

'I could have, yes,' he said. 'But I didn't.'

'Yngve...' She shook her head.

Hanstveit was the first person Yngve had told about Åse's illness. Not just because they had worked together for so long, but also because she was a breast cancer survivor. Every week, and after every test Åse underwent, Yngve had asked Hanstveit for her opinion, how *she* had felt at the same stages of her treatment. She always gave him an honest assessment. And, once she knew that all hope was gone, she was still honest with him. Honest but gentle. Hanstveit was probably the only person who had seen him at rock bottom, who – every day since he'd come back to work – had watched for signs of how he was coping, whether he was doing better or worse.

'We're getting help from four precincts,' she said now. 'Jessheim, Årnes, Eidsvoll and Lillestrøm are sending us a few detectives each.'

'Good,' Yngve said, trying to sound positive. 'When they get here, I want to set up somewhere they can interview as many people as possible ... and as quickly as possible. The handball court might be the best place.'

'Good idea.'

'We need to get Principal Brakstad to alert the parents,' Yngve continued. 'I'm sure he has a procedure for that. And we should have him tell the kids who were here last night to come to the handball court as soon as possible. We have to get a preliminary sense of who left when, who they were with, and what kind of relationship they had with the victims. More importantly, we need to find out if anyone saw anything.'

'We also have to make sure they have the opportunity to bring an adult along – parent, teacher, priest, whatever,' Hanstveit said. 'The last thing we need right now is someone screaming about their rights not being observed.'

'Of course,' Yngve said. 'We also need to start exploring the victims' friends and social networks.'

'I talked to Weedon about that,' Hanstveit said. 'I knew you'd need it. He's already on the job.'

'Good.'

They were silent for a moment.

A woman in a protective forensics outfit entered the building with a small suitcase in her hand.

'Did you know that Mari Lindgren was seeing Even Tollefsen up until a few days ago?' Hanstveit said. Yngve looked at her. 'The football player?'

'The very same.'

'Fuck,' Yngve said.

'Yeah, that's what I said as well. We need to talk to him. Fast.'

6

Fredheim High School was about three kilometres from our home on Granholtveien. No matter the weather, I always cycled. Fredheim was small – there were only about 7,500 of us living here. But the town was growing: the sawmill on the outskirts had attracted a lot of workers over the years, and we were only something like half an hour's drive away from Oslo Gardermoen Airport.

I'd always liked it here. It was where I was born and lived for the first seven years of my life. Then Dad had died, and Mum didn't want to hang around – seeing things that reminded her of him and everybody feeling sorry for her – so we moved to Solstad, another small town about thirty kilometres away. Imo, my uncle, stayed where he was because of his pig farm, but he still came to see us almost every day in his old, green Mercedes.

I liked it at Solstad, too, but Tobias got into some trouble at his school, so last year Mum decided it was time to move back. I don't know if she had finally come to terms with what happened to Dad, or whether it was because she'd inherited my grandmother's big house. Maybe it was because part of Mum had never really left Fredheim.

At first I really didn't like being back. I missed my friends. And it was so much easier to get to football training from Solstad. But Mum was intent on making this work, and it didn't take me long to make new friends. Now, just a little over a year later, it felt like I knew every inch of the place. Fredheim has a small-town cosiness, I supposed you'd call it. No tall buildings. Small shops in the centre. Cobblestones that make the cars drive slowly. Nice cafés that are always full in the summer. Forest surrounds the town on all sides. If you flew over it, it would look as if someone had carved a big, round circle out of the woods. And the smell: the whole town smells of sawdust, especially when the wind is coming from the east.

I had pulled my hood so tight around my face, the sounds around me were muffled. And in the rain, I could hardly see anything; only the sharpest colours stood out. That was probably why I stopped a few hundred metres away from the school. From a distance it looked as if someone had painted the clouds above it in deep, dark blue. Beyond the trees that separated the car park from the school, lights were flashing. Behind me I heard an urgent wailing – it was coming closer and closer.

I cycled up the hill that led to the school, but when I reached the forecourt in front of the main entrance, I had to get off my bike – the whole area was filled with people. Pupils crying, teachers with grim-looking faces. Uniformed police, ambulance men and women. The entrance itself was cordoned off with red-and-white tape. Something heavy pressed down on my chest, and I could feel the queasiness I'd felt when I first woke up return with full force. Everyone was staring at me. At least, that's how it felt.

Rain was pattering noisily onto my hood. I pulled it off so I could hear what people around me were saying.

'...there was blood everywhere...'

'...Tic-Tac called the police...'

A police officer lifted the cordon to allow two men and a woman, all dressed from head to toe in white plastic overalls, to come inside. One of them was carrying a small black case. They looked like something from a movie.

A voice cut through the chatter.

'...they found her in the music room.'

I looked around. People were still staring at me, I was sure of it. Then I saw Ida Hammer, Mari's best friend, as she threw her head back and let out a wail. Everyone's attention suddenly turned to her. She threw herself on the ground and howled, and for a moment that was all I could hear. Some of her friends stood around her, trying to stop her falling face down on the cold, wet asphalt.

I didn't notice when I let go of my bike. I only heard it topple to the ground.

7

NOW

'So you knew then that Mari had been murdered?'

Prosecutor Håkonsen looks at me like she doesn't really believe me.

'I didn't *know*, but seeing Mari's best friend cry her eyes out like that – I kind of guessed what had happened. But I didn't want to believe it. I kept saying to myself: *It's not her. It's not Mari. Someone else must have been murdered.*'

I sneak a look at the people in the public seats, trying to get a feel for what they think of my story. Hard to tell. Everyone is looking at me, waiting for me to continue.

'Right then and there, I wanted to forgive her for breaking up with me,' I say. 'It wasn't important anymore.'

'You wanted to *forgive* her?' Ms Håkonsen's voice is full of disbelief. I immediately regret what I've just said. I don't know what to say next. But I have to say something. I speak without thinking. 'I'm … I'm not going to lie to you, I was very angry with Mari. I wanted to … I don't know. Force the truth out of her or something.'

'You were going to demand an explanation.'

'Yes. But then, after seeing Ida, I didn't care anymore. I just wanted Mari to still be alive.'

I can feel a lump in my throat again. I try to swallow it away. Ms Håkonsen looks at me quizzically.

'OK,' she says. 'What happened next?'

'I threw up. Well. Almost. I leaned forwards, as if I was about to puke, but nothing happened.'

I try to get up, so I could show the court, but there's not enough space in the booth I'm sitting in. Ms Håkonsen gestures to me to sit down. I do as I'm told.

'Then Oskar came over,' I say.

'Oskar who?'

I think about how to answer for a few seconds. 'Oskar is one of my best friends,' I say. 'Has been ever since we were little. I asked him if he knew what had happened. He said he didn't, so I went and asked Tic-Tac.'

'Tic-Tac, the janitor?'

'Yes. He was sitting by the police car, smoking. He ... he told me that Mari and Johannes were dead.'

'How did Tic-Tac seem to you – when he told you this?'

'You mean what was he like?'

'That's what I mean, yes.'

'Shocked, I think, more than anything. Like he didn't know where he was or what he was doing. I guess we were all like that. He smoked kind of nervously. Like all the time.'

The prosecutor nods sceptically. 'Then what did you do?' she continues.

'I went home. Well, I ran.'

'You ran all the way home? In the rain?'

'It's really not that far.'

'You weren't nervous that people might think you were running away from the crime scene? Why didn't you take your bike? You'd arrived on it, hadn't you?'

'I didn't know what I was thinking at that moment.'

'Is that something that happens to you a lot?'

I frown. I don't know what she means.

'It sounds as if you almost blacked out...'

'No, I didn't,' I reply. 'I don't think I did. But I was upset. I just had to get out of there.'

'To be by yourself.'

'Yes ... something like that.'

'So you didn't think that everybody was looking at you the way they did because they thought you might have killed Johannes and Mari?'

'No. Not then.'

'But you thought so later?'

'Yeah, it ... it sort of crept into my mind quite quickly after.'

'Why was that?'

I sigh heavily. 'Fredheim is a small town,' I say. 'News travels fast.'

8
THEN

When my uncle knocked on the door, I was lying on my bed, staring at the wall. I could tell it was him – he always rapped on the door three times, short pauses between each knock. The final one always harder than the first two.

He opened the door before I'd had a chance to say 'come in'. I just kept staring at the wall.

'Hey champ,' Imo said. Then sighed.

I took a deep breath and released it slowly through my nose. My uncle didn't close the door behind him. He just stood there in the middle of the room. I could feel his eyes on me.

'I went down to the school as soon as I heard,' he said. 'But I couldn't find you. I guessed you'd come back here.'

I rolled over and looked at him, trying to stop myself from crying. He was wearing an open navy-blue jacket. Under the jacket, an unironed white t-shirt stretched over his stomach. He wore shorts, as usual with dark-grey woolly socks. Imo was one of those people who claimed they were never cold. As long as the temperature was above zero, my uncle always walked around in shorts.

He sat down on the bed. Put a hand on my shoulder, gave it a gentle squeeze. A few raindrops fell from his thick, dark hair and landed on the duvet cover.

'How are you?' he asked.

I didn't answer, because I didn't know what to say.

'Can I get you anything?' he said. 'A Coke, or ... whatever?'

I shook my head. Imo let go of my shoulder, stood up and went to open the window. Cool air filled the room in an instant. It made me shiver.

'Where's your brother?' Imo asked. 'I didn't hear him upstairs.'

'I don't know,' I said.

My uncle closed the window again, sat down on the armchair in the corner and picked up the guitar that was standing beside it. His thumb hit the E-string. It made a thick sound that spread around the room. Then his fingers began to dance over the strings. He didn't even look at the frets. Even though I knew he was improvising, it sounded like a proper song.

Imo stopped abruptly and put his hand over the strings to silence them. 'The police want to talk to you,' he said. 'I spoke to Yngve Mork at the school just a few minutes ago.'

'Of course they do,' I said.

'He's on his way here, I think. He's already called your mum. They need parental consent before they can question you. She's just called me. Asked me to tell you what's happening and be here when they question you. If you want me to, that is.'

I sat up. 'She called you?'

'Yes.'

She hadn't called *me*.

'Everyone's going to think that I did it,' I said.

'Why would they do that?'

I looked at him for moment, hesitating.

I picked up my mobile phone, which was lying on the bed. The display was full of messages I hadn't opened yet.

'Because of this,' I said, and showed Imo the text I had sent Mari the night before:

I'm going to find you sooner or later, Mari. And when I do, you're going to answer my questions, whether you like it or not.

Imo didn't say anything.

I couldn't help glancing at some of the messages I had received. My stomach felt like someone was squeezing it. 'God,' I murmured.

'What is it?'

Notifications were pouring in. I showed Imo the phone again. 'They all want to know if I did it. They don't say it, but I know that's what they're really asking.'

'Why the hell would they think that?' Imo demanded.

'They know that I was looking for Mari yesterday. At school and in Fredheim, later. I looked everywhere.'

'Mari wasn't at school during the day?'

'No, she wasn't. She was hiding from me, I think.'

Imo seemed to think about that for a moment. 'So what are your friends saying, exactly?'

I scrolled through the notifications. My finger was shaking a bit.

'They want to know how I am, why I ran away from school earlier and when I talked to Mari last. I bet they're already creating groups, talking about me.'

'You were here last night, though, weren't you?' Before I could answer, Imo added: 'So you couldn't have done it.'

I sighed heavily and swung my feet onto the floor. I covered my face with my hands for a few seconds. Had the police already seen the message I sent Mari? Had they started interviewing the others yet? If they had, I must already look guilty. Everyone knew that Johannes was popular with the girls. Everyone would be saying that Mari had fallen in love with him, and that I had killed them both because I was angry and jealous.

And then I realised: Johannes might be the reason Mari had split up with me.

'Just stick to the truth,' Imo said, 'and everything will be fine.'

Yeah, I said to myself. The truth. Somehow that didn't reassure me.

9
NOW

'So then the police came to see you?' Prosecutor Håkonsen looks up at me. 'Yngve Mork came to your house in Granholtveien 4?'

'Yes, he did.'

'But you didn't want Imo – your uncle – to be there with you?'

'No, I thought I could handle it myself. Besides, I hadn't done anything wrong.'

I glance at the public seats again. Still no sign whether they believe me or not. Just faces looking at me hard. Ms Håkonsen nods, as though she needs a moment or two to consider what I've just said.

'Just so we're clear, we're still talking about the morning of October 18th.'

'Yes. Well, it wasn't morning anymore when Yngve came around. At least, I don't think so. That day's all a bit of a fog.'

'I'd say you're remembering quite well, Even,' she says with a smile. 'According to police records the interview took place at eleven-thirty a.m.'

I nod. Why is that important?

'Did you already know Yngve Mork?'

'Everybody knew Yngve. He's lived and worked in Fredheim for years.'

'Did you like him?'

'Yes. Still do.'

I search for his eyes in the room. He gives me a blank look back. My mind drifts for a moment. His wife died four or five months ago. I wonder how he's dealing with it now. If he is dealing with it. He definitely looked a bit lost when he knocked on our door that day. Like he was still sad, but trying hard not to show it.

'According to the records, Chief Inspector Mork wanted to know if anyone could confirm whether or not you were alone the night before. The night of the murders. Could you tell the court what you replied?'

I take a quick breath in. 'I think I said that my brother might have been home. But his bedroom is on the second floor, and mine is in the basement, so I couldn't really tell for sure.'

'Your mother wasn't at home with you that evening?'

'No, she was at her boyfriend's. She usually was.'

'So on the whole, she wasn't there to take care of you and your brother?'

'Well, depends on how you look at it,' I say.

'Right now I'm asking you.'

I think about what to say for a second. 'Like I said before, my uncle was the one who brought us up really, and if he wasn't around, my brother and I knew how to take care of ourselves. Mum usually left some money on the kitchen sink for us to get groceries and stuff.'

'You don't find that strange?'

I shake my head and say no.

'Why not?'

'We were used to it. I suppose it stopped being strange a long time ago.'

'OK. We'll come back to that later. Would you say PCI Mork treated you as a suspect during that first interview?'

'No, I don't think so. He was very polite. Gave me time to think about my answers. If he already thought I was a suspect, he didn't show it.'

'He asked you about your relationship with Johannes Eklund, didn't he?'

'He did.'

'And what did you reply?'

'I said I knew him. That I liked him. He was a really good singer. We got on fine.'

'You played together in the school band, is that correct?'

'We did.'

'But you didn't play in the band on the night of the murders, did you?'

'No I didn't.'

'Why was that?'

'Mari had just broken up with me, and I was, well, depressed. I didn't think I could do it.'

'You didn't think you could *do it* ... you mean you didn't think you could perform?'

'Yes. That's what I meant.' My cheeks were getting warmer. 'I didn't think I could sit there on stage and play, and maybe see her in the audience. I knew she was going to be there.'

'How did you know that?'

'She told me. She was going to write a piece on the opening night for the school newspaper.'

'She had agreed to conduct an interview with Johannes Eklund after the show, hadn't she?'

'Yes. He was the star of the show.'

'Did that make you jealous?'

'That she was going to talk to him? No, not at all.' I try to sit up more straight. 'She was just doing her job.'

Ms Håkonsen checks the papers in front of her for a second, then looks up at me again.

'According to the police records, PCI Mork asked you about the grazes on your hand.'

Without thinking about it, I glance at my hand. They're gone now, of course, the grazes.

'Yes, he did,' I reply.

'You had hurt yourself?'

'On my way home from school that morning.'

'What happened?'

'I ran too fast.'

'You ran too fast?' Again, she sounds like she doesn't believe me.

'Yes. It was like ... my mind was racing, and my legs couldn't keep up. And I just fell forwards.'

I try to gesture with my hands, showing how I had just toppled over, how I had tried to break my fall. I can tell the prosecutor finds the whole incident strange. Which it was.

'It was a heavy fall,' I explain. 'On a hard road.'

'So you started to bleed?'

'Yes, but I didn't care. I ... I wanted the pain'.

'You wanted the pain...'

'I just wanted to feel something, you know? So it would hurt somewhere else besides ... besides in here.' I touch my chest.

She lets this sink in for a while. It's weird being so open about my feelings in front of so many people.

'So when Mork asked you how you had got those grazes, did you worry they might implicate you in the murders somehow?'

'Yes, I was afraid he'd think that.'

'And why were you afraid of that?'

'I knew what it looked like. And I knew my explanation – running and falling over sounded really stupid, like I'd made it up. Like when adults say they've cut themselves shaving, when everyone can tell they've been in a fight. I mean, I'm used to running. I run all the time. I never just fall on my face like that. And it was, what, less than half a day after my ex-girlfriend had been murdered. I knew I already had to be a suspect. I knew it didn't look good for me. But I didn't want to make up some bullshit story about my wounds, either. Imo told me to tell the truth, so that's what I did.'

'Imo told you that?'

'Yes.'

I think back to that day – Yngve asking me if there was anything I knew about Mari or Johannes that might help them solve the case. If Mari had been in an argument with anyone, for instance. I said no, because at the time I didn't really know. Then and there I really didn't know anything about the last days of Mari's life.

'Tell us some more about the school show,' Ms Håkonsen says next. 'You said you didn't play in the band. Who took your place?'

'Imo. My uncle. He was the musical director of the show anyway. I told him about Mari and that I didn't want to play. At first he tried to persuade me to change my mind, but I guess he understood what kind of state I was in, and then he said it was fine, he would step in for me. He'd written most of the songs anyway.'

'That's handy,' Ms Håkonsen says. 'That he could just do that.'

'Well, yes,' I reply.

She adjusts her round glasses. 'According to your statement that day, you didn't go out at all that evening.'

I think about my answer for a few seconds. 'I … thought I hadn't,' I say carefully.

'You *thought* you hadn't gone out?'

'No, I … Well, what I meant, is that, at the time, I couldn't quite remember what I did the evening of the…' I still find it hard to say out loud.

'The murders,' Ms Håkonsen finishes for me.

'Yes. But later I remembered that I'd taken the dog out for a walk. I'd promised my mother I'd do it.'

'So, again, you kind of blacked out that bit?'

'I didn't black out, no. I just didn't remember until later.'

'But you've blacked out before, haven't you?'

'I … what do you mean?'

'You've had episodes before where you've been so angry that you haven't remembered until later what you've done.'

I realise what she's talking about. I just didn't think she would bring it up in court.

'Yes,' I say quietly.

'Speak up, please,' the judge orders.

'Sorry. Yes. I … I sometimes lose my temper – when I play football mostly,' I say. 'I've seen red during a match a couple of times, and sort of blacked out, yes.'

Ms Håkonsen looks at me for a few seconds. 'So you admit to being angry on the night of the murders. You admit to blacking out from time to time when you're angry. And you didn't, at first, recall having left the house that night.'

I know how it all sounds, but I have no choice – I have to agree with her.

'What time did you go out with the dog?'

'It must have been around eleven.'

'And what time did the school doors close that evening?'

I wait for a moment. Then I say, 'They always close at eleven.'

10

THEN

Yngve Mork parked outside Fredheim High School, questions still bouncing back and forth in his head after the interview with Even. He really didn't know what to think. Even was clearly having a difficult time processing what had happened. But might he have answered Yngve's questions a little bit too well? And the grazes ... well, the explanation he gave for those really made an odd story.

Yngve also thought about the short conversation he'd had with Imo before going to Granholtveien 4. Imo had confirmed his arrangement with Tic-Tac about the door on the other side of the school. He had been allowed to park his car in the janitor's spot last night, but said that he'd left a lot sooner than he expected to – somewhere between 10.30 and 10.40. And he'd been true to his word: he hadn't told anyone else about the door being open.

Yngve got out of the car. Immediately he was met by a herd of reporters.

'Mork, what can you tell us about the killer?'

'Have you got any solid leads you're working on?'

'Do you have any suspects yet?'

'Will there be a press conference anytime soon?'

Yngve didn't answer any of them. He simply pushed forwards into the school building.

Inside, he was glad to see that Johannes Eklund's body had now been removed. Four crime-scene investigators were examining the staircase, taking pictures from every angle possible, recording every mark, every trace of blood, every scrap of evidence they came across.

Therese Kyrkjebø was standing a few feet away from the staircase, monitoring the work while sipping from a paper cup. Ginger tea, probably. She'd been suffering from morning sickness, and this certainly wasn't helping.

'There's coffee for you here, if you want it.'

'I'm fine,' he said. 'How are we doing?'

'I haven't asked yet,' she said with a shrug. 'I thought I'd wait for you.'

Yngve related what had happened in the interview with Even Tollefsen.

'So he wasn't here at all last night?' she asked.

'That's what he said.'

'Well, there goes *that* theory.'

'Yeah,' Yngve said. 'Maybe. Who's in charge of the forensics team?'

Therese pointed to a short woman at the bottom of the staircase. Yngve went over, Therese following behind, and introduced himself.

The woman stood up. 'Ann-Mari Sara. I'm in charge of the forensics division at Kripos.'

'Thanks so much for coming in on such short notice.'

'It's what we do.'

Sara was in her early fifties. The white full-body forensics suit made it impossible to tell what she really looked like. The only thing Yngve noticed about her was her high cheekbones, and that her eyes were rather close together.

'Have you discovered anything I should know about?' Yngve asked.

'A few things,' Sara said – her accent indicating she originally hailed from the far north. 'The victim on the staircase was beaten several times, probably with something sharp and fairly heavy.'

'No idea what kind of object?'

'None,' Sara replied. 'At least, not yet.'

'What about the other victim?' Therese asked.

'I haven't examined her closely yet, but she was most likely strangled. Someone tried to revive her afterwards.'

Yngve raised his eyebrows. 'Revive her?'

'We'll have to wait for the preliminary autopsy,' Sara said, 'but according to one of my colleagues, at least two of the victim's ribs were broken in a way that's consistent with someone trying to do CPR a bit violently.'

So the perpetrator regretted killing her, Yngve thought. While the opposite seemed to be the case with Johannes Eklund.

'Is it possible to say who was killed first?' he asked.

'Probably the girl,' Sara said. 'Whoever did this' – she pointed to the staircase – 'probably got blood on themselves, and there's nothing on the girl.'

That sounds about right, Yngve thought.

'One more thing,' Sara said. 'The female victim had a business card in her pocket.'

'Yeah?'

'It's for a reporter.'

Yngve looked at Therese.

'His name is Ole Hoff,' Sara said. 'You guys might know him.'

We do, Yngve thought to himself. He had spoken to Ole during the weekend about a stabbing that had taken place in the town centre.

He didn't have any more questions for Sara, so he thanked her for her time and watched her return to work. Then he turned to Therese.

'See if you can get hold of Ole,' he said. 'He and Mari had obviously been in touch.'

'I'll get right on it.'

'Talk to the janitor as well. See if the surveillance cameras on the outside were in use last night. Maybe we'll get lucky.'

'I'll do that, too,' said Therese.

Just as she walked away, Vibeke Hanstveit arrived.

'I've sent the extra detectives to the handball court,' she said.

'Good.'

'They're waiting for you.'

'Very good, I'm just going to...'

Åse was standing by the wall a couple of feet away from them.

You're always just *going to...*

Her voice, whether it was kind or scolding, was like a faint stream of light that always managed to break through the darkness. He both wanted it and didn't want it to linger.

'Yngve?'

He blinked. Hanstveit was staring hard at him.

'Yes?' he asked, rubbing his face.

Hanstveit looked at him for a few moments. Then, 'Are you sure you're up for this?'

'Up for what? How do you mean?'

'It's only been a couple of weeks since you buried your wife. Are you sure your head is in the right place?'

Yngve looked over at the wall again. She wasn't there anymore. He blinked a couple of times, quickly, in the hope that she would reappear. She didn't.

'Everyone knows how hard this is for you,' Hanstveit continued. 'But we have to do everything right, and do it fast. Especially now, when all of Norway is watching.'

Someone had said to him, after Åse had died, that he needed to talk to people. To his friends, his colleagues. You're not the only one having a rough time, they'd said. Others loved her, too. Staying silent is a symptom of grief and sorrow. Of darkness. Helplessness.

Yngve hadn't spoken a word about his grief to anyone, not even Hanstveit. He had shared so many of his anxieties with her that once Åse was finally gone, he'd found himself numb, unable to verbalise his pain.

'I'm fine,' he said and thought of the two people who'd been killed the previous night. The two *children*. 'Seriously,' he added. 'It's good for me to work. Good for me to think about something else.'

Hanstveit looked at him for a few moments. Then she said, 'Just promise me one thing: let me know if this is too much for you to handle right now. OK?'

This is too much for me to handle.

He blinked a few more times. Searched the walls, the ceilings, for her.

You've got to help me, Yngve. I can't take this anymore.
He swallowed hard.
You have to help me die.
'I'm fine,' he said without looking at Hanstveit. 'Really. I am.

11
NOW

'So it seems that things weren't looking good for you early on,' Ms Håkonsen says. 'Is that why you wrote what you did on Facebook, after Yngve Mork had left?'

She lifts her chin and looks directly at me. I think about how upset I was after Yngve Mork left. I remember going back to my room to have a lie down. I didn't know what to do. The messages kept pouring in. Whenever I looked at my Instagram account, there were pictures of Mari and Johannes. Among the *R.I.P.*s, the *I can't believe they're dead*s, and all the *I miss you so much*, there were comments about me.

—*Where is Even?*
—*Has anyone spoken to Even yet?*
—*I would SERIOUSLY like to know how Even feels about this.*
—*What if it's him?*
—*I KNOW it's him.*
—*I'm so going to KILL HIM if it is!*

And there I was, trying to come to terms with the fact that Johannes and Mari were dead. It didn't feel real. I remember wondering if that was why I wasn't bawling my eyes out.

I remember flipping through the pictures people were posting. Mari laughing. Mari looking at something on the horizon, but with half an eye on the camera. A typical school photograph. Mari as a baby. Mari with her arm around Ida Hammer.

The photos of Johannes were all very similar: on stage, microphone to his mouth, dry ice in the background, his index and little fingers doing the *let's rock* sign. Hundreds of people had liked those photos as well.

It didn't seem right to do nothing. To say nothing. I didn't really want to share my memories or my thoughts with anyone, but I kept on hearing Yngve Mork's questions in my head. And the feeling that the whole of Fredheim was assuming I was the one who'd committed the murders was overwhelming. That was why I decided to go to my Facebook page.

'Could you share with the court what you wrote, please?'

Ms Håkonsen approaches me with a piece of paper. I take a look at it. There they are. My own words. Looking at them again, I can't believe I actually wrote them. They feel like words written by someone desperately trying to convince people he's innocent.

I've never enjoyed reading out loud. But this is on a whole other level. At least two hundred people are looking at me.

I clear my voice before starting.

'Most of you know that Mari and I were going out until only a few days ago. And lots of you will probably be thinking that I was upset and angry when she dumped me. And I'll be honest, I was. But I could never – NEVER – have hurt her. I loved Mari. And I respected and looked up to Johannes. The world is a poorer place without them, and I will never forget them.'

My mouth has become as dry as sand, so I take a quick sip of my water and put down the piece of paper.

'What was the response to that post?'

'It was good. A lot of people liked it.'

'Did that make you feel better?'

'A little.'

'But you still weren't done defending yourself.'

I squint my eyes, not sure what she means.

'You agreed to do an interview with Ole Hoff from the local newspaper, on the very same day, didn't you? Wasn't that rather soon – after everything that had happened, after being interviewed by the police?'

She turns around slightly to look at the people around us, like they all agree that it was an odd thing to do.

'He called me,' I say. 'Said he'd come to my house to have a chat. Like it was just, you know, casual. I think I said yes because I wanted to talk about Mari. To try and sort out my own thoughts about her. Explain myself, maybe. And I knew Ole. He's my best friend's dad. And my mum wasn't home, so...'

'Your best friend – that's Oskar, correct?'

'Correct.'

'But Ole didn't *just* want to talk to you about your relationship with Mari, did he?'

I run a hand through my hair. It was getting a bit damp. 'No, he didn't.'

12
THEN

Before Ole arrived, I took another shower and put on some clean clothes. It made me feel a little bit better, but all the strength in my body seemed to have left me. Just walking up the stairs from my bedroom exhausted me.

Ole had worked on the *Fredheim Chronicle* for twenty-two years. Five more than my entire existence. I liked Ole – he was always cheerful, at least when I was around. He was quite strict with Oskar, but I thought that maybe real parenting should be like that.

We shook hands out on the front step, which felt a bit odd. Ole's hair was thinning on top and receding at the front, but otherwise he looked good for a man in his mid-forties. As we chatted and he came inside, I had the impression he was sizing me up, but not in the same way PCI Mork had. Ole seemed to be trying to work out how I was feeling, not whether I was a double murderer or not.

'Even,' Ole said, in a kind voice, 'We can do this another time, if you'd prefer.'

I said: 'No, it's fine.'

We sat down in the kitchen. Ole put his hands flat on the table and looked around.

'So, how's the football?' he asked.

I looked up. 'It's the off-season right now.'

'But you're still in training, aren't you?'

'Yeah,' I said. 'Three times a week.'

'So there's quite a lot of shuttling back and forth?'

'Yes,' I said and paused. Lillestrøm, my football club, was forty-two kilometres away from Fredheim. 'But I'm used to it. Besides, Imo usually gives me a ride, so it's fine, really. It'll be much easier when I get my driver's licence.'

'Are you still in the under-seventeens national team?'

'I don't know, to be honest. There hasn't been a call-up for a while.'

'You'll become a professional one day.'

I smiled. It felt good to smile.

'Which team would you like to play for?' Ole asked.

'United, of course.'

'You mean Leeds?'

I pulled a face. 'There's only one United, Ole. You know that.'

We grinned at each other. Neither of us said anything for a while.

'We don't have to call this an interview,' Ole said. 'If you find it uncomfortable.'

His reason for being there brought me back to reality with a bang. I almost began to cry and had to pull myself together.

'It's fine,' I said.

Ole wanted me to begin by talking about Mari. Anything that came to mind. I told him how we'd met at school on a very ordinary Tuesday. She'd come over during morning break and asked if she could interview me for the school paper.

'Me?' I said.

'Yes, you.'

'Why?'

'For a few reasons, actually.'

'A few?' I always stunned the girls with my cool, witty replies...

'You play football at a national level...'

I wobbled my head a bit in a yes-no gesture.

'...you play guitar in a pretty cool band...'

My face said, *well, I don't know about that.*

'...and...' She looked at me, slightly nervous, as though she wasn't entirely sure whether to carry on or not; '...you've lived in Fredheim before. A long time ago.' She bit her lip. 'I wondered what it's like to come back, especially...' she looked down '...coming back to the school where your dad worked.'

The fact that almost everyone at school, teachers included, knew who I was, was as much thanks to Dad as it was me playing football or being in a band. The car accident had left an imprint on the whole town. Everyone knew about it. People still talked about it.

Mari thought it could be a good story, a sort of portrait of the prodigal son. And I – Mr Smooth with the Ladies himself – I just stood there and couldn't say a word. I'd been interviewed before, so it wasn't *that*. It was just something about Mari that ... I don't know ... resonated with me somehow from the start.

She had pale skin and a heart-shaped face. Her hair was dark brown and messy, as though she'd just got up and hadn't bothered to brush it before going out. She wasn't trying to make me like her, which perhaps was one of the reasons why I did. And she seemed a bit nervous. Like it was the first time she was playing journalist and she didn't know how to go about it.

We met after school the same day, and that was when she told me her full name for the first time: Mari Elisabeth Lindgren. Like she was half Norwegian, half Swedish and maybe had a sister called Pippi.

I'd thought we would talk for about fifteen minutes or so, half an hour tops, but we ended up walking around the streets for about three hours. The weather was great that day, so warm and sunny, and it didn't get dark until late. She asked me all kinds of questions about all kinds of things. After a while, I started asking about her life, too.

She wanted to be a writer. Or a journalist. As long as she could write, she told me. It was so easy to talk to Mari. And the more time I spent with her, the more I liked her. She was about a foot shorter than me, and I loved seeing her head tilt up towards me, full of curiosity.

We said hello to each other the next day, before starting to exchange a few words whenever we met. Then we started to message each other. It wasn't long before I started to feel butterflies in my stomach whenever I thought about her, and I could tell that she felt the same way about me.

I liked her warm, shy smile. And when she laughed, her whole face changed – it opened up, her teeth appeared and her dimples looked so delicate. I wanted to touch them. I liked her hands, how small they were in mine. How warm they were. I liked her voice – hesitant whenever she asked me a question, confident when she answered one of mine. She never seemed to doubt anything she said.

And she was so sweet and nice.

A couple of weeks before the show I was ill. Not at death's door or anything like that, I just had a high temperature and a thumping headache. My whole body ached. So I stayed off school for a few days. Mari came to see me every afternoon, even if I told her to stay away so she wouldn't get the same bug. She insisted though, saying she never got sick. 'It'll be fine. Plus, your mum's never here. Someone has to look after you.'

One day she brought me some soup and basically force-fed me. I was two years old again. And when Mari, of course, *did* get sick a few days later, it was my turn to look after her, even though she didn't want me to see her pale and with dry lips, cold one minute, hot the next. But there was nothing I wanted more. And when she fell asleep in my lap one afternoon, I felt warm and good, deep down inside. It was a feeling I'd never experienced before.

I'd gone out with other girls. Mainly because I'd thought it would be cool to have a girlfriend. And sometimes I'd *thought* I was in love with them ... Mari was the first girl I was actually in love with though. For real.

When I finished telling Ole about Mari, there was a slight pause before he said: 'Even, do you know if...?' He hesitated again, before carrying on. 'Did Mari ever talk about ... *me* in the days before she died?'

I frowned.

Ole quickly produced a business card from his leather mobile phone cover. 'The police found one of these in her jacket pocket,' he said, and held it out to me. I took it and looked at it. 'Obviously, I've spoken to her over the years, but I've never given her one of my business cards.'

'No?'

He shook his head.

'You're sure?'

'One hundred percent. I would have remembered.'

I flipped it over. There was nothing written on the back.

'You didn't, by any chance, give it to her?' Ole asked.

'Me? Why would I do that?'

'I don't know, that's why I'm asking.'

One time when I was visiting Oskar, Ole had given me one of his cards. It was just before I went to play for Norway's under-seventeens team against Malta and Italy. Ole wanted me to call the news desk, or even better, *him*, as soon as the matches were over, so he'd given me the card. I had no idea where I'd put it after that, though.

'So Mari wanted to get hold of you, is that what you're saying?' I asked.

'It would appear so,' Ole said. 'I'm trying to find out why.'

I looked at him.

'Of course, it might mean nothing at all,' he added.

'Yes,' I said. 'Of course.'

Somehow, though, I got the feeling that maybe it did.

13
NOW

'So, Ole Hoff was involved in some way or another from the start?'

Ms Håkonsen coughs into her palm, then apologises. She looks at me, waiting for my reply.

My cheeks are hot. It's not easy, talking about yourself and what you did and felt, even if it wasn't that long ago. You feel so many eyes piercing you, making a note of every single remark you make. My chair is hard and uncomfortable. I glance at the clock on the wall, yearning for it to be over. It's not even half past nine yet.

I say sorry, and ask the prosecutor to repeat the question. While Ms Håkonsen does, everything that happened with Ole comes crashing down on me again. And I'm scared too – about what's coming up: soon we will be talking about Mum.

I have to pull myself together before I answer. 'You could say that, yes.'

'OK. So the interview is over, you get up from the kitchen table, and Ole Hoff is about to go back to his office to write up the story?'

I nod and say yes at the same time. 'Before he left, he said he would call me to go over my quotes. Just to make sure he didn't publish anything that wasn't accurate.'

'Noble,' Ms Håkonsen remarks.

'Apparently it's common courtesy.'

After a moment's hesitation, she seems to agree.

'Then what happened?' she asks.

'I walked him to the door. Ole was about to leave when...' I stop for a moment. 'When my mother came home.'

14
THEN

Ole was about to step out into the rain when Mum came walking up the short path from the road. I wasn't expecting her. She'd been staying at Knut's a lot lately. She was rushing along, huddled under her umbrella while pulling the dog along behind her. Their feet were like drumsticks on the ground. It took a few seconds before she noticed us, but as soon as she did, she stopped.

Once upon a time my Mum had been an attractive woman. I'd seen pictures of her when she first started going out with Dad. She really had been gorgeous. She had long blonde hair, and in every photograph she was smiling. Glowing, almost. She'd been tall and slim, too, and everything she wore seemed to fit her perfectly. Like her clothes were made just for her.

Now her clothes were hanging loosely around her body. She had dyed her hair black and cut it short, and she always wore a bit too much make-up. As she stood there on the path, scowling at Ole and me from under her umbrella, she looked like something from a horror movie.

'What the hell is *he* doing here?' she said to me, pointing her umbrella at Ole. GP, the dog, started to bark at this stranger in the doorway.

'Mum...'

I never enjoyed having visitors when Mum was home. All the questions, the fuss – I usually just wanted her to go away.

'Hi Susanne,' Ole said.

GP barked again.

'We were just having a chat,' I said.

'Why?' Her voice was sharp as she came charging towards us.

'Because...'

Mum reined GP's lead in close and quickly climbed the steps. She marched past Ole without looking at him, without saying hello, and she didn't allow the dog to greet him either. After what had happened, I would have thought that Mum might at least have stopped to give me a hug or ask me how I was doing. Certainly I would have expected her to say a few words to Ole; he was the same age as her, and well known in the town, after all. But she just pushed straight past us and opened the door. I hoped, no, I *prayed*, that Ole wouldn't notice the stink of alcohol that trailed in her wake like a bad perfume. Once inside she slammed the door behind her. We could hear GP still barking and growling.

'Sorry,' I said to Ole. 'My Mum, she...' I didn't know how to finish my sentence.

'Mothers, eh?' Ole said.

'Yeah.'

He waved a hand at me and said again that he'd call me later.

'Alright,' I answered.

'Be kind to yourself now,' Ole said. 'You hear?'

'I'll try,' I said. I just didn't know how.

15
NOW

Ms Håkonsen is looking at me again with those inquisitive eyes. Like she thinks I'm lying or holding something back. Every stare, every question, somehow feels like an attack, both on me and on my family.

I realise that I don't like her. I don't like her at all.

'So at that point you had already realised that your mother had a strained relationship with Ole Hoff?'

I look at my mother again. Even from a distance it looks as if she hasn't slept in weeks. Which probably is true. The bags under her eyes have grown. Her face is grey.

'Yes,' I say a little more quietly than I intended.

'But you had no idea why?'

I shake my head. 'Not at the time, no.'

16
THEN

When I went back inside, my mother was waiting for me in the hall. One of her feet was tapping impatiently against the floor.

'And what the hell do *you* think you're up to?'

For some reason she was still holding onto GP's lead. The dog came charging into me as usual. I squatted down to play with him a little.

'I'm not up to anything,' I said, stroking and scratching the beautiful little monster. He was making happy noises.

'You were talking to him ... that *reporter*.' She made it sound like a dirty word. 'Was he in here as well?'

'What if he was?'

'What *if*?' Mum rolled her eyes, as though it was the most awful thing imaginable.

'Do you have a problem with Oskar's dad or something?'

'That's none of your business.'

'OK then,' I said, shaking my head. This was getting stupid, so I stood up and walked past my crazy mother, towards the door to the basement.

'You, of all people, Even, should keep a low profile now that ... that ... Think of what...'

She stopped herself, but I knew what she'd been meaning to say. For my mother what everyone else thought or felt was always the most important thing, never mind Tobias or me. I just opened the door and started down the stairs, getting angrier by the second.

'Even, you're not going to your room now.'

I didn't answer, just kept on walking.

'Even!'

Finally downstairs, I slammed my door shut and sat down on the bed. I tried to breathe deeply, to calm down, but it didn't help. I whacked my hand against what I thought would be the mattress, but it turned out to be the bedframe. The impact made one of the scabs in my palm split open, and before I knew it, there was blood.

'Fuck.'

I got up to get some toilet paper. Then pressed it against my hand, thinking, what the hell was wrong with my mother? Why did she freak out like that because of Ole? A part of me wanted to run upstairs again and ask, but another part just wanted to leave her alone.

Half an hour or so later there were footsteps on the stairs. At first I thought it was Mrs Crazy, wanting to carry on arguing, but it was Tobias.

'Y'right?' he said, standing in the doorway.

'Hey,' I said, without getting up. My brother held back for a few seconds. 'I spoke to the police,' he said. 'They wanted to know where you were last night.'

I sat up, instantly feeling a knot tighten in my belly. 'And what did you say?'

He hesitated, then said: 'I said I thought you were here.'

'You *thought* I was here?'

'Well, yes ... I couldn't know for sure, could I? I was playing CoD. Had my headphones on. I was talking to Ruben at the same time.'

God, I said to myself. The police really did suspect me, and my dipshit brother hadn't exactly helped.

'Anyway, your friends are here,' he said, leaning against the doorframe. 'They want to know if you're up for a visit. I said I'd ask.'

'Is Mum still around?'

Tobias shook his head. 'I think she went back over to see The Moron.'

Knut went by many names in our house.

'So, what should I tell them?' he asked.

More than anything, I wanted to stay away from people, but then I thought that my friends might know something about what had happened and what people were really saying, so I said yes, send them down.

Oskar came in first. He opened his arms and gave me a hug. He'd grown recently and was now almost as tall as me. 'What's up?' he said, his voice faltering a little.

'Not much,' I said.

Fredrik and I bumped fists. He was about a head and a half shorter than me, and I used to muck about and tease him, ruffle his hair like he was a child. It didn't feel right to do that now.

'Jeez, this is mental,' Fredrik said.

'Tell me about it,' I replied.

Kaiss came in and gave me a good, hard hug as well and thumped me on the back. Kaiss always wore black and doused himself in aftershave, even though he didn't have a hint of a stubble. 'You alright, mate?' he said.

'M'alright,' I answered, though I was anything but.

I made room for them on the bed. Kaiss sat on the chair in the corner and picked up the guitar. He couldn't play a single chord, but I was happy for the distraction, as none of them seemed to know what to say. I didn't, either. Oskar got out his mobile phone. Fredrik did too.

I don't know how long we just sat there, but finally I said: 'So aren't any of you going to ask?'

They looked at me. 'Ask you what?' Oskar said.

'If I did it. If I killed them.'

I noticed Fredrik glancing at my scabs. At the bloody piece of toilet paper I'd thrown on the floor. Right then and there it almost felt like I had done it. Like the evidence was right there in front of their eyes. I didn't know how to explain the scabs and the blood, so I just said:

'I didn't.'

I saw them exchanging looks. 'We never thought you did,' Kaiss said, but it didn't feel like he meant it. 'Would we be here if we did?'

I didn't know what to say to that.

For a moment or two we just sat there listening to Kaiss strumming the guitar, lost in our own thoughts.

'The only positive thing about this is that the girls want to be hugged all the time,' Fredrik said.

It made me laugh. Fredrik was desperate for a girlfriend.

'So go on, then,' I said. 'What are the rumours? What are people saying? What are *the police* saying?'

'Well,' Oskar started, taking his time, 'the police aren't saying much. They want to talk to everyone who was at the show last night.'

'That's going to take forever,' Fredrik said.

'But what about the rumours – what's everyone else saying?' I asked.

'They...' Oskar exchanged looks with the others again. 'People ... don't know.' I could tell that he was lying. That he only wanted to spare me.

'Lots of people have liked your post,' he said, looking at his phone. I could tell that he was on Facebook. And then he frowned for a moment, and looked at me quickly.

'What is it?' I asked.

Oskar didn't seem to know what to say. So he just handed me his phone. I looked at the screen and saw my own post about Mari and Johannes. Eighty-eight likes and thirteen comments. A lot of hearts and R.I.P.s. I scrolled to the bottom, and my heart almost stopped. Just a few minutes ago a guy called Børre Halvorsen had written:

You're lying. I saw you.

17
NOW

'What did you think when you read that?'

The prosecutor has her arms behind her back as she walks slowly up and down in front of me.

'Well, I was shocked,' I say. 'Couldn't really understand why he would write something like that. Or believe it.'

'Did you know Børre Halvorsen well?'

'Not really. I knew he was one of the taggers in town – the kids who do graffiti. But no, I didn't *know* him. I'd never spoken to him. I suppose he might have known me, though. Because of the football, maybe. I'd been in the local newspaper quite a lot.'

Ms Håkonsens purses her lips. 'And at that point you still didn't remember that you had been out the previous night, walking your dog?'

I shake my head and say no. A quiet murmur spreads across the room. The lawyer doesn't look at me while asking her next question.

'How did your friends react to Børre's comment?'

I search for Oskar's eyes in the audience. He doesn't want to meet mine.

18
THEN

I looked at the screen, my jaw dropping. I couldn't get a word out. I just sat there and stared.

'What the actual fuck?' I finally muttered.

Fredrik and Kaiss got out their phones to check the feed themselves.

'It's not true,' I told them, in a much quieter voice than I had intended. None of my friends answered. 'It's not true,' I repeated, louder this time. 'He can't have seen me. I was here, in my room, all evening. Tobias was at home, he knows, he can...'

No, I said to myself. He couldn't.

I handed Oskar his phone. No one said anything, they just nodded, slowly. Seventeen people had already liked Børre Halvorsen's comment.

They believed him.

They fucking believed him.

'Want us to find the idiot?' Oskar asked. 'Find out what the hell he's talking about?'

I wanted to find Børre myself and beat the shit out of him, telling lies like that, but I knew that would be stupid, so I said: 'Yeah. Maybe.' Then: 'Yes. That would be great, actually.'

Oskar leapt up from the bed. 'Alright,' he said, looking at Fredrik and Kaiss. 'Let's go, then.'

Kaiss put down the guitar. I got up, hoping for a hug or a fist bump as they left my room.

'Talk later,' Oskar said. He was already in the staircase. Fredrik put his hands in his pockets and just nodded as he walked past me.

'Talk later,' Kaiss said too, and hurried after the others.

'Yeah,' I replied, my voice all quiet and slow. I remained where I was while my friends walked up the stairs without saying another word. I heard the front door open and then shut a moment later. The silence in the house made me realise that I'd never felt more alone.

19

Yngve placed his finger on the doorbell, but waited a few seconds before pressing it. This was the worst part of his job – talking to people who'd just lost a loved one. He'd done it many times, but nothing ever really prepared you for it. This time, with a child involved, it was worse than ever.

The tiny woman who opened the door seemed to jump at the sight of him. She said 'hi' in a voice that was a little too loud – as if she was happy to see him. She introduced herself as Kari-Mette Bjerkaas, Mari's aunt, Cecilie Lindgren's sister. She had a small mouth with thin lips. And she was so lean, she reminded Yngve of a long-distance runner.

'Come on in,' she said with a low voice, as if she didn't want to wake someone.

Yngve entered and untidied his shoes. 'How are they doing?' he asked, even though he knew the question was silly.

'Cecilie won't come out of Mari's room,' Bjerkaas said. 'She hardly speaks. Frode is out on the veranda.'

She led Yngve into the living room.

'Can you please ask your sister whether she could speak to me for a few minutes? It would be really helpful.'

'I'll try.'

Bjerkaas offered him a thin smile, before quietly ascending the stairs. Yngve took a look around while he was waiting. He noticed some photos of Mari on the wall – one in which she was wearing a swimsuit with a medal hanging from her neck. There were trophies on the mantel. A drawing of a house and a sun. It said *Mari, 8 years* in the bottom right-hand corner. Her confirmation photo was also there, right next to a picture of the family on a hillside somewhere, with fjords and clouds in the background. Another photo showed Mari when she couldn't have been more than a few months old, but Yngve could easily recognise her features. She was lying on her stomach, head slightly tilted from the floor. Hairless. Smiling. Beautiful.

At that moment, Yngve was glad he and Åse had never managed to have kids. If they had, he wouldn't be the only one grieving like he was right now. He would have needed to consider, to take care of someone else, too. It was more than enough to look after himself.

Not that they hadn't tried for children. Åse just couldn't get pregnant. At one point they discussed IVF treatment, and even adoption, but in the end they just decided that it wasn't meant to be. A silly thing to say, maybe, but it was like they somehow were going to war with nature. Maybe there was a reason why they shouldn't have children.

A draught from an open door made Yngve turn to the veranda. He could see the back of a man sitting out there. He wandered outside and found Frode Lindgren sitting on the stairs that led down to the lawn. His face was ash grey, and his eyes were red and swollen. His feet extended out from the stairs and onto the grass. His feet were getting wet, but he didn't seem to care. When he saw Yngve he stood up and began to remove his drenched socks.

'Have you found the bastard who did this?' he asked, standing on one foot and without looking at Yngve.

'Not yet,' Yngve said. 'But we're working as fast as we can. Which is why I'm here. It's imperative that I speak to you. Both of you. Think you can do that?'

Frode lifted his shoulders before lowering them again. He

opened his mouth wide, as if to bring the muscles in his face back to life.

'Yeah,' he said eventually. 'Let's try that. Whatever you need.'

He motioned for Yngve to go back inside.

As Frode closed the veranda door behind them, Cecilie came slowly down the stairs. She was holding on to the bannister, her sister beside her, trying to keep her steady. Yngve offered them all his condolences, but none of them replied.

Cecilie sat down on the sofa. Her sister removed a cup and a glass from the coffee table, and left the room. Yngve produced a notepad and a pen.

'I'll try to do this as quickly as I can,' he said. The three of them were sitting opposite each other, in a triangle, the table between them. 'We're trying to get an idea of Mari's movements the last days before...' He didn't finish the sentence. 'Who she talked to, where she was, whether or not something in particular was bothering her...'

Frode looked at his wife. She was staring at something in front of her. Her eyelids moved slowly, as if even the slightest movement required effort.

As neither of them spoke Yngve pressed on: 'I assume she was at school?'

'I think so,' Frode said. 'I haven't been around the last couple of days.'

'You haven't?'

'No, I've been...'

Frode didn't finish the sentence. He looked at his wife, who continued to stare distantly in front of her.

'Do you know if Mari had argued with anyone? Friends? School mates?'

Frode was now rolling his wet socks into a ball. 'Not that we know of,' he said. 'Mari was...' He looked away for a beat. 'She had a lot of friends,' he continued. 'Everybody liked Mari. At least, that was my impression.'

'What about you, Cecilie?' Yngve asked.

Tears were streaming down her face, but she didn't make a sound. She was moving her head slowly from side to side.

'She was seeing Even Tollefsen until recently?' Yngve asked.

Somewhere in the house a phone rang, but the noise stopped almost immediately. A heavy silence followed.

'Yes, she ... was,' Frode replied.

'Do you know what happened between them?'

Frode squeezed his socks so hard his knuckles turned white. He looked at his wife briefly, then shook his head.

'Did either of you go to the school performance last night?'

'I ... did,' Frode said.

'You went alone?'

'Yes, Cecilie didn't...' Again he didn't finish.

Yngve waited a moment before continuing. 'Did you speak to your daughter while you were there?'

'Only briefly. She was very busy.'

Yngve used the pause that followed to make a few notes, mostly to fill time. Then looked up again. 'We couldn't find Mari's mobile phone,' he said in a soft voice. 'Neither in her bag, nor anywhere else at school. Do you have any idea where it might be?'

'I don't know,' Frode said.'

'It's broken.' Cecilie's voice was quiet and slow.

'What happened?'

'I don't know. I just know that it's broken.'

'So where is it?'

'Repair shop, probably.'

'Do you know which one?'

She shrugged.

Yngve nodded and made a note.

'We couldn't find her keys, either,' he continued. 'Do you know if they're here?'

'I can check,' Frode said and got up. He seemed happy to have something to do.

Yngve tried to make eye contact with Cecilie while her husband was out of the room, but it was almost as if she was in a trance.

'They're not in the basket in the hall,' Frode said as he returned and sat down. 'That's where she leaves them.'

'Alright. Is there anything about the keys that would make it easier for us to identify them?'

'The keychain has a blue-and-white string on it,' Frode offered. 'I think it has three keys.'

Yngve made a note of that as well. Then waited a beat before asking: 'She had started to work for the school newspaper, is that right?' Once more he looked from one parent to the other.

'Yes,' Frode said and lowered his head again.

Yngve waited for Cecilie to speak, but she didn't.

'According to my colleague your daughter came by the precinct the other day, asking questions about a car accident. Do you know anything about that?'

Cecilie started to sob. Frode squeezed the socks again.

Yngve knew he had to press them. 'Do you know anything about that?' He turned towards Cecilie this time, as if addressing her directly.

Slowly she lifted her gaze, then whispered a dry no. She then turned towards her husband, whose cheek muscles were pulsing – on and off, on and off.

'No, we don't know anything about that,' he said quickly.

Again Yngve took his time writing.

'We also found Ole Hoff's business card among Mari's things,' he said. 'Did she talk to you about needing to speak to him about something?'

Frode stood up and took a few steps away from them. Cecilie followed his movements with tear-filled eyes. Frode had his back towards them, one hand on his hip, the other in front of his eyes.

Yngve waited.

And waited.

'I ... gave it to her,' Frode Lindgren finally said. 'Ole's business card.'

He turned to face Yngve. Fresh tears had formed shiny stripes on his cheeks. He wiped them away with the sleeve of his shirt and snorted at the same time. 'The other day, she asked me about that ... car accident.'

'Which car accident?'

Frode looked at Cecilie. All of a sudden his eyes seemed angry.

'The accident in which Jimmy Tollefsen was killed,' he said.

'Even's father,' Yngve said, for confirmation.

'Yes,' Frode said. 'I didn't know much about it, so I suggested she should go and ask Ole. He was already working at the *Fredheim Chronicle* back then.' Frode's voice had picked up some pace and intensity.

'So ... you *did* know that Mari was working on that particular story.' Yngve said it as something between a remark and a question.

Seconds passed before Frode said: 'Yes, I...' Then he shook his head. 'I'm sorry. This is all a bit too much for us right now. I hope you can appreciate that.'

'Of course,' Yngve said.

He waited a few seconds, then nodded and got up slowly.

'I want you to call me if you can think of anything that might be important to the investigation. Anything at all. I'm available around the clock. I'm usually awake, too, so it's really no bother if you call.' He handed Frode his business card. 'Thanks for agreeing to talk to me.'

Cecilie neither replied nor moved as Yngve headed for the hall and put on his shoes. Frode walked him out.

'Is it alright if I send a team over to take a look at Mari's room?' Yngve asked. 'They might find something important.'

'Yes, of course,' Frode said. 'That's perfectly alright.'

Yngve offered his hand. Frode took it with a firm grip.

'Take care of each other now,' Yngve said. 'You and Cecilie.'

Frode opened his mouth as if to say something, but he stopped himself and looked away.

'Just ... catch that son-of-a-bitch,' he said. 'You hear me, Mork? Just get that bastard.'

'We'll do everything we can,' Yngve said. 'You have my word on that.'

20

Yngve drove straight back to the handball court, which was located in a separate building a few hundred yards away from the school's main entrance. It was raining so hard as he arrived, it was almost impossible to see through the car windows.

Yngve parked right in front of the entrance to the court. He ran up the stairs to avoid the rain, but he was still wet through in seconds, and not for the first time today.

Inside he met up with Vibeke Hanstveit.

'We've conducted thirty-four interviews so far,' the police attorney said.

'Good,' Yngve said as he took off his police jacket and hung it up to dry. 'Anything interesting yet?'

'I don't know. I've only just collected them.'

A student – a girl with long, straight hair – came out of one of the changing rooms, a woman beside her. Yngve assumed it was her mother. Both looked at him nervously.

He fetched himself a cup of coffee, then sat down to look through the pile of interview transcripts. He flicked through them, looking for mentions of when the students had left the school premises the previous night, who they were with, and if they noticed anything out of the ordinary – anything the police could or should be aware of. About midway through the pile he stopped and looked at a quote from an interviewee named Frida Higraff.

Even Tollefsen says that he wasn't there, but I've heard that he was. If I were you, I would talk to him about this.

Beside, in the margin, the detective who had conducted the interview had written:

Check Facebook, and check <u>BØRRE HALVORSEN</u>.

Yngve was about to do just that when Therese Kyrkjebø entered the room. She stamped hard a few times, to shake the water from her shoes. Her hair was wet, too, as were her clothes, which strained across her growing bump.

'How did it go at Johannes Eklund's parents?' Yngve asked.

'As expected,' Therese answered with a sigh. 'They are in shock, obviously. Heartbroken. Johannes hadn't argued with anyone they could think of. He was a happy kid. Popular.'

Therese also got herself some coffee. 'How did it go at Mari's?'

Yngve told them how quiet Cecilie and Frode had become when he asked them about Even Tollefsen and the car accident.

'Which car accident?' Hanstveit asked, and Yngve filled them in.

'Mari came by the office the other day and asked if she could see the police report,' Therese said. 'She was writing a piece about it.' She blew on the contents of her cup. 'We don't usually hand out stuff like that, so I just said no, she couldn't.' She took a sip and made a face as if it was still too hot. 'But it's a bit more interesting now, of course. As Mari was seeing Jimmy Tollefsen's son up until a few days before her murder.'

Yngve told them how Frode Lindgren had initially said that he didn't know what kind of story Mari was working on for the school newspaper, but later admitted that he did.

'So he lied about it at first?' Hanstveit said.

'It would appear so,' Yngve said.

'Why lie about something like that?' Therese wondered.

'Why lie in general?' Yngve asked back. 'You do it to hide something. In an ongoing police investigation, in the case of their murdered daughter, I find that suspicious. Weird, in fact.'

There was a moment's silence.

'So ... do you think the car accident has something to do with...?' Hanstveit didn't finish the sentence. She didn't have to.

'I don't see how it can,' Yngve said at first. 'I worked that case myself over a decade ago. I remember it well, too. There was nothing suspicious about it. Jimmy had a turn of some kind. Susanne, his wife, tried to take over the wheel, but it was too late. Crash, boom...'

Another student entered the building, accompanied by a man. Hanstveit approached them and showed them where to go.

'But I guess it wouldn't hurt to look at that report again,' she said when she got back. 'Just in case.'

'By all means,' Yngve said. 'I don't think we'll find anything, though.'

They drank their coffee in silence for a little while. Yngve moved another piece of paper from the pile and started at the top of another interview.

'Johannes' parents wondered if we'd found his microphones,' Therese said after a beat. 'He always brought them in some kind of case. They were special, the microphones. Expensive.'

'Their kid's been murdered, and that's what they ask you?' Yngve said.

'They asked me all kinds of things, but as far as the microphones go, I think they had some kind of sentimental value to them; don't ask me how. They wanted them back, though, if we could find them."

Yngve tried to recall the crime scene. No, he hadn't seen a case anywhere. He put down his coffee cup and prepared to leave.

'Where are you going?' Therese called after him.

'To talk to the forensics team,' he said.

'Wait, I'll come with you.'

Back inside the school Yngve and Therese managed to find Ann-Mari Sara from the Kripos team on the second floor, outside the music room. Yngve asked her if they had found a microphone case. Sara consulted a large form inside a see-through plastic folder.

'Nope,' she confirmed. 'No case.'

Yngve turned to Therese. 'I want you to find out exactly what that case looks like,' he said. 'Pictures, preferably from all angles, would be perfect. If Johannes Eklund was careful about his microphones, it's likely that he had them with him when he was leaving the school premises last night. He obviously got into a fight with his killer,' he said, 'so the killer might have torn it from his hands.'

'And since we haven't found any cases here...'

'...then that may well be our murder weapon.'

21

I spent the rest of the afternoon in bed, staring at the ceiling, thinking about the murderer – who was still out there somewhere. I tried to wrap my head around what had happened, and why. My brain was working at full speed. It was impossible to shut it down. I kept seeing Mari in front of me. Alive and well. Sometimes my mind went crazy and imagined all kinds of ways she had been killed. I wondered what she had looked like when the police found her. The thoughts made me nauseous.

I pictured the scarf Mari always wore when it was cold – a big, fluffy red one. It was so huge it was like a blanket. I felt her hand in mine when we were at the cinema, her nails digging into my skin when she jumped at something scary in the movie. I remembered when she caught her finger in the door at home, and pretended it didn't hurt. She swallowed the pain, but the tears in her shiny, beautiful, brown eyes gave her away just a few seconds later. And then I had hugged her.

It was dark outside my basement window when Imo called.

'Hey champ,' he shouted into his phone. He was in the car. 'Get ready,' he said. 'I'll be there to pick you up in three minutes.'

'You're going to pick me up?'

There was a slight pause. 'Your mum didn't tell you?'

'Tell me what?' I asked.

My uncle sighed heavily at the other end. 'You're spending the night at my place.'

'I am?'

'You are. You need to be with someone tonight, and your mother … well, you know what she's like about death.'

I knew what he meant. When Gran died, my mother cried for days and days. I knew it wasn't just because her mother had passed – she'd been ill for years, after all, and Mum had said on more than one occasion that she hoped she wouldn't go on suffering for long. The reason Mum was so upset, I always thought, was because Gran's death, the funeral afterwards and all the attention Mum got in the days that followed, made her think of Dad again.

And now, death was here again – and it had come a little too close for comfort. One of the victims was my ex-girlfriend. A girl my mother had met.

'What about Tobias?' I asked.

'Oh, he had other plans,' Imo said.

I could only imagine what kind. He would probably put a pizza or two in the oven and then sit up in his room all night playing CoD or FIFA or whatever.

'Not sure I really want to do this today,' I said.

'No, maybe not, but you're going to anyway,' Imo said. 'It's not right for you to be alone tonight.'

I thought about it for a few moments.

'Come on,' my uncle said. 'I promised your mum I'd look after you. Don't be a spoilsport.'

I sighed and sat down on the bed, stroked my hair back.

'OK,' I said, 'Give me five minutes.'

Imo was sitting in the car with the engine running when I came out of the house. The window on the passenger side was open.

'Tell me you haven't eaten,' he shouted.

To be honest, I hadn't given much thought to food at all over the past few days.

'I haven't,' I said.

'Well, you've got something to look forward to then,' he said with a grin. 'Tonight, I'll cook you an Imo Special.'

An 'Imo Special' was nothing more than ready-made lasagne, garlic bread and a homemade salad, but it was a good meal. I'd had it plenty of times at his house.

I got into the car, which smelled fresh and clean for a change. Imo pulled me close. 'How are you, champ?' he said, while patting my shoulder. I sighed.

'Not good.'

I pulled out my phone and showed him Børre Halvorsen's Facebook comment. My uncle frowned as he read it.

'It's complete nonsense, of course,' I said. 'I was in my room all night.'

Imo said nothing for a short while. He looked like he was thinking. 'Just ignore it then,' he said at last, and put his hand on the gearstick. 'As long as you stick to the truth, there's no reason to worry.'

'I'm not really worried either,' I said, even though it felt like a lie. 'I'm more pissed off that he wrote what he did, and that people are liking it or thinking there might be some truth to it.'

Imo put the car into gear. 'Don't bother about it,' he said. 'It's probably a misunderstanding. It'll sort itself out.'

I decided to believe him.

It was still raining. I couldn't believe the amount of rain that continued to pour down on us. It was like God was angry or something. The streetlights made golden circles on the wet pavements. And even though it was windy, leaves were stuck to the ground.

There wasn't much traffic, but every time we met a car, it felt like the drivers and the passengers were staring at us, me in particular. The few people that were out walking also seemed to stop and follow us with their eyes. I watched them, wondering how much they knew about what had happened, if one of them was the murderer. I knew it was a stupid thought, but I couldn't stop myself.

As we headed towards the centre of Fredheim, I turned to Imo and said: 'Can we drive by the school?'

He looked at me. 'You mean now?'

'Yes.'

'Why do you want to go there, Even? I mean, now?'

I wasn't really sure myself, I just felt like I needed to see the place again. It was still so unreal, what had happened. Maybe I just needed to see if the nightmare was real or not. Imo gave me a long look. Then nodded reluctantly.

'Oh my God,' I said as we drove up the slope leading to the school.

Cars with media logos on their bonnets and vans with satellite dishes on their roofs were parked just outside the school perimeter. I saw men and women who presumably had never set foot in our tiny little town before, but were here in numbers, as part of their job. I saw faces I'd only ever seen on TV. Camera crews, radio journalists with microphones in their hands. Others who were checking the light on their cameras or talking to someone on the phone. It dawned on me for the first time that this wasn't something that only concerned us in Fredheim. It affected the whole of Norway.

The school building was still cordoned off. There were several police cars outside the entrance. I thought I saw people turning towards us, and I slid down in my seat. It was as though a wall of hate and suspicion had sprung up in front of me.

I looked over to the handball court, where we normally had PE. There were loads of people outside that entrance as well.

'That's where they're interviewing people,' Imo said. 'The police, that is.'

It was too far away for me to recognise anyone.

'Have they questioned you yet?' I asked.

'I haven't been interviewed formally yet, no. I did speak to Mork this morning, though. Briefly.'

'What did he ask you?'

My uncle took a deep breath. 'He wanted to know when I left the school, what exit I'd used, if I'd seen anything. Just a few basic questions really, to begin with. First they just want to work out who they need to talk to some more.'

'And you're one of them?'

Imo shrugged and said: 'I don't think so, but ... who knows?'

I moved in my seat so I could face him better. 'Did you see anything?' I asked. 'Did you see Mari?'

'I did,' he said. 'Straight after the show. She was going to interview Johannes.'

I stared at him, waiting for more. 'I was busy talking to people,' he continued. 'You know what it's like after a show. Everyone wants a word. I had some equipment to sort out as well, so I didn't really pay attention to anything. Then I went home.'

'How many people were still there when you left?'

He turned to me with a fleeting smile. 'That's what Mork asked me as well. Hard to say. I didn't count. Fifteen, twenty people, maybe.'

'Did you know them? Could you recognise them, do you think?

Imo sighed. 'I was tired. I really didn't think about anything apart from getting home.'

I could understand that. Imo had been working day and night in the run-up to the show.

'Have you seen enough?' he asked.

'I think so,' I replied.

'OK,' he said and put a firm hand on my thigh. 'Let's eat, then. I'm starving.'

22
NOW

'So you felt the net was closing in around you?' Ms Håkonsen asks with her back turned to me. She's looking into the audience, as if enjoying the attention.

'I did,' I say. 'Definitely.'

'At that point, how did you feel about your mother?' The prosecutor turns around to face me again. 'I mean, she'd picked a fight with you over a reporter, for no apparent reason, at least as far as you knew, and she shied away from her duty as a mother on a night that clearly wasn't easy for you, her son.'

It wasn't really a question, but she clearly wants me to say something in reply.

'Like I said before, I was used to Mum being weird and ... non-mummish, if that's even a word.'

Ms Håkonsen smiles. 'I'm sure it's admissible.'

I smile back. Then, like the flick of a switch, she's dead serious again.

'Did you know, at the time, that your mother had been to the school show that night?'

'I hadn't thought to ask if she had been, but I knew she had a ticket. I was supposed to play in the band, and Imo was the musical director – and I know she doesn't like to waste money, so I presumed she was still going.'

'Did you have any suspicions about your mother at that time?'

'About Mum being involved in the murders somehow?'

'Yes, that's what I'm asking.'

'No, I did not.'

Ms Håkonsen seems to think about that for a moment.

'OK. Take us through your evening with Imo. It was a rather special night, wasn't it?'

I breathe in sharply, then let the air out slowly through my nose.

'It most certainly was.'

23
THEN

Imo's house was about eight kilometres outside Fredheim, in the middle of nowhere. As well as being a musician, my uncle was a pig farmer. He had built a small music studio next to the pig shed. My friends and I were free to use it whenever we wanted.

He parked his big old green Mercedes outside the house, as close as possible to the front step. It was a lot darker here than in town. Trees of all kinds surrounded the farm. My uncle didn't bother with any extra lighting, except for a small lamp on the wall outside the house. A strong gust of wind made the leaves and the branches move, like they were dancing. It smelled of forest and mud as well. The rain had eased off a bit. Now it was just an icy drizzle.

I helped my uncle carry the shopping bags inside and couldn't help but notice that he'd been to the off-licence as well.

'First,' he said, putting the bags on the worktop, 'we'll fill our stomachs. Then...' he took out a bottle with the picture of a cactus on the label '...we'll get shitfaced.'

I raised my eyebrows.

'Come on, don't pretend you haven't been hammered before. And if there was ever an evening when you need it, champ, it's today. Tonight, I mean. Just don't tell your mum. She might be as fragile as a leaf these days, but boy, when she's angry, she's dangerous.'

He smiled and winked at me. I took a step closer and looked at the bottle.

'Tequila, Imo?'

'Mhm?'

He moved quickly around the kitchen, opening the fridge, turning on the oven, pulling out drawers and getting out dishes and plates and pots and pans. 'Have you got a problem with tequila?' he asked.

'I don't know,' I said. 'I've never tried it before.'

I didn't feel like drinking at all. The rage that I'd felt when Børre first posted his comment had drained away, but Mari was back in my thoughts again, and it was starting to really sink in that I would never ever see her again. I found it hard to think of anything but how it felt to hold her, how her head sometimes rested against my chest, how she liked to listen to my heart beating. It was suddenly difficult to breathe.

I tried to eat something, as I worried about how the evening might end if I didn't. Imo was right, I had had a few beers before, but I certainly wasn't a seasoned drinker. My friends sometimes teased me about it, saying I was always so serious about my football. *Come on, loosen up a bit*, they'd say.

When we'd finished eating, Imo poured some tequila into a small schnapps glass. 'The normal thing would be to drink this with salt and lemon,' he said. 'But normal is boring, so I normally don't bother.'

I looked at him. 'So ... you don't like boring, which is why you're doing something boring?'

He looked at me quizzically.

'You said you *normally* don't bother.'

He laughed at me and smiled. 'I knew you had a decent head on you. Go on, take a small sip, just for starters.'

I did as I was told. Even though I swallowed only a teaspoonful, it burned all the way down my throat. I coughed. My uncle laughed again.

'One more,' he said. 'You'll get used to it after a while.'

I could not for the life of me understand why people voluntarily drank this. And even claimed to like it.

'It's good, isn't it?'

I sent Imo a pointed look and took another sip. 'If you love barbed wire,' I said, having tried once more to swallow it. My head felt like it was on fire.

'I'll go put some music on,' Imo said. 'Let's leave all the washing-up. I can do that in the morning. The mice will be happy.'

Soon music was pouring out of the enormous loudspeakers in Imo's living room. As I sat on the sofa he put out a bowl of crisps, while humming to the music and doing a kind of dance. 'It sounds like he's playing seven guitars simultaneously,' he said.

We were listening to Tommy Emmanuel, Imo's favourite guitarist. He just couldn't stop moving to the music. He refilled my glass and spilled a little. I reluctantly took another sip. The tequila still made my throat and chest burn, but not as much as before.

We sat there for a while, just listening to the music, drinking. Imo sent a text to someone.

'Just checking that your brother is OK,' he said.

I looked at the bottle. We'd finished maybe a quarter of it. I was starting to feel the effects.

'So how come you never got married, Imo?'

He looked at me with a frown. 'Why do you ask?'

I really didn't know, and I said so. Maybe it was because it was impossible not to think of Mari all the time. Truth be told, before she died I had started to think of her as someone I would be with for a very long time. I knew it was silly – we hadn't been dating that long, and we were still young – but I just hadn't been able to stop myself.

'Well,' Imo started, then paused. 'It's never really been that important to me. And anyway,' he said, patting his belly as he burped discreetly, 'it would be a shame to keep all this Imo for just one person, don't you think?'

He laughed at his own joke. I smiled and took a sip. He did the same.

'Has there never been ... someone special?' I asked, pulling a face at the mouthful I'd just swallowed.

Imo angled his left ear to his shoulder, then did the same with his right. The bones in his neck cracked. 'Well, yes,' he said, and lowered his eyes. 'Of course there has.'

'So what happened?'

He let out a heavy sigh. 'Nothing,' he said. 'I guess that was the problem.'

Imo leaned forwards and emptied his glass. Poured himself another. There was still a fair bit left in my glass.

'She didn't want me, so...' He left the rest of the sentence hanging.

My phone rang. I glanced at the screen. Oskar. I stood up and went into the kitchen.

'What's up?' I said, and closed the door behind me. 'Did you find Børre?'

'We did,' Oskar said.

'And?'

He waited a moment. 'He said that he did see you yesterday evening.'

I snorted. 'And where would that have been, exactly?'

'At school. In one of the windows on the first floor.'

'That's bullshit,' I said angrily. 'I was at home the whole time. Sitting in my room. Jesus.'

Oskar didn't say anything. It felt like I wasn't talking to my friend. He was having doubts about me too. I could hear it in his voice.

'So...' I began. I didn't know quite what to say. Or believe. 'I didn't kill them, Oskar,' I said.

He still didn't answer. 'If you think I did, Oskar, just say it. Tell me straight.'

He hesitated.

'Come on,' I urged him. 'Tell me what you're thinking.'

'You have to admit, Even, it does all seem a bit weird.'

'Yes,' I said. 'It feels bloody fucking weird that you don't believe me when I say that I was in my room all last night.'

My forehead was burning. No just because of the tequila. I wanted to punch something again.

But I didn't. Instead, I just said: 'If you don't believe me, Oskar, why don't you just go ahead and fuck yourself.'

24

When I got back to the living room, Imo had topped up my glass. I grabbed it and downed it in one.

'Whoa,' Imo said. 'Easy now.'

I banged the glass back down on the table and tried to get the flames in my chest to die down. It took a while.

'More bad news?' Imo asked.

'You could say that,' I said, and swallowed. I explained about Børre and Oskar. Imo listened attentively.

'And you're absolutely sure you didn't go out last night?'

I sent him a hard look and said: 'Jesus, Imo, how could I *not* be sure about that? Don't *you* believe me either?'

'Yes, yes, relax. Of course I believe you. I'm just thinking about what everyone else might believe. If you say no, you didn't go out, and then later remember that you did, even if it was only to take out the trash or take that little dog of yours for a walk, then everyone will think you were lying about everything else as well.'

I took a deep breath.

GP.

My God.

I *had* been out last night. My heart started thumping in my chest. How the hell could I have forgotten about that?

I reached for the bottle and poured another shot, but I waited before downing it.

'Did Børre Halvorsen say *when* he saw you in the window on the first floor?' Imo asked. I shook my head and said no, before adding: 'And it wasn't *me* he saw.'

'No, no,' Imo said. 'Of course not.'

We sat there for a time, taking the odd sip. Imo got his phone out again and remained quiet for a while. I got out my own and found a news article about the police press conference. They were looking for a person who 'in all likelihood escaped through a window on the first floor sometime after 11 p.m. yesterday evening'.

My stomach started to swirl.

The police were also appealing for anyone who might know the whereabouts of Johannes' microphone case to come forward. I remembered that he was always very fussy about his microphones. 'They cost megabucks,' he used to say. 'That's why they sound so fucking good. My grandfather gave them to me.'

I checked my social media feeds again. I wanted to know if anyone else had seen me. I didn't see any new comments. But each time I saw a picture of Mari or Johannes, it was as if a rope tightened around my neck, squeezing life and energy out of me. Just stick to the truth, I reminded myself. You didn't do anything.

Imo and I took turns choosing what music to listen to – albums first, then single tracks. And I don't know at what point it happened, but suddenly the whole room was out of focus. My movements got slower. Any words I tried to speak came out as a mixture of spit and breath.

A sound far away ricocheted around in my head, and it took a few moments before I realised my phone was ringing again. For a moment I hoped it was Oskar calling back to apologise, but it wasn't. It was his father. Ole.

I stood up again and struggled for a few seconds while the room spun around me. I managed to find the green button then pressed the phone to my right ear. Or was it the left? I couldn't say for sure.

'Hi Even, it's Ole Hoff. I hope I'm not disturbing you.'

'No, no,' I said – shouted. Luckily they were easy words to pronounce. I closed a door. Didn't know exactly which one, but there was definitely less noise, and that was the most important thing.

'How are you?' Ole asked.

'Marvellous,' I said. And it sounded like I meant it too. 'Bloody marvellous,' I said, for some reason.

'So you haven't seen what they're writing about you on Facebook?'

I sighed. My mood nosedived. 'Well, yes,' I said, more subdued.

'What do you think about it?' he asked. Was there a hint of suspicion in his voice too? I wasn't sure.

'Well...' I said, 'I think that everyone probably thinks I did it. That I killed them.' It felt as though the words were all coming out of my mouth at the same time.

'So you're saying you weren't at school yesterday? That Børre Halvorsen couldn't possibly have seen you?'

I tried to arrange all the words he said so they made sense. 'Hm?'

Ole repeated what he had just said.

I thought for a bit. 'No,' I replied.

There was a short pause. Or was it long? I couldn't tell. Then he said: 'I've written a piece for the newspaper. Thought I'd go over your quotes before I send it to the printers. Is that alright with you?'

'Yes!' I shouted.

'OK, I'll start reading then.'

I realised that I had somehow managed to find my way into the kitchen. I held on to a chair while listening to Ole's voice, but I couldn't make out a single word he was saying. I have no idea how long it took before he stopped speaking, and I think maybe my eyes slowly closed towards the end. I came to again when I heard my name.

'Hm?'

'Does that sound OK with you?' he asked.

'Yes,' I said. 'No problem.'

Pause.

'Is everything OK, Even?'

'Everythingsfine.'

Another pause. There was some movement in my stomach. It felt as if something was making its way up towards my throat.

'Are you drunk, Even?'

'ME? NO!'

I let go of the chair, put down my phone, knocked over an empty bottle that was standing on the floor, and almost tripped on the rug in the hall. But then I caught sight of the door to the toilet. I managed to grab the door handle, which stopped me from falling flat on my face. I pushed it down and saw the porcelain in front of me and – lucky me – the toilet seat was already up, so I dropped down on all fours.

Somewhere on the way, my mind cleared momentarily and I wondered what Oskar's dad had really written. But then I thought of Mari's warm hands again.

A few moments later I heard someone laugh behind me.

'Amateur,' Imo was saying.

He helped me to my feet and flushed the toilet for me, making a face.

'Your mother's going to kill me,' he said, as the water sloshed around the toilet bowl.

'Hah,' I said, now able to focus for a second or two. 'Right now I wouldn't mind doing that myself.'

25

Well, this is eight minutes of your life you're never going to get back, Susanne Tollefsen thought. Eight minutes walking, incline level two, with nothing else to stare at but the wall and the basement window in front of her. She had almost given up, several times. All she could think of while she was moving forward, or not moving at all, depending on how you looked at it, was when it would all be over, when she could once more go up to Knut's apartment and mix herself a drink. Her tongue tingled just at the thought of it.

Thankfully she was alone. Not many people used this basement gym, the fifty-square-metre room in which she'd never thought she would ever actually find herself. Knut had insisted she got a key to the gym when they started dating a little over a year ago. 'Exercise helps,' the dimwit had said. 'Exercise is good for a lot of things.'

Easy for him to say; he ran 10k every other day. Exercise didn't do a damned thing for her. After a long day in the shop, her legs and head were heavy. She'd been walking back and forth between the shelves for hours, even though customers had been few and far between. She had seen some people inside the mall, though, people who had turned and pointed a finger in her direction when they thought she wasn't looking.

Some people who didn't know who she was had entered the shop, filled with anticipation and visions of what their soon-to-be-borns would look like in a light-blue babygro, a pink hat or a couple of delicate, fluffy socks. Susanne was happy for them. She remembered those days with affection. The certainty that they were *creating a family*. They were laying the foundations for the rest of their lives.

But instead of helping the parents-to-be, instead of supporting and sharing all her experience and wisdom as a mother, instead of telling them all about the wonderful times ahead, she'd found herself overwhelmed by the need to warn them. Stop, she had wanted to say. Go back, before it's too late. You have no idea what you're getting yourselves into.

But it *was* already too late. Everyone who entered the store was past the stage when they had shared the news of the pregnancy with their family and friends. And what the hell was she going to tell them anyway: that the likelihood of them going their separate ways in a year or ten was huge? That they wouldn't love each other anymore when the hardships of their everyday lives became too demanding, or when other temptations crossed their paths sometime in the future? That it was – that it *is* – incredibly difficult to raise one child, let alone two? That it was insanely, fucking hard?

She couldn't do that.

What good would that do?

Susanne had been glad that social services had managed to get her a job. She'd just wished it could be something different, somewhere else. She didn't need daily reminders of how good life could be. How good life once had been.

Nine minutes.

She was sweaty. Or maybe just warm, she wasn't sure. The sound of the treadmill almost hypnotised her. She found herself humming to the sound of it, trying to hold the notes as long as possible, just as she had when she had been singing in the choir with Cecilie and the others. Susanne hadn't sung in years, though, and she didn't have the breath for it anymore, either, nor the stomach muscles. So she stopped and watched the digital display instead, the white dot that was halfway through a 400-metre lap. She urged it to move forwards, one blip at a time.

She felt guilty about Tobias, who would be home alone once again. What difference did it make, though? Tobias was happy as long as he was left to himself in his room. He never came down to the living room to watch TV with her these days. It was the same with Even; when he wasn't at football practice he was hanging out with his friends. But at least he had them. Tobias didn't, except maybe that Ruben idiot from Solstad.

Susanne had realised a long time ago that it had been a mistake to move back to Fredheim. The house was too big, and everywhere she looked, she noticed things that needed fixing. Her mother had left tons of junk in the attic and the outhouse. It would take Susanne years just to go through it all.

But Fredheim was her home.

It was where she'd grown up, and for a long time she had loved it: singing in the choir, working at Myhrvold's garden centre, meeting people every day. Just hanging out with Jimmy and the kids. She had thought that coming back to her roots would do her a world of good, that it would be easier for her to find her true self again. She'd thought it would be easier for Tobias, too. She had hoped that he, that *they*, could start over.

Instead, everything in Fredheim reminded her of Jimmy, just as it had before they left. The car crash that ended his life had ruined hers too. But now that she had given Fredheim a second chance, she couldn't just leave again. She simply couldn't do that to her boys.

Sometimes the sound of the crash filled her mind – the smell of the trees they had hit, the burning stench from the engine reaching her nose as she came to. Sometimes as she woke up she could taste the blood on her lips. She would search for the tiny bits of broken glass that she first thought were diamonds.

Ten minutes.

Finally.

Susanne turned off the machine and got off the treadmill. Silence, at last. She exhaled and took a look at the mats, the weights, the ropes, the rubber bands. She didn't feel like using any of it; she just wanted a drink. Another one, to be fair – she'd had one before she came down into the gym. Alright, she'd had two.

There was Knut, obviously. Knut was company. He never demanded anything of her. And even if she knew she was never going to love him, Susanne was sure of his love, no matter what, even if she really couldn't understand why. There wasn't a thing in the world he wouldn't do for her. Maybe he just loved the memory of her, she thought. The girl he'd been head-over-heels with ever since junior high. Maybe she was just a nostalgia crush. Or maybe he thought he'd finally won his trophy.

She stopped in front of the punch bag and hit it, once. Not hard, but hard enough for her knuckles to hurt. She hit it again. She thought of Ole Hoff, and hit the bag again. And again. Now she could see parts of her skin starting to turn red.

You shouldn't have been so angry, she said to herself. Not with Even. It wasn't his fault that people were talking about him in Fredheim. That reporters wanted to speak to him. The police. She should probably talk to them herself soon. Everyone who'd been in the school theatre last night had been encouraged to talk to them voluntarily. But just the thought of Ole Hoff made her hit the bag again. Soon she was bleeding.

The door to the gym opened. Knut was standing there, as always dressed in his dark-blue cab driver's uniform. 'So this is where you're hiding,' he said.

'Hiding?' she spat back at him. 'I'm not hiding. I'm … exercising.'

Knut had been asleep on the sofa when she got home from work. She didn't want to wake him – he'd been working late the previous night. And when he had come to bed it had taken him ages to fall asleep. He'd been tossing and turning for hours.

'Off to work?' she asked.

'Yeah,' he replied. 'What are your plans for the evening?'

Susanne could feel the flames in her chest come to life again. She took a quick look at her red knuckles and thought: That, Knut, you really don't want to know.

26

Yngve locked his front door behind him, hung his jacket up to dry – again – and took off his shoes. Then he listened for sounds he knew he wouldn't hear. Her shoes weren't in the hall, either, of course. None of her coats were on their hooks. No smell of the perfume she used to wear.

He went into the kitchen and looked at the mess he'd left behind that morning: the newspaper, the plate with a half-eaten piece of bread spread with dark-grey liver paste. The glass of juice with sludgy chunks in it. He cleared it all away and then took a beer from the fridge. Decided to drink it in the living room. He didn't want the TV on. He just sat there in silence, and drank.

He was in the middle of a sip, when he noticed her standing in the doorway leading to the basement. She was wondering why he was so upset.

'Is it that obvious?' he asked.

She didn't answer, but took a step closer. Put her hands behind her back and leaned against the wall. She waited for him to explain, so he did. He told her what he'd seen and learned during the day, even though he knew she'd been with him the whole time. Sometimes it helped to say things out loud. Things became clearer. Easier to grasp or understand.

Åse looked at him with those big, beautiful eyes that never seemed to blink. Eyes full of blue life ... until they weren't anymore. She said that he was making sense of this, that the case would be solved, and if *he* wasn't the one to piece the puzzle together, he had people around him who could. Who were good people; who helped. That was the most important thing – that they got their answers.

Yngve finished his beer and went to work. In front of him, on the living room table, was the ten-year-old report he had filed after Jimmy Tollefsen's car accident on a road a few kilometres outside Fredheim. It wasn't a particularly thick file. Jimmy had fallen ill somehow and passed out, and although Susanne had tried to take the wheel, she hadn't been able to steer them clear of the trees along the side of the road. At least, Yngve said to himself, that's what she'd told him afterwards.

So what was it about the accident that had caught Mari Lindgren's eye?

The interviews that had been conducted at the handball court earlier today were also piled on the table. There were 112 so far. *There was something in Even's eyes*, one of the girls had said. *A blackness*. She had observed Even on the school premises earlier that day, when he was looking for Mari. It wasn't much to bring to the district attorney's office, but Yngve had seen the grazes on Even's hands, and he had wondered if the boy was a brilliant actor – his grief and his anguish had seemed so real. The part about Børre Halvorsen having seen Even at school – at a window on the first floor – Yngve had to admit he really didn't know what to make of that.

Once again he punched the number for Børre's mother, Filippa, into his phone. He had tried to call her several times earlier in the day, as Børre's own phone seemed to be disconnected.

She answered with a slow, sleepy voice. Finally. Yngve introduced himself and told her that he was trying to get hold of her son.

'What's he done this time?' she asked.

'Nothing,' Yngve replied. 'I just want to talk to him.'

'Børre isn't here,' she said. 'I have no idea where he is.'

'When do you think he'll be in?'

'He doesn't live here anymore', she sighed. 'Not regularly, at least. He comes by every now and then. When he wants money.'

Yngve heard Filippa Halvorsen take a long drag on a cigarette.

'So where does he live now, then?'

'With his lousy excuse of a father. Or ... with friends. I don't know.' There was a spiteful tone in her voice.

'How old is your son?' Yngve asked.

'Fifteen. No, sorry, he just turned sixteen.'

Yngve told Filippa Halvorsen to get Børre to call him back, if she saw him that evening. 'Or I can just stop by his school tomorrow.'

'Heh,' she snorted. 'Good luck with that.'

Yngve was about to ask what she meant, but Filippa Halvorsen beat him to it. 'They called me from his school last week and asked if I knew where he was. I didn't have a clue, I thought he was with his father.'

She didn't seem upset, Yngve thought. Just ... resigned. He repeated his request and hung up. Then went back to look at Børre's comment on Even's Facebook post. As he reread it, another message popped up, this time from a girl called Christina Theorin. She too had seen Even Tollefsen at the school on the night of the premiere. In the hall where the show took place.

'God, Even,' Yngve said out loud. 'What the hell have you done?'

He went back to the interview transcripts. He'd told the officers to ask the pupils when they had left the building, and who with. The closer to 11 p.m. they'd left, the more interesting their testimony would be.

A lot of people had stayed behind, waiting for those who had actually participated in the show to change. Mari and Johannes had been spotted going into the music room, apparently where Mari was intending to conduct the post-show interview.

This is moving too slowly, Yngve said to himself, as he thought about what they'd found so far. The forensic teams had focused mainly on the crime scenes, and yes, there were more than enough traces of blood to firmly establish the route the killer had taken after the murders. But they hadn't found anything on the roof or on the other side of the school. No torn-off piece of fabric from a jacket or a pair of trousers. Nothing that, with any degree of certainty, they could say had been deposited the night before. The heavy rainfall had ruined any chance of finding fresh, decent evidence.

Yngve's computer pinged. Incoming e-mail. Yngve pushed himself towards it. The victims' phone records. He had asked Weedon, one of the tech guys at the precinct, to retrieve Mari's mobile phone from the repair shop downtown. It had been deposited on Saturday, two days before her murder. The screen, according to Weedon, was completely shattered, but he was going to try and retrieve the data. She must have broken it some time after she'd texted Even, Yngve reasoned.

He opened the encrypted files from the phone company. He started to cross-check Johannes' list against Mari's, and discovered that no one had called both victims. It was easy, however, to see that Even had been eager to get in touch with his ex-girlfriend over the last few days of her life. Twenty-seven missed calls, from him to her. Yngve also noticed that Frode Lindgren, Mari's dad, had tried to reach his daughter several times that Saturday, and quite a few times the next day as well. She hadn't answered, which wasn't strange, since her phone was broken. But why didn't Frode know that? Cecilie, Mari's mother, apparently did.

Yngve identified the numbers of some of Mari's friends as well. She seemed to be a popular girl.

He went back to the pile of statements again. Martin Dietrichs, a boy in Mari's class, had said that he had seen her talking to her dad in the show's interval: *It looked as if they were arguing.*

Yngve sat up and dialled the kid's number straightaway. It took Martin Dietrichs a while to answer, but when he did, he immediately turned down the music playing in the background.

'Oh hey,' he said as Yngve introduced himself. He made a shushing sound to the others in the room.

'I'm just following up on what you said in your interview earlier today,' Yngve started. 'About Mari's argument with her father.'

'Oh yeah,' Martin Dietrichs said. '*That*. It certainly looked like they were rowing.'

'Can you describe what happened?'

'Well, during the interval I saw him walk over to her. She was standing with her back to him, talking to someone, I don't know who. When he came up to her, she turned away and waited for a second or two, then just walked straight past him. He tried to stop her, but ... she just tore herself away from him, if you know what I mean.'

'So ... he grabbed hold of her?'

'That's what it looked like to me.'

'Did you hear what they were talking about?'

'No, I was too far away for that.'

'Did you see where Mari went after that?'

'No, there were too many people around.'

'What about her dad – did you see where *he* went?'

'He stayed where he was, I think. I really don't remember. I wasn't really interested in him, you know. I was standing in line to get a Coke from the kiosk.'

Yngve made a few notes on his pad.

'OK,' he said eventually. 'Thank you for your time.'

'No problem. Hope I've helped.'

Yngve hung up. He thought about Frode Lindgren and what might have been going on in the Lindgren family before Mari was murdered. He contemplated calling Frode right away, but quickly decided against it. Not on a night like this. Parents argued with their children all the time. It didn't have to have anything to do with the murders.

Still, he couldn't get their odd behaviour out of his mind. The coolness he could feel in the living room of the Lindgren house, the distance between husband and wife – the way they sat far away from each other. And why did they act so strangely when he'd asked them about Jimmy's car accident?

She was back again. Standing against the wall.

'God,' he said out loud.

Just get a good night's sleep, she said, *and you'll be fresh and ready in the morning. You'll get the answers you're looking for.*

A good night's sleep.

Åse had asked for his help with a good night's sleep. The really long one.

You must help me. You can. Please.

'I couldn't do it,' he said to her. 'You know that.'

She didn't. Still, she didn't.

'It was never a question of wanting to or not, it was a question of whether I could,' he said louder. 'Even if I knew how much pain you were in, I just couldn't bring myself to do it.'

Yngve blinked, and hoped that she'd be gone when he opened his eyes again, but she wasn't. She just stood there looking at him. That's why he put a hand in front of his eyes. So she wouldn't see that he was crying.

27
NOW

'Have you been drunk like that a lot of times before, Even?'

Ms Håkonsen looks at me over her glasses.

'How do you mean?'

'I mean being sick.'

'Not a lot, no. I usually stay away from alcohol.'

'Because of your football?'

'Yes. And...'

I hesitate. I don't want to tell the court that my mother's drinking habits aren't something I'm keen to fall into myself.

'But it *has* happened?'

'Excuse me; what has?'

'You have been excessively drunk before?'

'Yes, it has happened a couple of times.'

'Ever get blackouts while heavily drunk?'

I'm not sure how to respond to that. 'I don't think so,' I finally say.

'That's not a very good answer, is it?'

'I guess not.'

'So what you're basically saying is that you don't know? You don't remember?'

I wriggle in my chair. 'I may ... I have forgotten some things when I've had too much to drink,' I say. 'That's pretty common though, isn't it?'

'I wouldn't know,' the prosecutor says. 'What I do know, is that apparently it runs in the family. Your mother has experienced blackouts, too. She said so during her testimony yesterday. She had blackouts both on the day of the car accident that killed your father, but also on other occasions when she'd been drinking.'

'I'm not my mother, though.'

'Of course you're not, but her blood runs through your veins, Even. You have her DNA. So it wouldn't be unfair to claim that the two of you are somewhat alike, at least in that respect.'

I pick at a fingernail. 'Is that ... Is that a question?' I stammer.

'No, it's just an observation. Do you remember what happened after you were sick that evening?'

I wait a beat before answering. 'No, I don't.'

'What's the next thing you remember, then?'

'I ... remember Yngve Mork standing over me.'

'Police Chief Inspector Mork was standing over you?'

'Yes. In my room. Or ... in my room in Imo's house.'

Ms Håkonsen is walking back and forth in front of me. 'And precisely *why* was he standing over you?'

I need to take a deep breath before continuing: 'Because there had been another murder.'

28
THEN

I was startled by a noise in the room. Then the flick of a switch made everything bright. I blinked ferociously for a second or two. Then I saw Yngve Mork bending above me.

At first I had no idea where I was or what had happened. Then I realised: I was at Imo's. Mork said my name so loudly that I jumped and sat bolt upright in my bed. My whole body protested, my head was thumping – it felt like it was in a vice – and I still had the taste of vomit in my mouth.

'What is it?' I asked, still trying to adjust my eyes to the light.

'Where were you this evening?' Mork asked. His question was curt – his voice, hard and authoritative. He reminded me of a teacher I'd had in primary school. I tried to pull myself together, but the room was still spinning.

'I was here,' I stammered. 'Why do you want to know? What time is it?'

Through the gap in the curtains I could see that it was still dark. But at this time of year that really didn't mean much.

'Is that true?' Mork asked, and turned round to face Imo, who was standing in the doorway. 'Is it true that he was here the whole evening?'

'Yes,' Imo said and nodded.

'The whole time? He didn't go out at all?'

'No.'

'Are you absolutely certain? You know for sure that he didn't go out after you'd gone to bed?'

'Well, I was here, wasn't I?' Imo said. 'I was working in the studio.' I could tell from his voice that he was getting angry. 'I sat up working for a while after Even had gone to bed. So yes, I do know. Plus, he wasn't exactly in a state to move about very easily.'

The policeman turned back to me. I must have looked like shit, because something in his expression changed. He seemed to be reassessing the situation.

'What the hell is going on?' I asked.

Mork took a deep breath and looked at me. 'Børre Halvorsen has been murdered.'

29

Yngve beat his hands against the steering wheel. His theory, which had seemed so valid just an hour before, was already crumbling.

Even had a solid alibi. At least, it appeared that way.

Yngve drove back to Fredheim, thinking about what to do next. It was almost two hours since the dead body of Børre Halvorsen had been discovered, and he'd lost valuable time searching for Even. First he'd been to the Tollefsens' house on Granholtveien 4. Tobias had answered, telling Yngve that Even was spending the night at Imo's. That trip alone had cost Yngve almost half an hour.

He parked up on the pavement at the foot of the bridge over the railway tracks. He wondered how many times in his life he'd walked or driven across it. Thousands, for sure. Now though – and forever after – he would think of the poor kid who had been found lying face down on the stony ground by a homeless man who sometimes slept down there.

Even though it was almost 2.30 a.m., people were gathered around the cordon the police had established when they had arrived at the scene. The steam pouring out of the crowd's mouths glowed in the streetlights, making it look like the onlookers were trapped in a fog that had issued from a troll's lair. It was as if they were extras on a dark, mysterious stage. Behind them, on the other side of the bridge, was Fredheim – quiet now, but it would soon be buzzing with angry, frightened voices.

Yngve wondered how long it would take for the complaints to pour in. At the press conference the day before he had said that, in all probability, the high-school murders were an isolated event. Now his credibility would be put to the test. The media would start to wonder whether he was the right man for the job. So would the inhabitants of Fredheim. Vibeke Hanstveit, the police attorney, would probably not question his level of commitment or his ability to get the job done, but as the person formally in charge of the investigation she would certainly be under a lot of pressure as well.

Better solve this thing quickly, he said to himself.

While Yngve had been looking for Even, Therese Kyrkjebø had taken charge of the crime scene. He found her under the bridge with the crime-scene officers. She was standing a few feet from the body, her hand placed on her slightly rounded belly.

'We have to ask for witnesses,' he said as he approached. 'Anyone who crossed the bridge some time after midnight. We have to check the trains as well; see if any were passing through after midnight. Get hold of potential conductors, passengers.' He sighed heavily.

'As if we don't have enough on our hands already,' Therese said. Her shoulders were raised almost to her ears. Her lips seemed blue against her pale face. The brutal death of yet another young person was hard to comprehend at the best of times, and in Therese's condition, it seemed somehow compounded.

'Are you cold?' Yngve asked.

'I'm fine,' she said. 'Just didn't put enough layers on.'

'Then you're *not* fine.'

'I'll be alright,' she insisted.

Thankfully it had stopped raining. But there was still a biting chill in the air.

He looked at the dead boy. A green cap with spots of blood on it was lying on the ground next to his head. His eyes were open, and he had several wounds on his face. His jacket was partly torn off – some of the seams were ripped open. Behind him, on the walls of the bridge, were spots of dried blood.

'It looks as if his head was smashed against the wall,' Therese said, pointing to red marks. 'Repeatedly, until...' She stopped herself and looked away, blanching.

Around them cameras were flashing, and one of the crime-scene technicians appeared to be filming the scene.

'If it's the same person who beat Johannes Eklund to death,' she continued, 'then it certainly seems that some kind of incredible, uncontrollable rage comes over him. He just can't stop until he's...'

'Or she,' Yngve said.

'You think so?' Therese asked, her voice a notch more agitated. 'You really think a woman or a girl could beat two teenage boys to death like this?'

Åse had asked him the same question last night. 'I don't know,' he said – the same thing he'd told Åse. 'If someone's angry enough, I guess they can do just about anything. But really, I have no idea.'

Therese didn't say anything. Yngve now noticed the homeless man – he was sitting on a large stone just outside the cordoned-off area. He had a grey blanket wrapped around him and was holding on to a mug, his knuckles white.

'Have you talked to him yet?' Yngve asked, nodding in his direction.

'Just briefly,' she said. 'I told him to sit tight and wait for you.'

'Good.'

The homeless man was Ulf, a character known to pretty much everyone in Fredheim. He walked about the town a lot, occasionally begging for pennies here or there. He was completely harmless, and despite being only in his thirties, he always looked like he was two months away from retirement. His tatty clothes seemed about to fall off him, and it didn't look as though he'd had a proper meal or a wash in months, which probably wasn't too far from the truth.

'Hey, Ulf,' Yngve said as he approached him. 'Sorry to keep you waiting. I'll let you go soon enough. Just wanted to know when you got here?'

Ulf blew gently into the cup and took a sip. 'I don't know,' he said in a weary voice. 'It might have been close to one.'

'And which direction did you come from?'

Ulf pointed to the tracks that led under the bridge to the train station a few hundred yards further on. It was possible to walk along the tracks, but not more than six feet on any side, as there were shrubs and trees everywhere.

'Did you see any cars in the parking lot in front of the train station?' Yngve asked.

'A couple,' Ulf said. 'I know for sure that there was a taxi sitting there. A couple of normal-looking cars, too.'

'Did you see anyone inside any of them?'

'No, sir.'

'No one moving away from the station as you got here?'

'There are always people around,' he said. 'But I didn't notice anyone special.'

Ulf took another sip. The smell of coffee reached Yngve's nostrils.

'Has he been here before?' Yngve pointed towards the body, now, thankfully, covered with a white blanket.

'Plenty of times,' Ulf replied. 'He doesn't drink or get high or anything like that. He just likes to hang out with us.'

'Alright,' Yngve said. 'Thanks for calling us out so quickly. And thank you for your patience.'

'Where the hell am I going to go now?' Ulf whimpered. 'You've cordoned off the whole area.'

'You don't have somewhere else you can stay tonight?

'I was going to stay here,' he said. 'My sleeping bag is just around the corner.' He wiped his lips and looked up at Yngve with an open mouth. There were more black teeth than white inside.

'I'm sorry,' Yngve said. 'I really can't help you with that right now.'

Once again he thanked Ulf for his help. Ulf got to his feet and retrieved his sleeping bag, before staggering up to the pavement. He began to walk slowly towards the town centre. It looked as if he was carrying the weight of the town on his shoulders.

Yngve went back to Therese, whose teeth were now chattering in the cold.

'Let's get it over with,' he said. 'Let's go and see his mum.'

They were about to return to their cars, when one of the crime-scene technicians called out to them. The man was standing close to the bridge wall, where Børre Halvorsen in all likelihood had been killed.

'What is it?' Yngve asked, walking over.

'This might be helpful,' the technician said, holding up some twee-zers, from which hung a piece of dark-brown leather.

'Looks like a piece of a glove or something,' Therese said.

'Yeah,' the technician said. 'I'm willing to bet on it, actually.'

30

For the next few hours, Imo and I just sat in his living room with our mobile phones out, constantly checking for updates. In between, I read interviews with people I knew and others I didn't know. Eve-ryone was telling the media how scared and sad they were. Their thoughts were with Mari and Johannes' families. Some were worried about their own children as well, about what they should do while the police carried out their investigation. Should they keep their children at home? Accompany them wherever they went?

It took a while for people to wake up, but once they did my social media feeds started buzzing. I checked Børre's Facebook comment from the day before, and noticed that even more people had joined in on the thread. A few had supported me, telling the others to give me the benefit of the doubt, but after Christina, one of Mari's friends, said that she'd seen me inside the school hall during the show that night, all the comments were full of hatred and disbelief.

I shook my head. This isn't happening, I said to myself. This isn't fucking happening. Someone had killed Børre. And given what Chris-tina had written, there would no doubt be people around town who would once again be pointing the finger at me. Børre had 'seen me'. Seen me do what? For fuck's sake!

I had no idea, though, what I'd done after I vomited. I presumed I had been asleep in Imo's bed. In theory, I could have gone out while Imo was working in his studio, but that just didn't make any sense. I hadn't been able to move. How the hell could I have made it to Fredheim and back again without being aware of it?

I wanted to tell Christina and the others that I'd already been questioned by the police, and that I hadn't been arrested. Wouldn't PCI Mork have brought me in or charged me if he thought I'd done it? I wanted to retaliate or tell my friends and the rest of Fredheim that I was innocent, but somehow I didn't think they'd believe me.

At one point I put my phone down and walked away from it. Every ping from each notification felt like a stab or an attack. But it was impossible not to go back and see what people were writing. They wanted to know where I was, where I had been. *Come on, Even, talk to us.* I turned off the sound. Put the phone away, then grabbed it again. More and more it felt like someone was trying to destroy my life. At the moment he or she was succeeding.

One of the news stories on the VG Nett site caught my attention. It was an interview with Oskar, my best friend – or former best friend. Apparently he was one of the last people to see Johannes alive. And Børre, I now realised. I had asked Oskar to find Børre and to confront him.

The thought gave me goosebumps. I clicked on the article. I was afraid to read on but couldn't stop myself. Oskar and some of Johannes' groupies had left the school together after the show, but Johannes had left his phone in the room where Mari had interviewed him. He went back to get it. 'If only Johannes had remembered his mobile,' Oskar said to the interviewer, 'he would still be alive today.' The headline read 'Chance Victim?'

Why the hell hadn't Oskar told me about this?

I took a shower and found some painkillers among the tablets in Imo's medicine cupboard. Washed them down with some water. They helped a little, but I still felt like I'd played three football matches in a row, without having a break in between. I had a training session later that day, but I just couldn't face going. I decided to give my coach a ring to explain, but I hung up before he had a chance to reply.

Afterwards, I sat on the bathroom floor, my back against the wall, thinking about Mari, Johannes and Børre, but mostly about Mari. I couldn't believe I would never get to see her again. Feel her skin against mine. Her lips. Her touch. What on earth had she said or done that was so bad she had to be killed for it?

'Your Mum called,' Imo said when I went back into the living room. 'She wants me to drive you home as soon as possible.'

'Why?'

'I think she wants to apologise for the argument you guys had yesterday,' he said.

'*I* didn't have a fight with her,' I said. '*She* had a fight with me.'

'Whatever.'

He moved one of the logs in the fire, which was about to go out. 'I said I'd give you some breakfast first, and then take you home. Are you hungry?'

I shook my head, a little too hard – it felt like nothing inside my skull was attached to anything. 'I don't think I'll want food ever again.'

Imo smiled and put his hands to his back as he stood up. One of his hands was shaking. I had noticed it before, too, but I didn't want to ask what was wrong – if he was ill or something.

'I'll make some breakfast anyway,' Imo said, walking towards the kitchen. 'You might change your mind.'

I wasn't looking forward to getting home. Mum quite often exploded for no reason, only to regret it when she had sobered up.

I followed Imo into the kitchen and forced myself to drink some coffee. I wondered once again what the people of Fredheim would think about the murders – and about me. I checked Facebook and the other feeds at regular intervals. The feeling of being slowly strangled got worse by the minute, as more and more people connected Børre's name to mine.

'They're having a memorial service at school later,' Imo said. 'Are you thinking of going?'

'Yes,' I said. 'I have to.'

'Are you sure that's wise?' my uncle asked me. 'I mean...' He stopped himself, but I knew what he was thinking.

'I'm not going to hide,' I said firmly. 'No fucking way.'

Imo looked at me for a few seconds. 'OK,' he said and held up his hands. 'I'm not going to try and stop you. More coffee?'

'No, thanks, I'm good.'

I decided to send a message to Ida Hammer, Mari's best friend. I kept it simple: just asking if we could talk. Of course, I wanted to know how she was – if she'd recovered from her violent reaction the day before. But I also needed to know how Mari had been in the days before she was killed. Maybe Ida knew why Mari had broken up with me and why she had Ole Hoff's business card in her pocket when she was found.

A minute passed then my mobile phone pinged. A reply from Ida: *Not really, considering.*

Right. I couldn't be bothered to ask for an explanation; I was pretty sure I knew it.

'You know Ole Hoff, the journalist?' I said to Imo.

'Mhm.'

Imo had been in the local paper a lot because of his music and Ole and Imo were about the same age. 'Do you know what Mum might have against him?'

'Against Ole?' Imo laughed. 'No, I have no idea. Why do you ask?'

'Yesterday, she wasn't happy about me talking to him.'

'Probably because he works at the *Chronicle*,' Imo said. 'Your mum doesn't like any focus on the family. And certainly not the kind of attention you'll be getting now.'

Maybe that was what she'd tried to tell me. I didn't know. I wasn't sure I even cared.

31

Yngve could tell that Therese wanted to say something as they were walking towards the entrance to the police station. But there was no opportunity: Yngve had tried to ward off the press, but they were hanging on to them like stray dogs around a bone.

'Let me just get inside and meet with my team,' Yngve said to the reporters, 'Then I'll come back out and talk to you. Briefly.'

Therese opened the door for him, as Yngve was carrying heavy bags of files and papers that he'd brought from home. Once inside, Therese finally spoke: 'There has to be another reason why Børre Halvorsen was murdered. Something other than saying he'd seen Even Tollefsen at a window in the school that night.'

'I've been thinking the same thing.'

They started up the staircase to their offices. 'And anyway that sighting doesn't prove anything,' Therese continued. 'Even if Even Tollefsen lied about being there that night, it doesn't automatically make him a killer.'

'No, but it weakens his credibility,' Yngve said.

'Still. And why kill him? It only makes Even look more guilty.'

Yngve had to agree with that.

'Are you going to tell the press about the piece of leather we found?' Therese asked.

'Yes I am. A single observation, someone seeing someone with a glove that matches the general description, could be enough.'

'We're going to get thousands of calls.'

'I know.'

'And we will have to follow up on every single lead.'

'I know that too.'

The detectives Vibeke Hanstveit had managed to round up had gathered in the large conference room. They were all drinking coffee or tea as Yngve entered the room. He greeted them all and thanked them for their efforts the previous day. By the looks of things, some of them had needed to vent a little last night. He could smell a faint odour of alcohol in the room. As long as they did their job, Yngve thought, he didn't care. They all had their coping mechanisms.

He gave them the same, tiring task as the day before: interviewing everyone at the school, this time the emphasis would be on their whereabouts the previous night.

The handball court was being used for the memorial service, which was scheduled for 11 a.m. So Yngve had asked for permission to use the arts centre in the middle of Fredheim, as it had several conference rooms suitable for interviews. What they needed now was word of the change of venue to get to the good people of Fredheim. Yngve was counting on Mr Brakstad, the principal of Fredheim High, to help out.

'I made some headway last night on the surveillance tapes,' one of the detectives from Lillestrøm said. 'I think I've found something interesting.'

'Very good,' Yngve said. 'I'll just give the press a quick briefing, then I'll come and look at it with you.'

The detective nodded.

'Therese, can you make sure the press gets a photo of that piece of leather we found?'

'I'm on it.'

Yngve went back downstairs. Rumours had apparently spread that he was going to come out and talk because there were now at least twenty-five reporters gathered around the entrance. Their microphones almost hit him in the face, and he noticed from their logos that journalists from Sweden and Denmark had now made their way to Fredheim as well. Vibeke Hanstveit had called him the night before to let him know that the town was making headlines all over Europe.

He gave them a quick update, which really didn't consist of any details they didn't already know. He reassured them that the police were taking every measure possible, and that he had every confidence they would be able to apprehend the person or persons responsible for the killings.

'Are the three murders connected?'

'Are you closing in on any suspects?'

'Mr Mork, are you going to call in specialists to help you out with the investigation?'

He didn't answer any of the questions that were thrown at him, but insisted that they were still in the early stages of the investigation, and that the press would be kept updated as soon as there were any new developments in the case.

'I'm sorry,' he added. 'That's all I can say at this point.'

As Yngve hurried back inside he found Åse waiting for him at the top of the stairs.

'I know,' he said. 'I could have handled it better.'

I think you managed quite well. I know you don't like large crowds, especially with cameras around. You even looked kind of handsome in front of all those reporters.

'Ha,' Yngve snorted. 'I most certainly did not.'

Inside Yngve left his jacket on his stool, before stepping into Weedon's office. The tech analyst was a ginger-haired, heavy-set man in his early thirties. When Yngve entered the room, the large man's face was so close to one of his three computer screens he was almost touching it. Behind him the surveillance tape detective from Lillestrøm was leaning in, watching over Weedon's shoulder. The room smelled of old food and sweat.

A picture on Weedon's screen was enhanced almost to the point of no recognition, but as Weedon zoomed out, the figure in the image became more and more clear. It was a man, and he looked to be of average height. He wore a jacket that might have been black, might have been blue, with no clear logos or notable designs on it. His trousers were almost identical in colour. A group of teenage girls were standing close by. The image was taken from one of the CCTV cameras outside Fredheim High School, and was pointing towards the entrance.

'Who's this?' Yngve asked.

The detective from Lillestrøm – Yngve now recalled his name was Davidsen – spoke:

'I watched the tapes, trying to determine whether everyone who went *in* between ten-thirty and eleven, also came back out. Everyone

is accounted for. Except this guy right here.' He pointed to the screen.
'He entered the school premises at ten forty-nine p.m.'

'And he didn't come back out?'

'Well, if he did, he certainly didn't come out the same way he came
in. I've triple-checked the tapes. He's not on any of them.'

The man in the photo had his back to the camera. There was something familiar about him, but Yngve couldn't quite determine what.
He was slouching somewhat. Skinny. Brown hair.

'A parent, maybe?' Weedon offered. He replayed the video tape,
frame by frame. On screen the man placed his right hand on the door
handle and pulled it towards himself. Then he entered the school.

'Can you zoom in on his hand, please?' Yngve pointed to the screen
again.

Weedon nodded, clicking and moving with his mouse. He then
reversed the tape and did as Yngve had asked. The image was grainy,
but the man's fingers were still visible.

'No ring,' Yngve said.

An image appeared before Yngve's mind's eye. Frode Lindgren,
squeezing his ball of socks. Yngve hadn't noticed it then, but now,
when he came to think of it, he was almost a hundred percent sure that
Frode hadn't been wearing his wedding ring that day.

Yngve studied the picture more closely. He couldn't really say that
he knew Frode Lindgren well, but there could be some resemblance, at
least in height and posture.

'Print out the best image you can find,' Yngve said to Weedon. 'Make
eight to ten copies to begin with, and then we'll bring everybody who
was still at school around that time in for questioning again.'

Weedon began searching through the recording straightaway.

'Let's see if we can identify those girls as well,' Yngve continued
and pointed to the screen, even though they weren't on it anymore.
'Find out if they noticed the guy as he was passing. Maybe one of them
knows who it is.'

'I'll see if I can pull a picture of his face from a reflection in the
window as well,' Weedon said.

'I'd be very pleased if you can,' Yngve said. 'Excellent work, gentlemen.'

Back at his desk he called Therese Kyrkjebø over and quickly briefed her on what they'd found on the CCTV recordings.

'I want you to try and get hold of some of Børre Halvorsen's friends,' he said. 'We need to know what he was doing the last days of his life. Whether he was having trouble with anyone – conflicts his mother wasn't aware of.'

'She wasn't aware of a whole lot of things.'

'I know. We also need to know if anyone saw Børre at school. If he did see Even Tollefsen there, then someone must have spotted Børre there, too, right? What was he doing there? It wasn't *his* school. He goes to Fredly Junior High. Where did they see him? Did he talk to anyone?'

'And if he did – who?' Therese seemed to understand where he was going with this.

'We need to find out exactly what Børre was doing between the show and last night. As of now, there is every reason to believe that his murder has something to do with the others, we're just lacking a common denominator. A common motive. And Even Tollefsen has an alibi for last night, so the Børre's sighting of Even seems to be irrelevant. At least for now.'

'I'm on it.'

'Good.'

Yngve fetched his jacket.

'Where are you going?' Therese asked.

'To see Frode Lindgren.'

32
NOW

'So Imo said he knew nothing about your mother's disagreement with Ole Hoff?'

'No.'

'And you believed him?'

'Of course. Why wouldn't I?'

'I guess you wouldn't.' Ms Håkonsen smiles at me briefly.

I can feel that I'm starting to lose my patience – both with her and with the whole trial. I didn't expect her to focus on every single piece of information, every single little detail. I'm hot, I'm sad, I'm thirsty, I'm ... I'm fucking exhausted.

'So you went back home to see your mother.'

'Yes,' I say, breathing out as I speak.

'Alright. Tell us how that went.'

33
THEN

It was a cold morning, but thankfully it was dry. Thick clouds moved across the sky, but there were patches of blue here and there, and some much-needed sunshine was breaking through, bathing the wet grass and leaves in a bright, golden light. A slight wind set the branches in motion, made them hiss as if they were trying to shake off the last few days of rain. To Susanne Tollefsen, it sounded like music.

She pulled her coat a little tighter around her, wondering when King Winter would arrive this year. Last year they'd had almost no snow at all. Not that it bothered her – she never went cross-country skiing or particularly liked the white stuff. The only good thing about winter, in her opinion, was that it was dark. She could stay inside all day long and not feel the slightest bit guilty about it. There would be no inner voice telling her to go outdoors, do some work in the yard or repair anything. She wouldn't have to clean the shed or throw away some of her mum's old stuff. Sometimes, though, like now, she did need to get out.

GP was shoving his nose into all kinds of rubbish at the side of the road. And every four metres or so he lifted his right leg and got rid of a squirt or two. This was their morning routine, consisting of a walk around the neighbourhood that took about fifteen to twenty minutes, depending on her mood or his nose. Today it felt good to get some fresh air. She'd gone to bed late the night before, and the morning had started a little too early. Knut had entered the bedroom, having just finished his late-night shift, and he had shaken her out of a morning sleep that, for once, hadn't been filled with noises and horrible images. Then he had told her what had happened under Fredheim Bridge.

Susanne had got up immediately and taken a shower. She'd had Knut drive her home, and she had called Imo and told him to get Even over as quickly as possible. She felt so guilty about not taking care of him the previous night. If she couldn't make up for it completely, she was certainly going to try.

Even and Imo still hadn't arrived when Susanne and GP got home from their walk. She decided to wait for them on the front steps. She fetched a cushion and sat down on the cold surface. GP placed himself at her feet. Soon he was asleep.

Susanne took a look around at everything that belonged to her now. The big house, the oak tree at the front, which stood in the middle of the circular drive. The garage, the outbuilding, which had once been used as a stable.

What the hell was she going to do with all this?

The urge for a glass to hold on to became strong, almost irresistible, but no, she wasn't going to go there now. Not yet anyway.

The sound of an engine made GP wake up and lift his head. Soon Imo's old green Mercedes stopped in front of the house. He parked behind the oak tree and turned off the engine. As always Imo got out of the car with an eager step. GP ran over to greet him, his tail waving back and forth like a metronome. Even needed a bit more time to get out of the car. It looked as if he was hurting somewhere.

Her eyes filled with tears. She hurried over to him and pulled him close. She could smell shampoo from his hair and peppermint from his mouth.

'How are you feeling?' she asked, once she had stopped kissing and hugging him. He looked so handsome. His chin was exactly the same as Jimmy's. He had his eyes, too.

'I'm good,' Even said. 'Well. As good as can be expected, I guess.'

'It's just...' She shook her and wiped away a tear. 'Awful.'

He looked so strong, she thought. Always had. Even when Jimmy died, Even had had a certain steelness to him. Like he wasn't going to let anyone see how much he actually hurt.

'Thanks for taking care of him last night,' she said to Imo.

'No problem. We had a pretty good night, didn't we, champ?'

Susanne looked at them both. There seemed to be a smile in Imo's face.

'I'd better be off,' he said. 'Call me if you need anything. Both of you.'

Susanne nodded and offered her thanks once more. She watched Imo take off. His car turned the corner, and there was silence.

'Shall we go in and make some hot chocolate or something?' She gave Even her best possible smile.

'I can't,' he said. 'There's a memorial service for Mari and Johannes at school. I ... have to be there. I mean, I want to.'

Susanne nodded and thought of Mari again. Mari Lindgren. Cecilie's daughter. Even had never told her directly that he'd found himself a girlfriend, but Susanne had sort of figured it out when she'd seen his sudden, blatant happiness, how he'd volunteered to take GP for a walk or help out at home more often. Still, it was Tobias who'd told her it was Mari, one evening when Even was at football practice.

First, she was happy for him. Really, she was. Then she started to worry about Cecilie – if they might have to start dealing with each other again.

'What is it with you and Ole Hoff, anyway?' asked Even.

The question caught her off-guard. She'd been in good spirits, with her firstborn finally home with her, but a black curtain descended over her eyes. She felt a fresh knot in her chest, too.

'Just leave it, Even,' she said. 'It's not important anymore.'

'Didn't seem like it yesterday,' he said. 'Is that why you're always so short with Oskar whenever he's here, too?'

Susanne looked at him. 'I'm not!'

'Yes, you are. You barely say hello to him, and you never smile or talk to him when he's around or ask how he is. Have you got something against the whole Hoff family? Is that it?'

Susanne didn't know what to say to that. Had she really behaved that way?

'I'm sorry,' she said. 'And I hope Oskar doesn't feel the same. That was never my intention. It's not *his* fault that...' She stopped herself. Looked down at the ground as she struggled to find a good way to finish the sentence.

'What's not his fault?'

She shook her head and closed her eyes, angry at herself for allowing herself to speak too freely. Then she opened them again and tilted her chin upwards.

'Oskar is welcome whenever he wants,' she said, and attempted a smile.

But this seemed to have no effect on Even. He had more questions, she could tell. Susanne braced herself.

'There's something else as well,' he said.

Susanne sighed.

'You know Cecilie. Mari's mum.'

She swallowed hard.

'Have you been in touch with her since...'

'No,' she replied.

Even frowned. 'You don't even know what I was going to ask you.'

'Of course I haven't been in touch with her since Mari died. For goodness' sake, Even, it's no more than a day since ... I'm sure that

Cecilie has more than enough on her plate without me...' Susanne stopped herself again.

'I wasn't thinking about *now*, Mum, I meant after we moved back.'

She took a breath, paused, then said: 'No.'

'Why not?'

'Well,' she said and hesitated, 'I just didn't feel like it.'

'But weren't you best friends once upon a time?'

She sighed again. 'Why are you asking about all this now, Even? Why is it suddenly so important to you?'

'I just think that it's a bit strange that the two of you don't have anything to do with each other anymore,' Even said. 'Mari and I talked about it. She found it weird too.'

'You know what?' Susanne said. 'So do I. But it's not my fault, I can tell you that much. Cecilie stopped talking to me at one point, and there's a limit to how many times you can be bothered to try, isn't there? To call, to suggest a coffee or a walk or ... something.' Susanne pulled GP towards her. 'You might as well get used to it,' she said and gave the dog an angry look. 'Friends come and go. There doesn't need to be any particular reason, it just happens. You drift apart. Then you get new friends, and you forget the old ones. You only ever keep a handful, if that, throughout your life. And that's if you're lucky.'

Even seemed to fade away into his own thoughts for a while.

'Wouldn't it be good to send her some flowers or something?' he asked. 'I mean now? She might need it.'

Susanne sighed. 'Yeah,' she said eventually, in a quiet voice. 'I guess I should do that.'

34

Because I'd left my bike at school the day before, I had to walk all the way back there, but I really didn't mind. It was good to stretch my legs a little, to use my body again. It was as if the fresh air cleansed me somehow, from the inside out.

I dreaded getting there, though. I knew a lot of people would be coming, and I was nervous about the kind of reception I would get. On my way to school my phone kept pinging. I'd been silly enough to turn the sound back on. There were notifications from threads I was tagged in, threads I *became* tagged in as I was walking, but even after I had untagged myself, someone added my name in a later response. It was as if people, boys and girls I had once considered friends, wanted me to know they were talking about me.

Roger Midtbø, a guy in one of my parallel classes, even said that he was going to pin me to the ground and force the truth out of me with his fists. So far his comment had got forty-eight likes and quite a few responses from others wanting revenge. I didn't think anyone would be foolish enough to actually jump me, but you could never really know.

The first thing I noticed as I got to the school was that the police cordons had been lifted. Only one police car was parked by the entrance. I knew it was probably still too soon for the school itself to open for classes, but at first glance everything looked normal. Almost as if nothing had happened.

When Mari and I were still together, the first thing I always did in the morning was look for her. Usually she was standing by the fountain, half listening to her friends' chatter, but I knew she was waiting for me to arrive. When I did, and she saw me, her smile reached into her eyes, and it made me warm deep inside my heart. Now, as I passed the fountain, which was turned off for the winter, it was as if she was still standing there, smiling at me. I had to force myself not to cry.

Even though it was well before 11 a.m., quite a few people had already assembled outside the handball court building. I spotted Elise, one of Mari's friends, standing next to two girls I knew by appearance, but not by name. Elise was one of the girls who'd tried to comfort Ida Hammer the day before.

I went over to her and said hello. She turned and stared at me, looking a bit shocked. I tried to ignore that.

'Do you know if Ida is coming later?' I asked.

'No,' she said, squaring her shoulders.

'No, you don't know if she's coming, or no, she's not coming?'

'I don't know if she's coming.'

'OK. If you see her, could you tell her I need to talk to her?'

'Why?' There was an edge to her voice that made me want to say something sarcastic.

'Just ... tell her what I said, OK?'

Elise didn't answer. I said thanks and walked away, feeling the ice from her cold stare on my neck. Others shot glances at me as well, before quickly looking away. *You haven't done anything*, I kept on repeating to myself. *Be proud. Stand tall.*

To keep myself occupied while we waited for the doors to open, I took out my phone. I saw that there had been a press conference about Børre's murder. Apparently the police had found a piece of a dark-brown leather glove at the crime scene. Yngve Mork didn't want to speculate about how that piece could have been torn off, but it wasn't hard to picture Børre trying to fight off his attacker, maybe biting him in the process.

I had just finished reading the article when someone called my name. I turned. Ole Hoff was coming my way.

'Oh, hello,' I said.

'How are you?' Ole asked. He seemed to be studying my face. I knew I looked like shit after last night's rendezvous with Imo's tequila bottle.

'I've been better.'

I told him about the drinking session – I wanted as many people as possible to know that I had an alibi for Børre's murder. 'I normally don't drink that much.'

Ole shook his head and told me he hadn't published the article about me yet. 'I wanted to go through it again with you when you were sober,' he said. 'There might still be room for it in tomorrow's paper.'

I thanked him for looking out for me. I glanced around; more and more people were arriving. Quite a few of them were staring our way, no doubt wondering what the hell we were talking about, and why I was even there.

'When I met you at your house yesterday,' Ole said, 'you told me that Mari had first approached you because she wanted to write an article about you. About your dad.'

I looked at him, frowning.

'She didn't just talk to *you* about your father,' Ole continued. 'She spoke to her own father about it as well.'

I shifted my weight from one foot to the other.

'She asked him about the accident, and he told her to come and see me,' Ole said. 'That's why she had my business card. He gave it to her. I've bought three cars from Frode over the last twenty years.'

I nodded slowly, trying to think what all this meant.

'Maybe she just wanted to know what I remembered about the accident,' Ole said. 'I covered it quite extensively.'

'Yes,' I said. 'Maybe.'

Mari's parents had always been a bit cold towards me, no doubt because I was seeing their daughter. But at least Mari's dad was interested in my football and what I wanted to do with my life. Mari always tried to stop him from asking me too many questions.

'Shush,' he always said, as a joke. 'I'm talking to the man who might be my son-in-law here.'

That always made her hot and bothered.

'Are you working on any special angle?' I asked Ole.

'Well', he said. 'I guess I'm just trying to make sense of it all, like everyone else.'

I wondered what he thought of the 'Chance Victim' article in which Oskar had been interviewed. I didn't ask, though, as I spotted my former best friend coming towards the handball court building with Kaiss and Fredrik. I turned away from them.

'How's your mother?' Ole asked me.

'Same as usual', I said. 'Hard to say what goes on in her mind sometimes.' I smiled briefly.

Ole nodded. 'I'll see you inside,' he said. 'And maybe I'll call you later, if that's alright.'

'Sure.'

At 10.45 the door to the handball court opened. I waited until I was sure my friends had gone in before joining the queue myself. I felt a push in my back. At first I thought it was just because of how squashed it was. Then it happened again. And again. Then someone threw something at the back of my head, possibly a small stone. It didn't hurt, but I felt it. I turned around to face the people behind me. No one looked at me directly.

I turned back again. Soon someone else threw something at me. Someone coughed behind me, too, and I was sure I heard the word 'murderer' muttered at the same time. I decided to ignore it. Didn't want to make a scene. But I could hear whispering, and I felt like running away. Hiding. Again I tried to steel myself and shut everything out. I kept looking straight ahead until I was finally inside.

In the middle of the handball court two A4-sized photographs of Mari and Johannes had been pinned on each side of a lectern. That was when it finally dawned upon me. It was true. Mari *was* dead. I just stood there staring at her picture. It was a school photo. She wore her hair in a ponytail, had her glasses on and her smile was a bit stiff. I felt something hard in my throat. It became difficult to breathe.

I decided to look at Johannes instead. He was posing, as he always did – like the rock star he was. I'd actually envied Johannes a bit, because he was so bloody good at everything. He was the natural centre of attention wherever he went.

Tic-Tac was walking back and forth with wires and extension leads for the loudspeakers. I found myself a seat in the back row, in the middle of a group of people I didn't know. Still, it was awkward and uncomfortable. It felt as if everyone was staring at me. Again I passed the time by looking at my phone. Every single news site was full of stories about Fredheim. I really couldn't hide from it anywhere.

Soon the principal came in. Mr Brakstad's dark-grey beard seemed to suit his mood. He was very tall, but now he seemed stooped, as though a heavy weight was pressing him downwards.

I really liked Mr Brakstad. He always made eye contact with me when we met in the corridor. He nodded and smiled and offered me a warm hello and a gentle 'how are you?' I always had the feeling that he really cared about us. Now he exchanged a few words with Tic-Tac, before standing behind the microphone, tapping it gently with a finger. A screeching noise ripped through the hall.

Everyone stopped talking and focused on Mr Brakstad.

'Hello.'

The sound was muffled. Tic-Tac adjusted some knobs on the amplifier.

'Could everyone find a seat and settle down please?'

The sound was better now. Sharper. Mr Brakstad looked over at Tic-Tac, nodded, and gave him the thumbs-up. Some people shushed others and soon everyone was quiet.

'Thank you.'

There must have been at least two hundred people in the hall – pupils and journalists. Some parents were there, too, but I couldn't see Mari's. I met Oskar's eyes briefly, before he looked away.

'I would like to start this memorial with two minutes' silence,' Mr Brakstad said. 'One for our dear pupil and friend, Mari Elisabeth Lindgren. And one for our dear pupil and friend, Johannes Eklund.'

I stared at the floor, at my feet. I'm pretty sure everyone else did the same. I tried to force myself not to think about what had happened, because I knew that if I let my mind wander, I would sob like a baby. I didn't want to cry, not here. Not in front of everyone.

From time to time I looked at the clock on the wall. I don't think two minutes have ever gone by so slowly. Around me people were crying, snorting. Coughing. Snorting again. When Mr Brakstad finally said thank you, it sounded like his voice was about to break. There was a heave of relief in the hall. It was almost as though no one had dared to breathe during the silence.

Mr Brakstad said something about how difficult this was, how hard it was to comprehend that an incident like this could happen in our little town.

'It's not easy to grasp the meaning of what's going on when you're in the midst of it,' he said. 'Humans, however, have a remarkable ability to get through even the worst of times, and move forward. However difficult that may seem right now, that's what we have to do as well. As a society. As a school. As a friend. We have to look after one another now. Help each other. The holes that Mari and Johannes have left behind will be impossible to fill, and we are not going to try to do that. We're not going to forget. We are not going to pretend that this never happened, because it did. We're going to talk about them, and remember them, for as long as we can breathe.'

He then gave the floor to a psychotherapist who basically just repeated what Mr Brakstad had said about talking about our beloved, departed friends. Her voice was dull and soft, so I faded out a bit. Soon Mr Brakstad was back at the microphone.

'I would like to finish this short memorial with a song that I know many of you like or maybe even love. I believe it's quite fitting for an occasion like this. In so many ways.'

I was afraid that Mr Brakstad had gone online to find a song about loss and sorrow that was popular in the charts. I should have guessed, though, which song our janitor would put on the PA system.

It was the one Imo had written for the school show. The song Johannes had performed. The show-stopper, the ballad that allowed Johannes to demonstrate the full range of his voice; that made everyone think what talent he had, what potential. It was a song about Fredheim, about how much he loved the place where we lived, how happy he was whenever he came back, how much he'd missed it when he was gone. As soon as I heard the first notes – the chords I had played on my guitar, the ones we had practised as a band – I couldn't help myself. I started to cry. And when I listened to the lyrics Imo had written, it was as if they were meant for Mari and Johannes instead.

35

Just like the day before, it was Cecilie Lindgren's sister who answered the door when Yngve rang the bell.

'Is Frode here?' he asked.

'Um, no,' Kari-Mette Bjerkaas said.

'Where is he?'

'I don't know.'

That made Yngve frown. 'Did he spend the night here?

'No, he didn't.'

'OK, so ... your sister, is she around?'

'Yes, but—'

'I need to speak with her.'

Bjerkaas hesitated for a beat, before opening the door and letting him in.

'Stay here, let me go upstairs and get her for you.'

Yngve waited in the hall for Mari's mother to come down. When she finally did, Yngve thought she looked like a living corpse – thin, with dry lips, her hair undone. Cecilie Lindgren looked like she hadn't slept a single second in a very long time.

'Sorry to bother you again,' Yngve started, and she stopped a few feet away from him. 'I only have a few questions, if I may.'

Cecilie crossed her arms, waiting for him to start.

'I'm trying to get hold of your husband,' he said. 'Do you know where he is?'

She wet her lips with her tongue. 'No.'

'You have no idea?'

It took a few seconds for her to respond. 'I think he may be in Oslo with his brother.'

'What's he doing there? Now?'

'I ... don't know.'

That's a lie, Yngve thought. 'Why isn't he here, Cecilie? With you?'

She closed her eyes and kept them like that for a few seconds, before blinking rapidly. 'Frode and I, we ... we were perhaps on the verge of leaving each other before...' She stopped herself. 'I don't know. This is all so...'

She couldn't finish the sentence. Maybe she didn't even have the answers, Yngve thought. It dawned upon him that the Lindgren family weren't just dealing with one tragedy. They were dealing with two.

'I need a few words with your husband,' Yngve said, regretting that he had to ask. 'He's not answering my calls. Do you have a number for his brother in Oslo?'

Cecilie wiped her tears. 'I'll get it for you.'

She turned and shuffled into the next room. Soon she returned with a yellow post-it note. Yngve could clearly read the numbers and the name: Reidar Lindgren.

'Like I said, I don't know if Frode's there, but ... it's a place to start, if nothing else.'

Yngve said thanks, then: 'How long has he been gone?'

'He left on Saturday.'

'What time?'

She sighed heavily. 'I don't know. Twelve-ish, maybe? Why – is it important?'

'Guess not,' he said. 'Just wanted to know.' He smiled briefly. He was about to leave, when he changed his mind and turned towards her once more. 'Cecilie, do you know if...?' He searched for the right words, realising they probably didn't exist in a situation like this. 'Frode talked to Mari in the interval between the first and second parts of the school show on Monday night. Or ... it looked as if he tried to talk to her, but apparently, she didn't want to. Do you know why?'

Cecilie's eyes narrowed. 'The problems in our family have nothing to do with what happened that night.'

'Are you sure?'

'Of course I'm sure,' she said harshly. 'Do you think my husband killed her? Is that what you're saying? Is that why you want to talk to him? You think he killed her?'

'No, it's not...'

'He loved her!' she shouted. 'He loved ... *me*. Us. Our family. He could never have hurt Mari.'

'I apologise, I didn't mean to—'

'Please leave,' she said. Her voice was trembling. Fresh tears had formed in her eyes, too. 'Don't you people have a killer to catch?' Her lower lip was shaking. 'I'm sure it's Even who did it. That's what everyone thinks, and you're standing here, saying that...'

She put a hand up in front of her mouth. Tears were streaming down her face.

'I'm sorry,' Yngve said, as softly as he could. 'I didn't mean to insinuate that...'

Cecilie stared at him with blood-shot eyes.

Yngve held his hands up in front of him. 'It was ... I'll go,' he said. 'I'm sorry. I'll go now. Thank you for ... thank you.'

🗗

You can't really blame her, Åse said. She was sitting on the back seat, looking at him in the mirror. For some reason she was wearing her nightdress.

'But I didn't...' he started. 'I didn't mean to suggest that Frode had killed her.'

Losing someone the way the Lindgrens had was completely different from what he'd gone through. He was able to prepare for his loss. Cecilie and Frode hadn't received any warning. They had probably gone to work that morning, thinking about nothing and anything, only to have their world shattered in the blink of an eye, the flick of a switch. He muttered an apology again, hoping that Cecilie, in some way, would be able to hear him.

Yngve took a deep breath and dialled the number she had given him.

A man answered straightaway.

Yngve introduced himself. 'I'm trying to reach your brother. Is he with you?'

'I don't know,' Reidar Lindgren said. 'Not right now, anyway. He's been staying at my place for a few days, but I'm at work, so I don't know if he's there right now.'

'A few days, you say. Since when, exactly?'

'Um ... Saturday? Yes. Saturday. I was going to a reunion party that night. Twenty-five years. Can you believe it?'

'Are you far from your apartment?'

'You mean as we speak?'

'That's what I mean, yes.'

'A little.'

'Would you mind going home to check?' Yngve said. 'I really need to talk to him. Could you have him call me? He's got my number.'

'Has something happened?' Reidar Lindgren asked. 'Something else, I mean?' He sounded unsure.

'Depends what you mean,' Yngve said. 'But I have some questions for him, and at this stage of the investigation, it's imperative that I talk to the person who might have known Mari best.'

A loud bang in the background seemed to make Lindgren jump. 'I'm at a construction site,' he explained. 'But I'll hurry home. See if I can get hold of him for you.'

'I appreciate it, thanks.'

□

Back at the office, Yngve met Therese Kyrkjebø by the water dispenser. She drank a cup, then filled it again. She placed a hand on her growing belly, as if to make sure everything was OK.

'I've spoken to a friend of Børre Halvorsen's,' she said. 'Victor Ramsfjell is his name. He didn't hang out with Børre the night he was killed, but Victor says Børre told him he'd seen Even Tollefsen through one of the school windows on the night of the murders.'

'Did he know which window?'

'The one on the far right,' Therese said. 'The one you climbed through. According to Victor, Børre was sure that it was Even he'd seen.'

Yngve gave this some thought for a few seconds.

'This case gets weirder by the minute,' he said.

'I know,' Therese answered.

'I better go and see if we've had any tips come through on the hotline. Any leads on the leather glove?'

'None yet,' Therese said. 'Except that half the population owns one, apparently.'

36

After the memorial, it seemed as if lots of people needed some kind of distraction. On my way out, I heard online gaming sessions being organised. Others were going to one of the cafés in the town centre, just to chill. A few of them mentioned needing a smoke. I wasn't sure of what.

I was on my way to my bike, which had been propped up against a lamppost, when a familiar voice behind me called my name. I turned and saw Oskar, Fredrik and Kaiss coming towards me.

I took a deep breath as they stopped in front of me. At first, none of them spoke. Kaiss tapped one of his feet on the ground. Oskar ran a hand through his hair, and looked everywhere but into my eyes. Fredrik fiddled with his fingers.

'What's up?' Oskar said, after a while.

'I don't know,' I said. I could hear the anger in my voice.

'Right,' he said. I wasn't going to make it easy for him, so I just stood there, staring at him, waiting for him to go first.

'So, I spoke to my dad,' he started. 'And he said you were pretty shitfaced last night.'

'Lucky bastard,' Kaiss muttered.

Oskar was still having trouble stringing his sentences together, but he went on: 'So if you were pissed when Børre was killed, you ... couldn't have done it,' he said quickly, without looking at me.

'Is that your idea of an apology?'

'I guess,' Oskar said. '

'We know you couldn't kill anyone,' Kaiss offered.

'Do you?' I asked. 'How can you possibly know that? How can anyone possibly know what they're capable of doing, if the wrong buttons are pushed?'

I had no idea why I just said that.

'Are you saying—?'

'I'm not saying anything,' I interrupted. 'I just know that everyone is jumping to conclusions in this town, and I'm stuck in the middle of the shitstorm. Do you have any idea what that feels like? Do you have any idea what it feels like to have your own best friends doubt you?'

None of them said anything.

'It's not a good feeling, I can tell you that much,' I continued. I could feel my cheeks turning red.

'We're sorry anyhow,' Fredrik said. 'If you want us to go, we can go. We just ... we wanted to help, in any way we can. If you need some help, that is, or if you...'

'Fredrik,' I said. 'Stop talking.'

He looked at me with some uncertainty. I sighed heavily. 'Just ... OK. Thanks. I appreciate it.'

We just stood there for a few moments. The air was cold, but nice against my red-hot face.

'I just can't believe this shit,' Kaiss said.

'Me neither,' Fredrik added. 'Especially that Børre was killed right after we talked to him.'

I looked at them, one after the other. 'How...?' I wasn't sure what my question was. 'How did Børre react?' I asked. 'Could he have been lying?'

My friends exchanged quick glances.

'It didn't seem like he was,' Kaiss said. 'I mean, there really wasn't any reason for him to, right?'

I shook my head. 'I don't get it,' I said. 'I just don't. Not any of it.'

A group of girls walked past. Fredrik sent them an appraising look, but none of them looked back.

'It must have been someone else, then,' Oskar said. 'There's no other explanation.

I nodded, but couldn't think of who that could be.

For some strange reason, I thought about something Imo had said about my mother. *She might be a bit frail these days, your mother, but when she's angry, she's dangerous.* She had been to the school show that night.

I hadn't even thought to ask her about it. About when she left. What she saw. Who she talked to, if anyone. I just hadn't thought it was important.

'What is it?' Oskar said. 'You're as pale as a ghost.'

'Am I?' I said. I could feel my heart racing.

Thinking about Mum had made me think about Dad, too. The car accident. Mari was looking into it. She'd talked to her father about it. She was going to do the same with Ole. And my mother had been in the car that day.

'It's nothing,' I said. 'I just haven't been eating much lately. Did any of you see Ida in there?'

They all shook their heads.

Thinking about my mother made me want to get home and speak to her – see what she knew. But I had something more important to do first.

37

'Alright, thanks for your call.'

Yngve hung up and rubbed his eyes. The man who'd just phoned the hotline had informed him that his next-door neighbour used to wear his leather gloves every day when he went out to pick up the morning newspaper, but today that hadn't happened. 'I don't know if it's any help or not, but ... I thought I'd just mention it...'

Yngve was prepared for a lot of nonsense, but he'd hoped for some substance at least. One woman, probably in her late seventies, had even called in to suggest that the murders of Børre Halvorsen might have something to do with the high-school killings.

His mobile phone rang now. It was Reidar Lindgren.

'Frode isn't in my apartment,' he said. 'I don't know where he is. He hasn't left me a note or anything.'

'So he has a key to your apartment?'

'Yeah, I gave him one last night, before he went out.'

'Do you know where he was going? Last night, I mean?'

'No, but ... I had the impression that he was going out-out. You know, for a night out. He asked if I could think of any cheap bars in the city. I don't go out much, but I do know a few. Everything's so damned expensive around here.'

It wasn't uncommon to drown one's sorrows in alcohol, Yngve thought to himself. After Åse died, he'd downed a few bottles as well, but he'd preferred to do it on his own. People dealt with death in different ways.

'Why was he with you in the first place?' Yngve asked.

The phone went quiet for a beat. 'I don't know what had happened,' Reidar Lindgren said eventually. 'But I think it had something to do with the family. With Cecilie. They'd had a falling-out of some kind. At least that's what I thought.'

'Had there been any problems in the marriage before?'

'Not that I know of. Nothing major, anyway. This time, though ... I've never seen him quite like this. So ... angry. So distraught.'

'Did you ask him why?'

'Yes, but he didn't want to talk about it. I respected that.'

'OK,' Yngve said. 'Thanks for calling and helping out. If you see him, can you have him call me?'

'Will do.'

'Thanks.'

So Frode Lindgren was angry, Yngve thought. At his wife, first and foremost. But even if he was mad at Cecilie, Frode had still made the trip back to Fredheim two days after he'd left the family home, in order to go to the school theatre show. He did have a number of missed calls to his daughter as well, so maybe that was why. He wanted to talk to her. But she, for some reason, didn't want to talk to him.

The preliminary autopsy report came in a little later. Mari had died of asphyxiation, and she had also suffered three fractured ribs, not two, as the chief of the forensic team had first suggested.

There was another detail that struck Yngve as odd.

Mari had been beaten before she died. Not particularly hard, but hard enough for her to suffer a small rupture in her upper lip. It probably hadn't been more than a punch. Afterwards the killer had put his hands around her neck and squeezed. Everything suggested that the murderer had become angry and then violent, and that he'd later regretted what he'd done. Nothing similar had happened to either Johannes Eklund or Børre Halvorsen.

Mari's murder is the key to all of this, Yngve thought. It has to be.

Johannes Eklund's autopsy report didn't reveal anything they hadn't already been able to deduce themselves. He had been beaten to death with a sharp, hard object, but so far they hadn't had any solid leads about where his microphone case might be.

The man on the CCTV footage was still unidentified, but a lot of people still hadn't been interviewed for the second time. Slowly, but surely, they were moving in the right direction. At least, that's what Åse kept telling him.

Eighteen people – eighteen tickets from the opening night – were still not accounted for. They'd either not made contact with the police yet – perhaps because they didn't think they had anything in particular to offer, and so were of little interest; or they *were* of interest, because they hadn't hurried to help. That might mean they had something to hide, or they were protecting someone.

The hotline phone rang again. Yngve braced himself for yet another 'valuable tip'.

He sat up straight, though, when the caller said his name: Ivar Morten Tollefsen. *Imo.*

After a pause, Imo spoke. He said: 'There's something I have to tell you.'

38
NOW

The prosecutor, Ms Håkonsen, is walking up and down in front of me with a glass of water in her hand. My own glass is empty, so I fill it.

'So even though Ida Hammer had refused to meet you or talk to you, you still went over to her house?'

'I did.'

'Why?'

'She'd been Mari's best friend. I thought she could help me.'

'And did she?'

I think about Ida for a second. I haven't seen her in the courtroom. I know she had a rough time after Mari died, and after...

I clear my throat and say: 'Well yes. And no.'

39
THEN

I had been to Ida's house once before. It was a few weeks after Mari had interviewed me. She wanted me to go with her to a party there. It was the first time I'd properly met her friends. I had seen them, of course, in school and around Fredheim, but they weren't part of my group; but after that night, all of a sudden they were.

I had a football match the next day, so I stayed away from the booze, which was flowing freely. I really couldn't stay late either. It was an important match against Ham-Kam, the top team.

Mari and I sent each other looks all evening, and it felt as if we both knew that something was going to happen later that night. When I had to go, she left with me, and the looks she got from her friends, the ones saying 'we want to know *everything*', only confirmed what I'd been thinking.

I walked her home.

There were a few drops of rain in the air that night, but it wasn't cold. Thunder rumbled in the distance, with the odd lightning strike breaking through the dark clouds. It felt as if somehow the sky was reflecting the electricity between us. And somewhere along the road our hands met.

We stopped outside her house and talked for hours. Quietly, because we didn't want anyone to hear what we were saying. And that's where we kissed for the first time. A little, careful kiss to begin with, then more and more intense. My insides rose and fell on the swell, and as I walked home afterwards – a lot later than my coach would like – it felt as if my whole body was smiling.

I lay in bed thinking of Mari. I relived the kisses, the warmth of her body, her tender, sad voice when she said she had to go, as she should've been in bed a lot earlier. *My dad's going to kill me*, she said.

Now, no one answered when I rang Ida's bell. I stepped back and looked up at the windows. No twitching curtains. No sound from inside.

'Ida?'

I coughed and tried again, a bit louder this time, before ringing the bell once more. I heard someone fiddling with an upstairs window lock.

Ida stuck her head out. Her eyes were red and swollen.

'Hi,' I said, a bit awkwardly. Ida didn't answer, but her eyes darkened with anger.

'Can I talk to you?' I asked.

'About what?' Her voice was always a bit nasal, but it sounded worse now, coming from above my head.

I shrugged. 'What do you think?'

She didn't answer.

'I didn't kill them.'

'And why should I believe you?'

'Why shouldn't you?' I stared up at her. 'I really liked Mari, you know that. I think maybe...' No, I couldn't use the word I was about to say. It was so easy to use big words about people who were dead.

'Someone said they'd seen you at the school.'

I sighed. 'It's not true. I was at home all night.'

Ida didn't answer.

'Please come down,' I begged. 'I need to talk to you.'

It didn't look like she was going to close the window. Not to begin with at least. I looked up at her with pleading eyes. I wasn't planning on giving up. Then something in her hard mask changed. Her face softened, and she rolled her eyes.

'Hang on a minute, then.'

It took more like five for her to open to the door and stick her head out. I realised that she'd done herself up. Her eyes were more shiny and she'd put on some foundation. She was wearing a different top as well. I had to stop myself from staring at her breasts; they seemed to have been stuffed inside a bra that was far too small for them.

She didn't open the door fully, or invite me in. She seemed to want to keep me at a distance, so she could shut the door quickly if I suddenly decided to attack her.

'What do you want to talk about?' she asked.

'Mari, obviously,' I said with a sigh. 'I'm trying to find out what happened.'

Was that really what I was doing? I wasn't sure.

'Isn't that what the police are supposed to be doing?'

'Yes, but I need some answers too. And you knew her best.'

Ida just looked at me.

'Can't we at least talk about it?' I pleaded. 'See if we can think of anything new?'

Again, it was like she looked me up and down. Assessed me. I knew that she liked me, really. Finally, she opened the door and let me in.

'Do you want anything?' she asked, when I'd kicked off my shoes. 'I think we've only got Coke and milk.'

'No, thanks,' I said.

'Let's go out the back, so I can have a cigarette.'

I followed her through the house and out onto the veranda. It looked like this was where Ida had been sitting all day, under a blanket. Her mobile phone was on the bench. There were cushions on one of the chairs. The ashtray was close to overflowing.

Ida found another cushion for me, and we sat down.

'What the hell's going on, Ida?'

She let out big sigh. 'I don't know,' she said.

'She must have said something to you about ... something. About why she split up with me, just like that, out of nowhere. Why she wouldn't speak to me after.'

Ida looked at me briefly, tapped her cigarette packet to get one out. She lit it. 'I thought it was a bit harsh, to be honest.'

I waited for her to continue.

'And a bit odd that she didn't want to say anything.' She exhaled the smoke. 'But I promised to help her to...' She sighed.

'To what?'

'To keep you away from her.'

I felt my eyes widen. 'What do you mean?'

'The last few days before ... she was killed, she was here, with me.'

'She was?'

'Yes.'

'So...?' I couldn't decide which question to ask her first. 'Did she stay overnight as well?'

Ida nodded and took another drag on her cigarette.

'I don't think she was on good terms with her parents. Or ... I don't know.'

'So she was ... here, when she should have been at school?'

'Yes,' Ida said.

'But ... was she ill?'

'No. She didn't seem to be.'

'Bu why wouldn't she talk to me? Did she tell you?'

Ida took a deep breath. 'I don't really know,' she said. 'But hey, she was my friend. If I could help her in any way...'

I needed a few seconds to absorb what Ida had just told me.

'Was she scared of me? Is that it?'

'It was nothing like that. I think she just didn't want to talk to you.'

'There wasn't ... anyone else, was there?'

'Do you mean – was she in love with anyone else?' She smiled when I nodded. 'No, Even. She wasn't. She would have told me *that*.'

Ida took another drag on her cigarette. For a few moments we just sat there in silence.

'She was very different, those last few days,' Ida said at last.

'Different, how?'

'As if ... well, as if she wasn't quite with it, if you know what I mean.'

Ida blew the smoke straight up in the air. I watched what little wind there was catch it and whisk it away.

'She really lost it at one point.'

'How so?'

'All the calls – from you. Her dad. She didn't want to talk to anyone, and her phone just wouldn't stop ringing. Suddenly she just threw it against the wall. The screen broke almost completely, and something else inside it must've bust, too, because she couldn't turn it back on later.'

I slumped into my chair. I couldn't imagine Mari acting like that. Why hadn't she just turned the phone off?

Ida rubbed her eyes, as if the smoke was making them hurt.

'When was this?' I asked her.

'The day she broke up with you.'

Saturday, I said to myself.

'She regretted it afterwards. Started crying and everything. Made me take her phone to the repair shop for her.'

'She didn't want to do it herself?'

'No, she didn't want to leave the house. My room, even.'

'Because she was afraid she might run into me, was that it?'

'Yeah,' Ida said. 'Something like that. Or her parents. I don't know.'

'What was going on with her parents?'

'I don't know. She didn't want to talk about it. Cecilie even texted me to ask if I knew where Mari was.'

'Did you tell her?'

'Of course I did. I had to. I told her about the broken phone, too, so Cecilie wouldn't worry about not getting a reply.'

Ida's phone vibrated. She checked to see what it was, but didn't respond to the notification.

'Were you at the show that night?' I asked.

'Yes.'

'Did you speak to Mari afterwards?'

'No, I knew she was going to interview Johannes, so me and Elise, we just left.'

'You ... didn't notice anything suspicious on your way out?'

She shook her head. 'The police asked me that as well, and I've tried to think. But nothing happened – nothing was different. Everyone was happy. It was a fun show.'

I moved a little in my chair. 'It must have been one of the last people left then,' I said. 'Unless someone forgot something and went back inside.'

'Possibly,' Ida said.

I thought about something Yngve Mork had said in the press conference – about the killer leaving through one of the upstairs windows.

'Who would have stayed behind, other than the guys who were part of the show?' I said – to myself more than Ida.

'The janitor, maybe.'

I looked at her. 'Tic-Tac?'

She nodded. 'He was there that night. I saw him. And he's got keys to everything.'

I thought about that. And remembered that I'd seen something in his eyes the morning I'd arrived at the school and seen Ida collapsing to the floor. I'd thought it was shock, but could it have been something else? Fear? Remorse? Nervousness?

Tic-Tac was the kind of guy I could imagine eyeing up the girls at school. Had he seen Mari that evening, spoken to her and then ... tried it on in some way?

There was no way of knowing.

'How well do you know Mari's parents?' I asked.

'Well, you know,' Ida said, 'I was there all the time. Cecilie's like my second mother.'

'I think I might go to see them,' I said. 'Want to join me?'

40

Ida, for some reason, had to change her clothes yet again. When she finally joined me she said that she really didn't want to go, but she knew she'd have to see Mari's parents at some point, so why not get it over with?

I was dreading it, too. I wondered how Frode and Cecilie would feel about seeing me again. If they could even face talking to me. I was glad I had Ida coming along with me.

As we got closer to their house, I thought about the first time Mari had invited me over for dinner. As we'd sat down and started to eat – oven baked cod with peas, potatoes and bacon – they were all watching me carefully. It was only after the meal that I understood why.

'You really shouldn't hold your cutlery like that,' Mari said, teasing me.

'How do you mean? Like what?'

'Like you are skiing and the knife and fork are your sticks.'

'Oh, do I?'

Mari had laughed.

Apparently my parents had never bothered to teach me properly. I'd make sure I got it right the next time I shared a meal with my girlfriend. I hadn't been invited back to their table, though, and every time I went there to pick Mari up or just visit, I could always feel a certain distance from her parents. Cecilie, in particular, never said much.

'You're different, you and Mari,' I said to Ida, as I walked beside her, pushing my bike. Mari wasn't at all interested in blogging or fashion; she was serious about her schoolwork and she already knew what she wanted to do with her life. Ida's biggest worry, it seemed, was what she should be wearing, and whether it would make her look sexy enough.

'How do you mean, different?' she asked.

I tried to find the right words – ones that didn't sound condescending or disrespectful.

Ida came to my rescue. 'I guess we are,' she said. 'Or ... I guess we *were*. But isn't that a good thing? I mean, that you can be completely different and still like each other?'

I thought about my friends for a moment. I was the only one of us who played football. Fredrik was an only child, and a very spoilt one at that. Kaiss was a devout Muslim. Oskar was a cross-country skiier.

Yeah, it was a good thing.

'So tell me,' I said, 'what were you guys doing at school recently?'

'Why do you want to know?'

'I guess I just want to know what Mari did those last few days...'

She thought about it for a moment. 'We were studying *Ghosts* in Norwegian literature.'

'Ibsen.'

'Yes, I think that was the dude's name.' She rolled her eyes. 'Sooo boring.'

I smiled.

'We were doing some grammar bullshit in English. And we were doing blood samples and stuff like that in biology. Did blood tests on each other. Yuck!'

I remembered doing that the previous year. I'd actually enjoyed it.

Soon we were at Mari's house. I took a deep breath and tried to steel myself. Like Ida said, better to get it over and done with.

After we'd rung the bell, a woman I'd never seen before opened the door.

'Hi,' Ida said. 'I was wondering if Mari's mum and dad are in? I'm Ida – Mari's best friend.'

'Oh, right,' the woman said, before sending me a long look, as though she was wondering why *I* was there, too. If she didn't already know who I was, I wasn't going to tell her.

'Frode's not here right now,' she said, 'but I'll ask if Cecilie can talk to you for a second. Hang on a minute.'

The woman closed the door. Ida and I exchanged glances. Neither of us knew what to expect. I'd heard some people say that losing a child was the worst thing that could happen to anyone. That it was impossible to imagine the grief unless you had actually experienced it yourself.

We waited for a few minutes, then the door opened again. Cecilie was standing there in front of us. At first she only had eyes for Ida, tears welling up. Then she started to sob, and Ida did too. They stepped towards each other and hugged for what seemed like a good minute or more. It looked as if they both were hanging on to each other for dear life, crying and hugging. I just stood there on the bottom step, not knowing where to look or what to do.

When they let go of each other, Cecilie wiped Ida's tears from her cheeks and tucked a stray lock of hair behind her ear.

Then she saw me.

And everything changed.

She pushed Ida away. The overwhelming sadness gave way to a rage that seemed to grow with every second. She struggled for words as she stared down at me. Like a boxer waiting for the bell to ring. I wanted to say something, to find the right words to soothe the hurt I could see in her eyes. A pain she thought I'd caused her.

Cecilie just looked at me with horror, then at Ida – as though she could not comprehend how Ida – *Ida* – could betray her this way.

'Cecilie,' I said. 'I didn't—'

'Go,' she said, her voice trembling. 'Just leave. Both of you. Go away!'

'Cecilie,' Ida tried as well, but Mari's mother gave her the same hard look as she'd given me.

Ida held up her hands and retreated down the steps. 'We're leaving,' she said. 'We just wanted to...'

She stopped herself. Mari's mother sent me another look filled with hate. Then she went inside and slammed the door.

41
NOW

I need to pee, but I know there is still a long way to go before I'm finished. I push the thought away.

'Really,' Prosecutor Håkonsen says. 'What did you expect was going to happen? That Mari's mother was just going to open her arms to you, too? You didn't think she'd heard the rumours?'

'I admit, it was a stupid thing to do,' I say. 'But I was looking for answers, and I really thought that Cecilie might be able to help.'

'Even in her moment of grief?'

'Well, yes. And I felt it was the right thing to do.'

'The right thing to do,' Ms Håkonsen repeats, as if she can't quite believe I've just said that.

'I know it sounds silly, but I was hoping she would be able to look me in the eye and *see* that I couldn't have murdered her daughter.'

'Sounds a bit naïve, if you ask me.'

'I realise that now. But back then I thought that if she would only just see me and talk to me, she would understand. A cold, evil murderer wouldn't go to his victim's parents like that.'

'And that wasn't you.'

'That wasn't me, no.'

'How did her reaction make you feel?'

I let out a long breath. 'Like shit. Sorry,' I quickly add. 'I was hurt and sad. Of course I was. Slightly shocked, too, however weird that sounds.'

'But the shocks for you that day were far from over, isn't that correct?'

I realise she's talking about Imo. I nod and say:

'Yes, that's right.'

42
THEN

Ida and I barely spoke on the way back.

'Do you want to come in?' she said when we were outside her house again. 'I make a mean smoothie, if you fancy it.'

The tone of her voice suggested there was more to her question than just concern and the need to be with someone. I tried to read the expression in her eyes.

'I thought you only had milk and Coke?' I said.

Ida smiled back.

'Another time, maybe,' I said. 'I need to go home now.'

Ida put her arms round me and held me for a long time. It felt really good to get a hug. And it was good to hold Ida. She smelled nice, and she was soft.

'Thank you for walking me home,' she whispered in my ear.

'No worries,' I said, gently pushing her away. 'Thanks for coming with me to...' I nodded towards the road we'd just come down.

'Don't be upset by what Cecilie said,' Ida said. 'She's just a bit crazy because of what's happened.'

I nodded, even though I didn't know how I couldn't be upset about being branded a murderer without the chance of even speaking in my own defence.

'Oh, and another thing,' she said, just as I was getting onto my bike. 'Mum and Dad are out this evening, so I thought I'd have a small party – for some of Mari's friends. And Johannes' too,' she added quickly. 'If you and your friends would like to come, just ... well, come.'

I hesitated.

'It's not a party-party,' she added. 'More a get-together ... to talk about what's happened and to hang out.'

'Thanks', I said. 'I'll think about it.

Ida smiled – a big, beautiful smile. Then she went into the house. She didn't seem sad anymore.

◻

I could smell the cheese on toast even before I went into the kitchen. Sometimes it seemed like Mum never ate anything, so I assumed that I would find my brother in there, guzzling, eyes glued to his mobile phone.

'Hello?' Mum's voice was bright and breezy. I wondered if there was a glass somewhere in the house with ice cubes in it.

Before I got to the kitchen door, I heard GP's paws scratching across the floor. He barked, and as soon as I opened the door, he jumped up at me, wagging his tail. I gave him a good stroke and pat and told him how cute and lovely he was.

Tobias was anything but. He was sitting on a stool with his baseball cap on back to front, bent over his food. He was chewing with his whole face. Mum was leaning against the worktop beside him. She had a radiant smile and, yep, a glass in her hand.

'Where have you been?' she asked.

'Here and there,' I said. 'Is there any more cheese on toast, or has that lard-arse eaten it all?'

I nodded at my brother. He raised his head and gave me an exaggerated smile, food still in his mouth.

'God, you're disgusting.'

'There's one left,' Mum said and pointed to the stove. 'I can make some more, if you like. Are you done, Tobias, or shall I make some more for you, too? It's really no bother.'

My brother didn't answer.

The cheese lay melted, thick and delicious on the toasted bread. I grabbed it and took a bite. Perfectly done, just the right amount of ketchup under the ham, and a light sprinkle of oregano on top. God, it was good to have something to eat again without feeling my insides turn over.

I chewed, observing my brother for a few moments. He was at least a head taller than Mum now. I wondered how he was getting on. If he was happy. He didn't seem to care that his clothes were often a bit dirty and that you could smell the sweat on him from a few feet away. He lived his life online, sitting in his room all day, gaming. I knew he chatted to his friend Ruben almost every day, but I had no idea whether he had any other friends – ones he actually talked to face to face.

You should be taking care of him, I thought. You should be taking him out, introducing him to people. But it wasn't easy. Travelling back and forth to Lillestrøm several times a week took up a lot of my time. And then there was Mari and my mates. The day only had so many hours. Still, I felt bad for him. And guilty.

My phone rang. It was Imo.

'What's up?' I said.

'Even,' he began. There was an edge to his voice.

'What is it?' I asked, suddenly anxious.

'Before I say anything else, it's important that you listen to me now. Can you do that, Even?'

I was confused. Imo never talked like this. 'Yes, of course,' I said. 'What is it? What's happened?'

'Don't get wound up, but the police are coming round to see me.'

'The police?' I said. 'Why?'

I felt a huge knot form in my belly.

'It's not what it sounds,' Imo said. 'But you know the leather glove the police are looking for?'

'Yeah...'

It was a few seconds before Imo spoke again:

'That leather glove is mine.'

43

'What the hell are you saying, Imo?'

It had become hard to breathe. I noticed that Mum and Tobias had turned to look at me.

'Well, at least I think it's mine,' Imo continued. 'I just called the police to tell them.'

'So...?' My thoughts were all over the place. 'So, were they stolen or something?'

'Maybe,' he answered. 'I just know that I wore them before the show, when I carried the keyboard and all the other stuff inside the school, and that I couldn't find them later when I was going home. I don't know if anyone actually stole them. And I really didn't look that hard for them, either. I thought I would find them the day after. I really just wanted to get home.'

I waited for him to tell me more.

'I thought it best to be open and honest with the police,' Imo said. 'So I thought it was best to tell you too, in case, you know, rumours start to spread. You know how things get around here.'

I did have a good idea, yes.

'Don't worry, champ,' Imo added. 'It's all good.'

'Let's hope so.'

'It is. It will be.'

After we'd hung up, I filled Mum and Tobias in on what Imo had told me. Tobias finished his glass of milk and then went upstairs, without saying a word, while Mum seemed to retreat – to somewhere deep inside her mind. Her eyes faded, and she had a worried look on her face.

'I want to know something,' I asked her.

She needed a moment or two to realise that I'd spoken to her. 'Hm?'

'When did you leave the school that night?'

She looked at me, bewildered. 'I left right away,' she answered.

'You went straight home?' By 'home' I meant Knut's apartment.

She seemed to understand. 'Mhm...'

'When did you get there?'

'I don't know,' she said. 'I didn't check the time. Why do you ask?'

'Did you walk home alone?'

'Yes. What is this? Why do I feel like I'm being interrogated all of a sudden?'

I didn't know how to respond to that, so I just said: 'I was just wondering.'

She snorted. 'You'll make an excellent cop one day.'

I wondered if Yngve Mork had talked to her yet, or if she had volunteered to go to the station. I was about to ask, but she downed the rest of her glass and turned to mix herself another drink.

🗗

When Oskar rang the bell a little while later, Mum was all smiles again. I could tell she was tipsy. She met my best friend in the hall with a broad smile.

'Oskar,' she almost shouted. 'How nice to see you again. How are you?'

I sent her a quick look that said 'don't overdo it, Mum', but she clearly didn't take the hint. She wanted to know what we were going to do now, what we were going to do later. I don't know how many times I said 'Mum' in a sharp voice, but it didn't stop her. I finally managed to drag Oskar away from her and down to my room.

For an hour or so we just ate crisps and played Call of Duty. It felt really good to do something ordinary and normal again. We stayed away from group chats though, as I didn't want to communicate with anyone.

Oskar's phone rang after we'd been playing for a while. He looked at the display, but decided to ignore it. 'Just my Mum having a go again,' he explained.

'Having a go about what?' I wanted to know.

Oskar sighed heavily. 'With everything that's happened, she ... she thinks I should just stay home.'

'She's afraid.'

'Yeah, and...' He looked at me quickly, then back at the monitor.

She's afraid of *me*, I thought. She's afraid that I would do something to her son.

I couldn't quite believe it. But then again, I couldn't really blame her, either. According to a lot of people in Fredheim I was capable of triple murder. I thought about that for a second, about the things I'd said to my friends earlier in the day – about anyone being capable of killing someone. Was that really true? Could my mother, for instance, do that? Could Oskar? Could I?

I really didn't know.

And that was maybe what scared me the most.

44

The largest conference room at Fredheim's arts centre was equipped with everything a good police investigation required. A whiteboard, pens in various colours, a projector, monitors and, most importantly, a coffee machine that took capsules of various sizes and strengths, and that only needed a refill of water every now and then.

Yngve Mork had gathered his detectives around a large table. He stood at one end, looking at a host of coffee mugs, water bottles, mobile phones, note pads, car keys and key chains, all belonging to a group of people who were waiting for him to take the lead. He was looking at men and women he didn't know, officers and detectives who'd been transferred in from their districts, away from other pressing matters. Here they had been told what to do for the past day and a half by a sixty-three-year-old grieving widower they'd never met before. It was a demanding situation for all of them. For Yngve this was the first time he'd had a team this big under his command.

'It's almost strange,' he started with a careful smile. 'We've been working together for thirty-six hours or so, and this is this first time we've all been gathered in the same room for more than thirty seconds.'

His jovial tone – Åse's idea – didn't catch on in the way he'd hoped. 'I'd like to thank each and every one of you for your efforts so far. They've been impressive. But there are still a lot of questions to be answered, so I thought we could go through them one by one. Maybe talking it through will help make things a little bit clearer.'

Some of the detectives leaned forwards.

'Alright, let's consider Mari Lindgren and Johannes Eklund first,' Yngve continued. 'Ann-Mari Sara from Kripos is as sure as she can be about Mari being the first victim. Her death also differs from the others, because she was murdered in a non-violent fashion – if that's even a term we can use. What I mean is that she was strangled first. Then someone tried to bring her back to life again, which indicates remorse. Is our killer a close relation, perhaps? Now, a lot of people in this town seem to *know* that Even Tollefsen is the perpetrator, because he used to be her boyfriend. In other words, they believe it was an act of jealousy. Johannes Eklund may have become a victim because he was in the wrong place at the wrong time. He might have seen what happened, and in order to protect that truth from getting out, he had to die. Alternatively, jealousy might have been involved. Were Johannes and Mari becoming close?'

Yngve sought Therese Kyrkjebø's eyes. She and the others seemed to be paying careful attention to what he was saying.

'Even, however, vehemently denies being at the school premises that night, even though several witnesses claim otherwise. One of them is Børre Halvorsen, the sixteen-year-old who was found dead with half his head smashed in under the railway bridge.'

Cold, Åse said to him. *That was uncalled for.*

He immediately regretted his choice of words, and he could see the surprise in some of the detectives' faces. He cleared his voice and decided to just press on.

'It could be suggested that Børre's sighting of Even was a potential motive for his killing. But Even has an alibi for the night in question.

And if we do believe the sighting in itself is a motive, that would mean the others who also claim to have seen Even at the school that night might be in danger too. I really don't think anything will happen to them as well.'

'Question,' one of the officers in the room said. It was Davidsen, the man from Lillestrøm who'd gone through the CCTV recordings. He had tipped his chair a little backwards, so that it rested only on two legs. 'Do we have anyone else's word besides this Emo fellow that Even, in fact, did spend the night at the pig farm place at the time of Børre Halvorsen's murder?'

'Imo,' Therese corrected.

'No, we don't,' Yngve said. 'But—'

'I guess what I'm really asking is if he's trustworthy,' the officer continued. 'I mean, this thing with his gloves disappearing and having the janitor leave the door on the other side open for him and everything. Are we one hundred percent certain he's telling the truth?'

'It's hard to be one hundred percent sure of anything,' Yngve said. 'But I know Imo well. He's a good man, and he's done a lot of good for this community over the last twenty-five years.'

'That doesn't have to mean anything.'

'I know, but as far as *I* know, he's not in the habit of lying about … stuff. And what would his motive be for giving Even a false alibi?'

'The usual,' the detective continued. 'To cover for his nephew.'

'So you're saying that Imo knew that Even killed Mari and Johannes, and that Imo – knowing that – thought it was OK for him to take another life? "Go ahead, son, I'll cover for you next time as well"?'

The detective didn't respond, neither did anyone else. 'Even was still drunk when I woke him last night,' Yngve continued. 'I find it hard to believe that a teenager in such a state could make his way to Fredheim Bridge – an eight-kilometre hike – in the middle of the night, without anyone noticing him. Not to mention the fact that he would have to get back, too. A total of sixteen kilometres. In the middle of the night.'

Again a moment's pause in the room.

'It was just a question,' Davidsen finally said.

'And questions are good,' Yngve said enthusiastically. 'So we can chew over this thing properly. And we musn't rule out that Børre Halvorsen's murder might not be related to the other two at all. He's been known to graffiti a lot of houses and buildings in the area over the last few years. He's definitely pissed a lot of people off.'

'It's still a hell of a thing to do,' Vibeke Hanstveit said. 'Beat a sixteen-year old to death over some spray paint.'

'I don't disagree with you on that,' Yngve said. 'Which means that we need to find motives for all the murders. And because Mari was killed first, I think it might be a good idea to focus on her first. At least until we hit a dead end. Um, no pun intended.'

He knew that Åse would be frowning, but he quickly put her out of his mind.

'If we can find the motive for her murder, I believe the other bits and pieces will fall neatly into place. So let's talk about Mari.'

Yngve quickly brought the task force up to speed on the steps Mari had taken to find out more about the car accident that had ended Jimmy Tollefsen's life. Yngve added that he'd taken another good look at the report he wrote after the accident, but hadn't found anything irregular.

'There was nothing wrong with the car, and he didn't have any alcohol in his blood. Everything suggests that Susanne Tollefsen's story checks out: Jimmy had a turn of some kind. He passed out. That's why they skidded off the road.'

'But we only have her word for it, right?' The question came from Therese Kyrkjebø.

'Yes,' Yngve said.

'So maybe we should bring her in again,' one of the other detectives argued – a man with caramel-coloured hair and a big belly.

Yngve thought of the interviews he had conducted with Susanne ten years before. It had taken days for her to answer even the simplest of questions, as she was being treated for a fractured collarbone and some other minor injuries.

'Was she at the school show that night?' the same detective asked.

Vibeke Hanstveit produced a sheet of paper with a lot of names on it. 'Doesn't look like it,' she said, as she scanned it. 'She hasn't come in for questioning.'

'If she was, and she hasn't come forward, I say we get her in here right away,' Therese said.

'I've been meaning to have a sit-down with her anyway,' Yngve said. 'No one knows her son better than she does.'

'You think Even still might have something to do with all this?' Vibeke Hanstveit asked.

'I don't know,' Yngve said. 'That's what I'd like to find out. And I'd like to question her again about the car accident, too. Is there any way she could have had a motive for killing Mari? Mari was going to write a piece about the car accident, but that isn't something you would kill three teenagers over. Unless, of course, Mari had discovered something that wasn't uncovered ten years ago. Something that suggests Susanne lied to us. I find it very hard to believe that Mari had, though.'

'Why?' Hanstveit asked.

'She wasn't privy to a single piece of physical evidence, for one. It's not my impression that she'd talked to Susanne about the accident, or even talked that much to her at all – even though Mari was going out with her son.'

The room went quiet for a moment.

'I'll head over to her house after this meeting,' Yngve said. 'In the meantime, let's look at other possible motives as well. Let's hear them all. There are no stupid ideas. No silly thoughts.' Yngve searched the room with his eyes. 'Come on,' he said. 'There must have been *something* that has struck you as odd or weird.'

'Maybe someone else had a thing for Mari,' one of the detectives suggested – a woman with long, fair hair. 'Maybe they thought that Mari was on the market again after her break-up with Even, which apparently was done very publicly. But she refused them and they reacted angrily.'

Yngve thought about it. 'That would suggest that someone had time to make a move on her in the few minutes it took Johannes Eklund to leave the music room, go downstairs with his friends, realise that he'd misplaced his phone, and then come back up again. I don't think that would have taken him very long.'

'There *are* people like that,' she argued, 'who get straight to the point. Without any fuss.'

Again the room went quiet. No one seemed to support her suggestion.

'Alright,' Yngve said. 'Let us move away from the motive a little.'

He asked if they had managed to identify the man who had entered the school by the main door at 10.49 p.m., and who hadn't come back out the same way.

'I talked to the group of girls who were standing outside at the time,' another detective said. 'They hadn't noticed him.'

Yngve thought of Mari's father, who he still hadn't managed to get hold of. His absence from the town – from his wife's side just after their daughter had been killed – was beginning to look more and more suspicious.

'What about Børre Halvorsen's movements between the show and his murder. Do we know what he was up to, besides not going to school?'

'I spoke to his father earlier,' Therese said. 'He had no idea where Børre had been.'

'God, didn't *either* of his parents have any kind of control over this kid?' Hanstveit asked.

'Poor lad,' one of the others offered.

Therese pursed her lips and shook her head slightly, before stroking her belly.

'The door-to-door around the area close to the bridge,' Yngve continued. 'Did that give us anything?'

The man with the caramel-coloured hair coughed into his fist. 'There aren't many houses with a direct view of the bridge, so no, not really.'

'There's a CCTV camera at the train station,' Therese said. 'I've requested the footage, if there even was any, but I haven't got a reply yet.'

Yngve ran a hand over his head. 'How are we doing on the microphone case?'

'Nothing solid as of yet,' Davidsen said.

'Alright,' Yngve said and started to walk up and down in front of the table. 'Priority number one: find the man on the CCTV footage of the school and ask him what he was doing there. Next: find out as much as we can about Mari's life – her interests, her friends – there must be something we've missed. Same goes for Børre Halvorsen. We need a list of the people he was in contact with between the night of the school murders until he was killed himself.'

Some of the officers made notes.

'Anyone have anything to add?' Yngve asked.

No one spoke.

'OK. Then let's get to it.'

Åse remained in the room as the task force left it. She thought he handled it well. 'I don't know about that,' he said.

'What's that?'

He turned to look at Hanstveit. She was standing in the door, looking at him.

'Hm?'

'You were saying something.'

'Oh, was I?'

'Yes, you were.'

He tried to laugh it off. 'I'm an old man,' he said with a careful smile. 'I was just talking to myself.'

45

When we rang the bell at Ida's house, Oskar and I could already hear the music playing inside.

Elise opened the door for us. 'Even!' She was sloshed already. 'Come in!'

Gone was the blatant suspicion from earlier in the day. I wondered if Ida had had a talk with her about me. She pulled at my arm without saying anything to Oskar. A strange mixture of perfume and alcohol followed in her wake. I thought Ida had said that this wasn't a 'party-party'.

Inside there were people everywhere. I half expected to see Mari sitting on the sofa, stealing a secret look at me. The only looks I was getting were sneaky, suspicious ones. But no one said anything to me. I tried to relax.

Oskar and I were looking for Fredrik and Kaiss, when Ida popped up. Like Elise, she called my name loudly. I noticed that several people in the room turned towards us. But that didn't stop Ida from throwing her arms around me, leaving me no choice but to accept the hug.

Ida held me tight and breathed in my ear: 'I'm so glad you came!' Her voice pierced my brain which was already thumping with the heavy rhythms of a song I didn't like. I was a bit put out when Ida kissed me on the cheek as well, but I just smiled and tried in vain to stop my face flushing red. Again, I noticed some looks from the room. People clearly found Ida's behaviour odd.

'Where are your parents?' I asked. I wondered if there was ever a better question to kill a party.

'It's their wedding anniversary today,' she said. 'Or ... something. They went for dinner somewhere. They promised not to be back until late.'

Let's hope not, I thought. I tried to picture what the house would look like in a few hours' time. Ida was dancing – half on her own, half with me. She was still holding my hand.

'Come on,' she said. 'Let's get you something to drink.'

She didn't wait for a yes or a no, just pulled me with her. I thought of GP. So this was what he felt like, being dragged along all the time.

The music wasn't as loud in the kitchen, but a group of people were standing around a machine that was humming and whirring. One of the guys – I didn't know him from before – looked at me with a sneer on his lips. I decided to ignore him.

'We're making smoothies,' Ida said. 'I make insanely good smoothies.'

'So I've heard.'

There was a tall, glass blender on the worktop and lots of fruit, yoghurt, juice and alcohol. Ida pulled me over and started to throw kiwi, banana, strawberry and avocado into the blender. Then she poured in some juice. She was about to open a bottle of vodka as well, when I said: 'No alcohol for me, please.'

'Oh, come on,' she said. 'Don't be such a party pooper.'

Then she poured in the vodka, as though it was water, and started the machine. The noise was swallowed by the laughter and music from the living room. I wondered how this was honouring Mari and Johannes – if anyone else was even thinking of them at all right now. Ida let the blender do its thing for about thirty seconds, then she poured the red-green-whitish sludge into a glass and handed it to me.

'How many of these have you had so far?'

'Why do you ask, *Daddy*?'

I gave her a sheepish smile.

'Taste it.'

I did as she said, and decided that 'insane' was actually the best way to describe her smoothie. The combination of fruit and vodka was strange, initially nice and sweet, but then followed by a taste like nails and poison. I took a tiny sip for the sake of appearances. 'Very good,' I said.

'Well, hello there!' Fredrik's voice cut through the noise behind me.

I turned around and we did our usual handshake-hug thing.

'Where's Kaiss?' I asked.

'He had to go to trombone rehearsal,' Fredrik said.

'Trombone?'

'Yep, he's started playing the trombone.'

I tried to picture it. Kaiss. Trombone. Instead of a party. 'You're joking?'

'Nope, he's having a blow or seventeen.' Fredrik pretended to do the sliding back and forth thing with his arm.

'Well, that's as close as he'll ever get to a blowjob,' I said.

We all laughed. I noticed Ida sending me looks that were a bit too long. I took another sip of the nails-and-poison smoothie. The other boys had almost finished theirs already.

Someone in the next room called for Ida. She rushed out.

'Don't go anywhere,' she said before she left, giving me a stern look. I held up my hands. Oskar and Fredrik did the same. Then we lowered them, one by one.

'I need some air,' I said.

We went out onto the steps at the front of the house. I looked around and then emptied three-quarters of the smoothie onto the flower bed.

'Thank you and goodnight,' Fredrik said to the flowers, while putting some *snus* under his lip.

'Need any help?' Oskar asked.

I wasn't sure what he was getting at.

'To keep Ida away?' he continued.

I snorted and made a face that said, *Oskar, you idiot.* 'She's just drunk,' I said.

We went back inside. While the others continued to pour Ida's fruit-nail gloop down their throats, I stuck to Coke. After about an hour, I had to go to the loo. Leaving the upstairs bathroom I found Ida outside the door. I hadn't seen her in a while. I had assumed she was lying asleep somewhere, half drowned in her own vomit, but her eyes were surprisingly clear and focused. It felt like they were sucking me in as she moved slowly towards me like a panther closing in on its prey.

'Hey,' she said. Her voice was soft and sensual. Seductive. 'Mari was lucky,' she said. 'But then again, she usually got what she wanted.' Another step closer. She was right in front of me now. 'Question is: did *you* get what you wanted?'

She put a hand on my chest. Let it rest there for a while before sliding it down over my stomach muscles. Looking me in the eyes the whole time.

I blinked.

Swallowed.

She kissed me, tentatively. 'I bet she didn't do this to you.'

Her voice was almost a whisper. Her hand started to fiddle with my belt. She opened the door to the bathroom behind me with the other. Then she pushed me inside.

'Ida...'

'Shhhh.'

My belt was undone. She pushed me gently to begin with, then with more and more force.

'It's not dangerous,' she said.

Dangerous, no. But...

Ida had her hand pressed on my crotch. I could smell the alcohol on her breath. We were in the bathroom now. Bathtub and shower, a floor big enough for dancing. A gigantic mirror. Ida locked the door behind us.

'Ida,' I said again.

'Don't say anything,' she said while looking at me. 'You don't need to say anything. No one needs to know.'

I swallowed again.

It wasn't that Ida wasn't attractive. She was. She was gorgeous. And God knows I'd dreamt about a gorgeous girl doing exactly this to me, in a bathroom. But all I could see was Mari – her eyes, her hands, her hair – and that stupid text message she'd sent me, the one about me being the best and all, but that she couldn't be with me any longer.

I guessed Ida could tell, because she suddenly stopped what she was doing.

'So ... Mari could have you, but ... I can't?'

I stood there watching the change in her eyes from one moment to the next. No more seduction. No more lust.

'Ida, I...'

'No one says no to me.'

I didn't know what to say.

'You're going to regret this,' she said.

I tried to think of the right thing to say, something that might repair the damage that had just been done, but nothing seemed right.

'I'm sorry,' was all I said.

'Get out,' she said.

'Ida,' I tried. 'Don't...'

'Just get the FUCK OUT!'

Her scream was so loud I thought someone might hear it, even if the music was still thumping downstairs. I fastened my belt and hurried out. But I didn't like what I'd seen in Ida's eyes when she screamed. She'd frightened me.

46

Susanne had seen the text messages, but she'd ignored them. She didn't have anything to say to the police – she'd said everything ten years ago, over and over again. While she was having the worst time of her life. She didn't have a single thing to add. End of story.

But when she noticed his car coming up the driveway, she didn't know what to do. She put down her glass, then changed her mind, grabbed hold of it once more and swigged it down, feeling that lovely, beautiful warmth in her chest. She took a deep breath, thinking about what she was going to say, how she was going to handle it. Handle him.

She decided to meet the bastard at the door.

'So you *are* home,' Yngve Mork said as he walked up the porch steps.

'I'm sorry,' she said with a smile that felt as fake as a plastic Christmas tree. 'I was just about to call you back.'

'Really. Been busy?'

'Well,' she said. 'Yes. Sort of. There's been a lot to do and ... a lot to think about lately.'

'I know the feeling. Can I borrow two minutes of your time?'

She thought about that for a second. 'Will I ever get them back?'

He laughed at that. 'I guess you won't. I need to speak to you, though.'

'Well, why didn't you just say so?'

He didn't have an answer to that. 'Can I come in?' he said.

Susanne waited another beat before pushing the door open for him. 'Don't bother with the shoes,' she said over her shoulder. 'It's already filthy in here.'

'Don't be ridiculous,' he said. 'My boots are as dirty as ... well, let's just say that they are very dirty.'

Susanne was about to protest again. Why, she really didn't know – she hated grimy floors. She always gave her boys a hard time whenever they walked in with their shoes on. She watched Mork undo his laces and place his boots next to the others. Neatly. Manners, she thought. So that's what that looked like.

'So what can I do for you this time, officer?' She tried to sound inviting, but didn't think she'd pulled it off.

'I need to talk to you about ... Can we sit down somewhere, please? Your kitchen, for instance, is really nice. I was there yesterday with your son.'

'I'm sure it looks a mess.'

'I'm sure it's fine.'

'Well, don't say I didn't warn you.'

She went inside first, clearing away some glasses and plates, before showing him to a chair. 'Can I get you anything? Coffee? Tea? A drink, maybe? Oh, I forgot. You're on duty.'

'I am,' he said with a smile. 'And I'm fine, thank you.'

'Suit yourself.'

She poured herself a glass of tap water, before sitting down opposite him at the table. She realised she was fidgeting with her fingers, so she stopped.

'So how are things?' he asked.

'They're awesome,' she said, immediately regretting her choice of words. She wasn't a teenager. She wasn't Tobias. 'And I'm a bit busy, so...'

'Alright, then,' Mork said. 'How well did you know Mari Lindgren?'

The question took her by surprise. She thought of Cecilie for a second, then pushed her out of her mind.

'I only talked to her a couple of times,' she said. 'Briefly. So no, I really didn't know her at all.'

'Did you, by any chance, talk to her on Monday night?'

'No, I left with everyone else right after the show was over.'

He held her gaze for a moment. 'So you did go to the show?'

'I just said that I did.'

'Why didn't you tell us?'

'Hm?'

'We've been asking everyone who attended the show that night to come forward. To contact us. You might have seen something important.'

'I didn't know about that.'

'You didn't?'

He doesn't believe me, she thought. 'No,' she said firmly. 'I didn't. I've had more than enough on my plate to...'

She stopped herself. She *had* seen Mork's call for help. She'd just decided not to heed it.

'Besides, like I told you, I left right after. What possible interest could *I* be to the investigation?'

He didn't have a response to that. He waited a moment before asking his next question. Susanne felt scrutinised. Invaded. Like he was looking for something deep inside her. She could feel her face becoming hot. Or maybe it was just the drink. My God, she'd had quite a few, hadn't she? She just hoped it wouldn't show. That she wouldn't say something she'd live to regret.

'You went straight home?'

'I did.'

Then she laughed.

'What's so funny?'

'It's just that Even asked me the same question earlier today.'

'He did?'

'Yeah,' she said and rolled her eyes. 'Little mister police.'

Mork seemed to give that some thought. 'Mari was doing a feature for the school newspaper about your son and his father before she died,' he continued.

Susanne felt a sharp pang in her chest. 'Did she ever talk to you about that?'

'No.'

'You're sure?'

'Of course I'm sure.'

'She didn't ask you about your car accident, either?'

She looked at him. 'And why would she do that?' She could hear the steel in her own voice.

'I'm just asking.'

'No,' she said quickly, and a tad too loud. 'She didn't. And I know you,' she continued. 'You're not *just* asking. What the hell has Jimmy's death got to do with any of this?'

'I don't know,' he said. 'That's what we're trying to find out.'

'Why don't you tell me what you really want to know, officer? Do you want to know if I killed her? Is that it? Let me save you the time and the trouble. I didn't. You think I'm crazy? You think I'm evil? I may be a lot of things, detective, but I'm no fucking murderer.'

A voice inside her head wanted to say something, but she managed to push it away. She could tell that she'd given him some food for thought, though.

'Was there anything else?' She pushed her shoulders back a little and lifted her chin.

'Did you leave school with anyone?'

She sighed heavily. 'No.'

'What did you do last night?'

She snorted. 'Depends on what you mean by "last night".'

'How about around midnight.'

'I was at Knut's.'

'Any chance he can verify that?'

She laughed. 'Probably not. He was working, as always. But I sure as hell wasn't under the railway bridge, beating a kid my own son's age to death.'

He nodded slowly. Then waited a while, before getting up.

'Thank you for your time, Susanne,' he said. 'And it really wasn't more than two minutes.'

'It felt like a whole lot more.'

47

'So let me get this straight,' Imo said. We were sitting in his living room. I had a glass of Coke in my hand, Imo a cup of tea. It was half past eleven, but I was anything but tired.

'A super-hot girl more or less offers you full service and you ... you said no?'

I gave a feeble smile as I replayed the whole incident again in my head. I needed to process it, which was exactly why I had ridden my bike straight here after I'd left the party. I could always talk to him about anything.

He shook his head in disbelief. 'When I was your age, Even, it was hard enough to even get some titty-action. We're talking Fort Knox. Locked and sealed from head to toe.'

I laughed. 'Things are a bit different nowadays, Imo.'

'God, what I wouldn't give to be seventeen again.'

He drank some tea and crossed his legs. 'Two things,' he said, raising his index finger. 'First, life doesn't often offer you many gifts that will provide you with wanking material for as long as there's steam in your rocket. Take them. With both hands. Whenever you can.'

I grinned, then started laughing.

'Two.' Imo held up another finger. 'A gentleman never tells.'

He was being serious now. 'Keep this between you and Ida. Even though this sort of thing will never be bad for *your* reputation, it's not the same for her.'

I knew what he meant. Rumours spread fast, especially in a place like Fredheim. Her outburst did make me wonder how genuine Mari and Ida's friendship had been, though. It was almost as if she was jealous of Mari, not necessarily because of me. And if Ida really *was* jealous...

No, I said to myself, stopping the thought right away. Ida could never have killed her best friend. She could never have been a match for Johannes on her own. Or Børre, for that matter.

Or could she?

People were capable of a lot of things when they were angry enough.

'There are three things you must never do to a girl, Even,' Imo said. Clearly this was the night for my uncle's gems of wisdom. 'One, you don't spread false rumours about a girl. That's mean. Two, you stick to one girl at a time. And three...' he held his third finger in the air and paused for effect: 'You don't hit them. Not under any circumstance. A guy picks a fight with you, sure, you stand your ground. Not with a girl. Not ever.'

I nodded slowly.

'You've lived by these rules all your life, Imo?'

'I have, yes.'

He took another sip of his tea. 'You've still got a lot to learn, champ.' His hand was shaking again.

'How did you get on with the police?' I asked. I hadn't thought about Imo's leather glove all evening.

'Well ... I think it went well,' he said. 'They're still looking for my gloves.'

'So you don't think they suspect you of...?'

'No, no,' Imo said, without hesitation. 'Not at all.' He smiled. Then he got up and said: 'It's late, and you've got school tomorrow, right?'

I nodded.

'Your mother will kill me if she finds out you've been sitting here nattering until midnight.'

I looked up at him. 'You always say that, don't you?'

'What?'

'That Mum will kill you if this or that.'

'You don't think she would?' Imo said, and winked at me. 'Go on, now. Off you go.'

⌐

It was pitch-dark outside when I left for home. Thankfully the main road back to Fredheim was lit. As I cycled along, I thought about Ida and her ferocious scream, but then the humming of a car behind me caught my attention. Traffic wasn't uncommon, even at this hour, but I noticed that the sound of the engine didn't change – it didn't come any closer.

I looked over my shoulder. The car was about a hundred yards behind me. Only the parking lights were on. And I was right, it *was* keeping pace with me. The distance made it hard to see what kind of car it was, especially as new cars all looked the same to me. But it was definitely a car, not a van or a truck.

I slowed down. So did the car.

I stopped completely. Put my feet on the ground.

The car stopped, too.

I tried to get a good look at the driver, but the windscreen was too dark. I considered turning and cycling back towards it, just to see what would happen, but decided not to. Too risky. Instead, I got back on my bike and cycled as fast as I could towards Fredheim. Every now and then a car would come in the opposite direction. I wondered if I should call Imo, have him come to my rescue. For days now people had been saying more or less to my face, albeit online, that they were going to get justice for the dead, one way or the other. I hadn't thought anyone would actually do anything. Now I wasn't so sure.

The effort was starting to make my thighs burn, but I was making good speed and progress towards Fredheim. Behind me the car was still keeping its distance. But then I was sure it was coming closer – I could hear it picking up speed. There was nowhere for me to go. No track at the side of the road to turn down. The roar of the engine got closer and closer, and finally, a car sailed past me.

It wasn't the same one.

It was a BMW. The air pressure almost sent me into the ditch alongside the road, but I managed to hold on tight to the handlebars and stop before I fell. As the car passed, I felt something wet hitting me in the face. It was cold and it smelled of alcohol. It took me a few seconds to realise I'd been sprayed with a generous helping of screen wash.

'Fuck me,' I said as I dried myself with the sleeves of my jacket. It must have been on purpose, but the question was whether the idiot driver knew it was me, or if he would do something like that to any cyclist. I'd heard it happen before.

I looked back. The same car that had been following me earlier had closed the gap. I wondered if I should wait for it, but decided instead to keep going.

When I got to the petrol station on the outskirts of town, I felt relief. There would be people there – it was open twenty-four hours.

I turned off the road and into the station. A man was filling his car. Another was coming out of the store, eating a hot dog. I stopped behind one of the pumps and waited as the car behind me passed and then picked up some speed. I got a good look at the licence plate: CJ45025. I got my phone out and did a search for the number. It was registered to a car dealer here in Fredheim.

I only knew one person who worked at a car dealer's in this town.

Frode Lindgren. Mari's father.

Had he been following me?

When I was sure the car was far enough ahead of me, I got back on my bike. I was just about to cross the bridge, when my phone rang. I stopped and pulled it out of my pocket.

It was Oskar.

'Bro,' he said, when I answered. 'Take a look at the thing you posted on Facebook yesterday.'

'OK...' I said, immediately feeling my heart starting to race.

Oskar was not the bearer of good news, I could hear it in his voice.

'Check out Nina's comment,' he said.

'OK,' I said again. 'I'll call you back.'

I scrolled down. It didn't take me long to find the comment Oskar was referring to. When I read it, my jaw dropped.

And Even says he wasn't there that evening? Check this, 1:23 into the clip.

Nina was a girl in my class. She had even tagged me; she wanted me to see the comment. Some people had responded to it: *Shit*; *FFS*; *Knew it. I fucking knew it!*

I swallowed and pressed play. The video was from the show. It started in the middle of Johannes' solo number, his declaration of love for Fredheim. The sound was rubbish because the video was taken from the back of the auditorium, behind the rows of seats, but it was easy enough to see and hear that everyone was listening. No one was messing about, whispering to each other or answering a text. Johannes was really in his element up there on stage.

I watched the time. One minute. I waited impatiently for it to get to 1:23.

1:10 became 1:20.

Then 1:23.

And that was when I saw him.

There wasn't much light at the back of the auditorium, so it was hard to see his face, but the camera itself gave off enough light for me to see the back of someone's head, a boy wearing a baseball cap and a denim jacket.

Thoughts bombarded me from all directions.

'Jesus,' I whispered.

It was ... me.

At least, it certainly looked like that way. It was my jacket, or one that was almost the same. The person was the same height as me. Had the same kind of baseball cap as the one I sometimes used. I rewound the recording a few seconds to see if I could get a better look at the face. No. His head was turned towards the stage.

I stopped the clip again and scrolled down through all the comments. My eyes stopped sharp at a reply from a girl called Ylva. I had no idea who Ylva was, but what she'd written made my heart jump.

Idiots. That's not Even. It's his brother.

48
NOW

'Let me stop you right there.'

Ms Håkonsen waves her hand in the air, like she's a cheerleader or something. It almost makes me laugh, but the seriousness of what we're talking about quickly pulls me back.

'Did you know that your brother was going to be there that evening?'

'I really thought he wasn't. A while before the show my mother asked him if he wanted to come along, but he just laughed unkindly and said no. Shows like that weren't his thing.'

'And yet, there he was.'

'Yes. He was.'

'What did you think about that, when you saw the video?'

I think about my answer for a second. 'Well, it made me realise how people could have thought they saw *me* there. I mean, from a distance my brother and I aren't too different. We're about the same height. And we did have almost the same kind of denim jacket. The same baseball cap. A lot of pieces fell into place for me when I saw it.'

'Did you, at that point, think that your brother could have been the one behind all this?'

'Well, the questions did hit me pretty quick. What was he doing there? Did he kill them? I guess it was only natural.'

Ms Håkonsen nods slightly. 'Then what did you do?'

'I went home. To confront him.'

49
THEN

I was standing on the outskirts of Fredheim, not far away from where Børre Halvorsen had been murdered. My thoughts were running riot.

I pressed play again and watched the video to the end, but I couldn't see where my brother went. I did see Mari, though, to the far right of the screen. And I almost sank to my knees.

It shouldn't have taken me by surprise. I knew she'd been there. But still, it was weird to see her again. It was like she was still alive. She had a camera around her neck. Seemed focused on the work she was there to do. As she disappeared out of view, I let out a loud sob.

There she was, only an hour and a half before someone killed her. I wondered if she'd had any idea she was in danger as she went around, trying to behave like a professional journalist. Had she been afraid of anyone? Had she known that something might happen? Probably not. She was going to conduct an interview. Then go home and continue to hide from me.

My thoughts went back to my brother. Yes, he'd turned up at the school looking a bit like me; but wasn't it a huge leap to then think he'd killed my ex-girlfriend and the star of the school show? As I cycled home, I tried to work out how I was going to confront him. I thought about phoning Imo, just to get his advice, but I decided against it.

When I pulled up in front of our house, I looked up at Tobias's window. A bluish light flickered across the walls of his room. I went inside, poured myself a large glass of water, drank it all down, then went to knock on his door.

'Go away!' Tobias yelled.

'It's me,' I said.

Behind the door cars were crashing and smashing into something. Grand Theft Auto, probably. Tobias didn't answer. I knocked again and tried the door. It was locked. The noises stopped: he'd paused the game. I heard him coming to open the door.

'Hi,' I said.

I looked him straight in the eye. Had Tobias killed my girlfriend? Could he really have done such a horrible thing?

'What is it?' he asked. His look told me he didn't appreciate being interrupted.

'Why do you lock your door?' I couldn't think of anything else to say.

'Don't want Mum just barging in,' he said. 'You want something?'

I looked over his shoulder. His room was, if possible, even messier than mine.

'Just wanted a word with you,' I said, holding his gaze.

He let out an exaggerated sigh. 'What about?'

I waited a moment, before I said: 'The school show.'

Tobias tilted his head slightly as though trying to work out what I meant, how he should respond.

'I thought you didn't like school shows,' I said.

Tobias just stared back at me. I half expected him to launch himself at me, but he stayed where he was, not saying a word. The expression in his eyes was back to weary and bored – as if it made no difference whatsoever if I was there or not. He looked like he might fall asleep at any moment.

'Can I come in?' I asked.

He thought about it for a few seconds, then opened the door wide with another sigh, as though being with his brother was the worst thing in the world. He slouched in behind me and sat down in his favourite chair. There were plates on the floor beside it. Glasses, bottles, a scrunched-up crisp bag. I counted four pairs of trousers on the floor. It looked like he'd just stepped out of them all.

'You really should get some air in here,' I said.

Tobias didn't reply.

I didn't know when it started – or why – or if we'd ever really been close, me and Tobias, but I couldn't remember the last time we'd actually talked about something real and serious. Something other than kill streaks on Call of Duty or what kind of pizza we wanted to order. We'd never talked about Mum, for instance. Or Dad. Or Knut, the knucklehead who sometimes slept in our house.

I was still standing in the middle of the room. 'Why did you go to the show, Tobias?'

He looked up at me. 'Do I need a reason?'

'Normally, no. This time, though, you do.'

'I don't need to explain myself to you.'

'Yes, you do, because most people around this town think that I killed my ex-girlfriend, and one of the reasons for that might be the fact that they saw *you* there. They thought you were me. Børre Halvorsen had even seen you in one of the windows – the window the police think the murderer escaped through. I need to know what the fuck you were doing there, Tobias.'

My brother grabbed the controller and started to play GTA again. I snatched it out of his hands and threw it against the wall. The controller smashed into God knows how many pieces.

'What the fuck?!'

Tobias stood up. I knew this could get messy. We'd had our fights over the years, Tobias and me, and I'd probably knocked his ass to the ground forty-nine times out of fifty. Things were different now, though. Tobias was bigger. Stronger. No doubt he'd stocked up plenty of reasons to get one back at me. The question was, who was angrier: him or me? And then a nasty thought sent a prickle of fear over my body: which of us was more capable of doing something really violent? What if my brother really was some kind of psycho?

'I saw a video of you,' I said, forcing myself to step forward so I was right up in his face. 'So talk to me.'

If I'd prodded his chest with my finger, he would have exploded. Things would have gone from bad to worse. I could almost feel the sparks flying out of my eyes, though, which might have been the reason why Tobias pulled back a little.

'Alright, I was there,' he said, finally. 'So what? I wanted to see the show. What the fuck is wrong with that?'

'I don't believe you,' I said. 'It's not your kind of show. Not your kind of music. So *why* were you there, Tobias? I know Mum didn't buy you a ticket.'

He lowered his eyes.

'Answer me!' I screamed so loud he almost jumped.

'I went for a walk,' he said, 'and I kind of found myself at your school. I knew that Mum and Imo were there, so I thought I'd see if I could get in. And I did. No one was watching the door. I didn't think anyone would notice me. No one normally does.'

'You walked straight past someone filming the show, you fucking twat.'

He didn't have an answer to that.

'Did you talk to Mari?' I asked.

Tobias said nothing, just kept his eyes down.

'Did you?'

I took a step closer. He still said nothing.

'How long were you there?' I asked.

'Don't remember,' he said, with a shrug.

'Did you leave before the show was over?'

Again he waited a beat before saying: 'Yes.'

'How did you get home?'

'I walked.'

'Straight home?'

'Can't remember.'

'You can't remember.'

I couldn't believe my ears. I looked at him, trying to work out whether he was telling me the truth or not. It was difficult to tell. But he wasn't making much sense – not remembering even the most basic details.

'My girlfriend was killed that night, in case you've forgotten,' I said. My voice was trembling. 'If I were you, I'd try a little harder to get my facts straight.'

He retreated a step, and nearly fell backwards onto the bed.

'I walked around for a little while, then I went home. It might have been around midnight. I don't know. That make you happy, Sherlock?'

I ran my fingers through my hair and sighed heavily. So Tobias had been out more than long enough to kill Mari and Johannes. And he had been at the school.

I stared at him for a second. 'I don't believe you, Tobias. Not for a second.'

He responded by looking at the floor again. And I thought: Is this the moment? Is this when he is going to confess?

'I ... I broke into a car.'

My mouth fell open. It was like someone had stuck a pin in me.

'Jesus, Tobias.' That was all I could say.

But when what he'd actually done finally sank it, I was angry again. 'What the hell did you do that for?'

Tobias hesitated, then said: 'There was ... an iPad on the seat inside.'

My jaw dropped again. 'An iPad?' I didn't know what to think or say. I looked around his room.

'But you've already got an iPad...'

'Yes, but...' He looked away. Wrung his hands. 'I needed the money.'

'Money? For what?'

'None of your business.'

'Er, I think it is. It is now, anyway.'

He straightened up and pushed back his shoulders.

'So, are you going to tell me?' I pressed.

'No.'

I wanted to punch him. Beat the truth out of him, but I managed to control myself.

'So, you sold it? Is that what you're saying?'

'Yes, I did.'

'Who to?'

'Does it really matter?'

I looked at him for a few seconds. So that was the lay of the land. My brother was a thief. He was a fucking thief.

I turned and walked towards the door.

'You owe me a controller, for fuck's sake!' he shouted after me.

I just slammed the door and went down to my room and sat on the bed. Børre had seen my brother in one of the windows at the school. He must have been in there, looking for something to steal, I thought. The bloody fucking thief.

I was sure the rumours had spread further now – everyone would know it was Tobias at the school. I didn't want to go online to see. All I could hope was that no one had told Mum yet, but I knew that was only a matter of time.

I put my headphones on and tried to listen to some music for a while, hoping it would block out the whirl of thoughts. But when I turned it off again, none of the songs I'd been listening to lingered in my head. Instead, it was Johannes' voice, singing a song that felt all the more touching now that he was dead. I guessed they would be playing it at his funeral.

God, the funeral.

I hadn't even thought about the fact that Mari and Johannes would have to be buried. I wondered if there would be a joint service, or if the families would want them buried separately. And I wondered what Mari's parents would say if I showed up. I wanted to say goodbye to her properly, too. Was I not going to be allowed to do that?

And if I wasn't, what else could I do? Doing nothing would be agony. I would try to find the one who killed her, I thought. Not just to clear my name, but because it was what Mari deserved. Truth was, I shouldn't really be interfering. The police should be left alone to do their job. But it wouldn't hurt to look around, I said to myself, to keep my eyes open. And I still wasn't one hundred percent sure that my brother was telling me the truth. About anything.

I'll have a look in his room, I thought. Tomorrow, after he's gone to school.

God.

Just the thought of going through his things, looking for clues or signs that he might be a killer, made me nauseous.

50

The face of Weedon, the ginger-haired tech analyst, appeared on Yngve's computer screen in a pop-up box. He was live messaging – rather than walking round the corner to have a chat.

'Hey boss. I thought you'd still be working.'

Åse looked at him from the chair on the other side of the table. It was hours since she'd told him to go home, but he'd ignored her and started going through the interviews again, looking for remarks or clues they hadn't dug into deeply enough. So far he'd come up with nothing fresh.

'I've managed to fix Mari's phone,' Weedon said.

'OK, good. Found anything interesting on it?'

'Er ... are we really allowed to look at texts and go through her apps and stuff like that? Don't we have to write to Facebook or Apple and...'

'Yes,' Yngve said. 'I'm sure we do. But it'll take forever to get an answer, and we might not even get a yes.' Yngve ducked away from Åse's gaze. 'Just take a quick look,' he said. 'Mari didn't have a working phone the last forty-eight hours or so of her life, and it might be critical for us to know who she communicated with on Facebook or Messenger or whatever the hell they're called – these apps the kids use nowadays.'

Weedon hesitated for a moment, then looked away from the camera. There was a tapping – he was typing at his usual high speed.

'Start with WhatsApp,' Yngve said. 'If she used it.'

'She did,' Weedon said. 'Do you want me to read you the names of everyone she was in contact with?'

'Just the most recent ones first,' Yngve said.'

'OK.'

Now Weedon was moving his thumb across Mari's phone. 'She had quite a few chat groups,' he began. 'There was a lot of activity on the day of the school show, but Mari didn't get involved. At least not in this particular group.'

Yngve looked at his clock. Almost midnight.

'There are ... one, two, four, six, eight ... *twelve* people in the next group,' Weedon continued. 'All girls.'

'We have a fairly good idea of her female friends,' Yngve said. 'Concentrate on the boys.'

'Alright.'

A few seconds passed.

'I'll just say them out loud as I go along,' Weedon said.

Yngve was getting impatient. It didn't help that Åse was still looking at him. Her eyebrows were raised.

'Stick to those she was in private chats with,' he said.

'OK.'

While he waited, Yngve found a pen and started clicking it on and off, on and off.

Finally Weedon said: 'On the day she died, she chatted with Johannes Eklund...'

'About what?'

'Let me see...'

Another beat. 'Nothing important, it seems, only some stuff about the show. She wanted to confirm that they were going to do the interview afterwards. Johannes agreed. With a smiley, even.'

'Alright,' Yngve said. 'Who else was she chatting with?'

'Let me see...'

Yngve drew a big circle on his notepad.

'Her father tried to reach her,' Weedon said. '*Hello. You're not answering my calls, so I'm trying to reach you in here instead. Can we meet somewhere? Talk about it?*'

Talk about what? Yngve wondered. 'When was that?' he asked.

'Sunday. The day before she died,' Weedon answered, scratching his head.

'Hm,' Yngve murmured. Getting hold of Frode Lindgren was becoming more and more imperative. He still hadn't returned any of Yngve's calls.

'She had been chatting to Even Tollefsen a lot,' Weedon continued. 'There must be thousands of exchanges between just the two of them. But on those last two days, though, she's not responding to him. He's ... pretty desperate, it seems, to get answers from her.'

So far Even's story checks out with the findings on her phone, Yngve thought.

'Huh...' Weedon exclaimed.

'What is it?' Yngve asked.

'She did have a private chat with another Tollefsen.'

'Who?'

'A Tobias.'

Even's brother, Yngve said to himself. 'What the hell were *they* talking about?'

'Let me see...'

Again it took Weedon half a minute to comb through the communication.

'It started a little while ago,' he said. 'Five or six weeks or so. She contacted him because she needed some pictures of Even for an article she was going to write.'

The one for the school newspaper, Yngve thought as he waited for Weedon to continue.

'She says that she's reluctant to ask Even directly, because she doesn't just want *his* favourite pictures of himself. She wants some pics from his childhood, preferably some embarrassing ones, because she wants the story to be fun. She's hoping that Tobias might get her some photos that are fun for everyone – apart from Even. Then there are a few smileys and that kind of thing. She also wants to know if Tobias can get her a picture or two of Jimmy. Their father.'

Nothing irregular about that, Yngve thought. The article Mari was writing was about Jimmy as well.

'Tobias says he is going to try. Then a couple of weeks go by before Tobias says that he has found some really cool ones. Mari gets excited. They agree to meet.'

'When was this?'

'A little over a week ago.'

'Nothing more recent?'

Weedon's thumb moved over her phone screen display again.

'Well, yes.' A couple of seconds passed. 'He wrote to her last Friday – that would be three days before her murder – that he'd found out what kind of blood type Jimmy had.'

'What?'

'That's what it says.'

Yngve scratched the back of his head. 'So she asked him for that information?'

'I don't know. It doesn't say.'

Maybe they had talked about it when they met, Yngve thought. That was the only plausible explanation.

'They were also in touch on the night she died.'

Yngve sat up in his chair. 'What are they saying?'

'*She's* not saying anything. It's Tobias who wants to meet her. He asks her a couple of times, without getting a reply.'

'Hm. Anything else?'

'No, that's it.'

Yngve asked Weedon to go through Mari's other apps as well. But he didn't find anything in particular of interest.

After Weedon had disappeared from Yngve's screen, Åse continued looking at him. 'I know,' he said. 'It's not the proper way to go about it.'

She smiled. Because she liked it, she said – him not following protocol. Being naughty. He smiled back. 'This is the new me,' he said. 'I don't know if it's a good thing or a bad thing.'

In the years that had passed between Åse first being diagnosed with breast cancer and the day she actually died, they had tried to prepare themselves for the inevitable. They had talked about death at length, but always in an arm's-length way, as if it were something theoretical. Mostly it was Åse reminding him of the practical things he had to do, like oiling the workbench in the kitchen every two years, or remembering to change the gas hose on the grill.

Of course, there were the physical signs of her slow but steady decay, but they had both somehow accepted her death with a kind of serenity – something that had come as a great surprise to him. It was almost as if they really didn't think it would happen, that it was all some kind of a prank, and that they would somehow be able to get through this as well. Like they did everything else.

Four weeks ago, on the day she died, it was as if though reality finally hit him. He had held on to every hour, every minute she continued to live, even though he wanted her suffering to be over. He knew this was life – the way of the world – but he cursed it. This wasn't how it was supposed to be. It made no sense to him that some people would live to be a hundred, while others merely made it to sixteen or sixty-two.

Yngve had wanted to scream then, because it was so bloody unfair. He had wanted to shout, because *fate* was so unfair. He hadn't been able to stop crying. But maybe that was what had kept him going. Without his tears the fire that was raging in his chest would have consumed him.

He looked over the desk at her. Her smile had faded. But their love never would, and neither would his grief. It was just going to change, and he was fine with that. Åse was, too. She had said so many times.

I will just be there, with you, around you and in you. And you will feel my hand in your heart instead of on your chest.

She vanished into thin air, as she did these days, with no warning.

Yngve made a decision. He needed to put her away for a bit. He needed to close the door to the room where all the colours were dark. He wasn't going to lock it and throw away the key, no. He was going to keep it around his neck, as close to his heart as he could. And when the time was right, he was going to open it again.

Now he just needed to work.

It simply wasn't his moment to be mourning.

51

Mum was already in the kitchen when I got there, reading the paper, drinking her morning coffee. I hoped it was alcohol free. GP lay at her feet with his tongue hanging out, hoping to catch a titbit or two. She ignored him.

'Good morning,' she said.

'Morning.'

'They say they've got a strong lead.'

'Hm?'

'The police. They say they've got some new evidence in the case.'

I wondered what kind of evidence it was, or if that was something they just said to the media.

'Any details?' I asked.

'No. There's some stuff about how difficult this case is, though.'

I wondered when Yngve Mork would get in touch with me again. I had a feeling it would be soon.

'Working today?' I asked.

'Yes,' Mum sighed. 'I have to leave in a minute or two.'

I looked at her. I couldn't see any signs of last night's drinking. There were bags under her eyes, but then again, there always were.

'Is that brother of yours going to make an appearance today?' She looked up at the ceiling, as though Tobias might suddenly come bursting through it.

'Don't know,' I said. I guessed he probably wouldn't come down until I had left.

Mum looked at the clock on the wall. 'I'll go and see what he's up to.'

I heard her feet on the stairs, GP eagerly following, paws scratching against the steps. Then a knock on my brother's door.

'Tobias, time to get up!'

She got no answer. She knocked again. Called his name once more and made another point of how late it was. Still no answer. Again she knocked, harder this time. Same result.

I went upstairs too. When I got there, Mum was trying the handle. It was locked, just as it had been the evening before. GP was jumping around her ankles, wagging his tail.

'He's started to lock the door,' Mum said, more to herself than me. She tried the handle again. 'Tobias!'

I put my ear to the door. Couldn't hear a thing. No music. No movement. 'Tobias!' I yelled. 'What's going on?'

I tried to push at the door. It didn't budge. I looked at Mum. 'Do you have the key?'

Mum shook her head frantically. I put my shoulder to the door but still it didn't move, not even a little bit. It was old and heavy. I stepped back and took a run at it. I just bounced off. GP barked. I took a look around for something to hit the handle with. Spotted the fire extinguisher by the wall. I picked it up, then slammed it down on the handle with all my might. It didn't break.

I tried the same again. No luck. And even if I did manage to get the handle off, I thought, the door would still be locked. The whole thing would have to come off its hinges. I had to kick it in.

GP was jumping around my ankles, wanting to play.

'Keep him away from me!' I shouted at my mum.

She grabbed the lead and got him to sit still. Give it all you've got, I said to myself, like they do in the movies. Then I began to kick. I kicked and kicked and kicked. But still nothing happened. I attacked it again, targeting the same spot, and finally I felt something give, the door was about to give way. This gave me more strength, and I kicked again, as hard as I could. Slowly, gradually, the door was coming apart.

For a moment I was afraid it might fall on my brother, that he'd fallen asleep while playing GTA during the night, and that he was still sitting in the same place. But the door just fell on an empty chair. Tobias wasn't even in the room.

52

While Even was kicking down Tobias's door, several possible scenarios raced through Susanne's mind. Tobias had fainted. He'd somehow passed away during the night. He'd taken his own life. She had been worried sick for years, thinking that he spent way too much time on his own, that he didn't have any friends. That he didn't care about anything. Somehow, though, she hadn't been prepared for this. An empty room.

The window was shut, so he couldn't have climbed through there.

He hadn't got up early, either, she'd been awake since quarter to three. He must have left the house some time during the night.

But where had he gone? And why?

Even ran downstairs, phone to his ear. Susanne went after him. She needed to hold on to the bannister to stop herself toppling over. For a moment she caught a glimpse of herself in the big entrance-hall mirror. This thin, despicable creature of a human being, face drained of colour, eyes big and round. She looked like a witch. A raving, mad witch.

'Fuck, he's not answering,' Even muttered, as he pressed some more buttons on his phone, putting it once more to his ear. 'Hey, Imo,' Even said, before explaining what had happened. 'So he's not at your place?'

Susanne was too far away to hear what Imo replied, but she could see Even cursing, then thinking to himself. It felt as if something, or someone, was choking her. She couldn't breathe.

Tobias was gone.

Had he run away?

Had someone asked him to come over in the middle of the night, and then...?

Susanne closed her eyes and tried to shake the thoughts that hit her with full force.

'I'm going to his school' Even told Imo. A short beat, then he shook his head. 'It'll be quicker if I go by bike.'

He said something else as well, but Susanne couldn't tell what it was. She went back upstairs again, back into Tobias's room. He wasn't there this time, either. She walked back down and called his name, half expecting him to just appear, like he'd been playing a prank. She went down into the basement. Couldn't find him in the laundry room. He wasn't in the larder either. Not in the bathroom. Not in Even's bedroom.

'Mum,' Even said as she came back up again, her face hot.

She searched for Tobias in the hall, the living room; she looked out of the windows, but he wasn't in the garden or out the front.

'It'll be alright,' Even said behind her. 'We're going to find him.'

'His coat,' Susanne said and went into the hall again, to the pegs where his outdoor clothes normally hung. 'It's still here,' she said, pointing to it. 'His shoes, too. He ... he must have worn his trainers. He complained about them being too small, but he ... he must have taken them anyway...'

Even took a step closer and put a firm hand on her shoulders. 'The best thing you can do right now, Mum, is to sit down and wait by the phone. Have yourself a cup of tea or something. I'll call you as soon as I've been to his school.'

Susanne looked at him, but couldn't focus on his eyes. She could see his mouth moving, but couldn't make out the words it was making. Yes, he was saying something about a phone and Imo being on his way.

'OK,' she whimpered.

'Call Knut,' Even said. 'Tell him what's happened, and get him to come over. He can help.'

Tears were running from her eyes, but she couldn't make a sound.

'But don't stay too long on the phone,' Even shouted. 'In case I'm calling.'

Susanne nodded, carefully at first, then more and more vigorously. Even pulled her close and gave her a hug. Then he hurried out.

53
NOW

'Did you really think you were going to find your brother at his school?' Ms Håkonsen asks.

'Not really,' I reply. 'But I had to do something. School was the obvious place to look for him first.'

She nods. 'Do you remember what you were thinking on your way there?

'How do you mean?'

'What were you thinking about your brother's behaviour?'

'I remember thinking that maybe Tobias had run away. That maybe he thought the net was closing in on him or something.'

'And why would that be?'

'Because of the videotape. And the fact he'd been seen in the school newspaper room – the place the police said the killer had left the building that night, and the fact that he really didn't have a good explanation as to why he was there in the first place.'

Ms Håkonsen nods again. 'And *was* your brother at his school that morning?'

'No, he wasn't.'

'But you did talk to people?'

'I did, yes. The other kids. Teachers. I even got one of them to help me look for him. But we couldn't find him.'

'The teacher who helped you; what was his name?'

'Tom Hulsker.'

'You didn't know him from before, did you?'

'No, I didn't.'

'But he knew you.'

'Well, yes. He knew me because of my dad.'

'We'll get back to Mr Hulsker a little later,' Ms Håkonsen says. 'When you couldn't find your brother at school – what did you do?'

'I called Mum. By then, she was hysterical, so I spoke to Imo instead. We agreed about what to do next.'

'And what was that?'

'We were just going to go around town, looking for him. Me on my bike, Imo by car. The plan was to ask if anyone had seen him. Bus station, train station, shops he liked to hang out in, the mall ... We tried to cover as much ground as we possibly could, as quickly as possible.'

'But you didn't find him.'

I shake my head and say no.

'Then what did you do.'

I find Yngve Mork's eyes in the audience.

'We called the police.'

54
THEN

Back at the house I found Mum on the sofa in the living room. Knut was sitting beside her with his hand on her forehead.

'I've given her a little something to calm her down,' Knut said quietly.

I had no idea how Knut had got his hands on pills like that, but it wasn't really important right now. Mum seemed to be relaxed. At least she wasn't screaming and crying anymore.

'Everything's going to be fine, Mum,' I repeated. 'We'll find him.'

I thought about my original plan for the day. I was still tempted to go up to Tobias's room and have a look through his things.

Knut looked at me and said: 'Could we ... eh... go somewhere for a chat?'

Knut had never asked me anything, except maybe to pass the salt during dinner.

'Sure,' I said, slightly bewildered. 'Let's go into the kitchen.'

I got a lemon yoghurt from the fridge and leaned against the worktop, waiting for Knut to speak. It took a while before he finally did.

'I'm worried about your mum.' He looked at me. 'Before you got here, before I gave her that pill, she said she couldn't take it anymore. She was beside herself. Said that if anything happened to Tobias as well, she wouldn't be able to deal with it.' He stared at me with grave eyes.

'Wouldn't deal with it?' I said. 'What are you saying? That she wouldn't be able to stop herself from committing suicide?'

Knut held my gaze for a few seconds. 'That's how I interpreted it, yes. I think she might need some help. Professional help.'

'She's just being dramatic, Knut. You know how she gets. She's not suicidal, she'd never do that to me – or us.'

'Maybe you're right. I'm just worried about her.'

I nodded. 'Let's just wait and see,' I said forcing down the yoghurt. 'Right now she's clinging to the hope that Tobias will come back, and there's still every chance he just might do that.'

'I'll look after her in the meantime,' he said. 'Perhaps I should take her back to my place?'

'Good idea,' I said. It was a sensible move, as she would probably freak out even more if the police came by.

⌷

Yngve Mork was not in uniform when he arrived. The female officer with him was, though.

Imo, who'd arrived a short while before, went out to greet them. He showed them into the kitchen where it was warmer.

'This is Therese Kyrkjebø,' Mork said, turning to the female officer. She held out her hand for me to shake.

Mork turned to me. 'Still no sign of your brother?'

'No,' I said. 'Not yet.'

'What can you tell us about him, Even?'

I took a deep breath. 'He's a couple of years younger than me,' I said. 'About the same height. Shoulder-length hair, similar to mine. Brown eyes.'

'Good to know, thanks,' Mork said, as Kyrkjebø took notes. 'But I was thinking more about his personality. What kind of person is he?'

I looked over at Imo as I thought about what to say. I wondered if the police officers knew my brother's reputation from Solstad. A couple of weeks before we moved back to Fredheim, a girl called Amalie had shown some interest in him. According to my brother they were going out, but Amalie saw it differently. She hadn't been honest with him, either. It turned out that she only wanted to get close to Tobias so she could get closer to me.

Tobias was furious when he found out. I didn't witness it myself, but apparently he'd grabbed Amalie in the playground during break, in front of everyone. It made a lot of noise at his school, and my mother freaked out. Because Gran was dead and her house was standing empty, my mother saw it as a sign – an opportunity to get Tobias away from a school and a community that viewed him as potentially violent.

Now I simply told the officers that my brother didn't have great social skills, that he didn't have a lot of friends.

'What about ... his relationship with girls?'

I swallowed a couple of times, before meeting Mork's eyes. 'He hasn't had any girlfriends here, if that's what you're asking.'

'Do you know if he has any contact with girls other than at school?'

'Don't know,' I said, with a shrug. 'Tobias hasn't been easy to talk to recently.'

Kyrkjebø made a note of some kind. Mork waited a moment or two before he asked: 'Even ... did you know that your brother had been in touch with Mari recently?'

I looked at him, at Kyrkjebø. At Imo.

'They texted on WhatsApp.'

'What about?' I asked, before Mork had a chance to go on.

'Well, it started when she asked for his help a little while ago. She wanted him to find some photos of you and your dad for the article she was going to write for the school paper.'

I looked at them one by one again. I couldn't understand why Mari had gone behind my back like that. Why hadn't she just asked me?

'And did he help her?'

Mork nodded. 'We think so. That's certainly what it looks like from their communication.'

So Tobias must have met up with her. To give her some pictures. I shook my head in disbelief.

'He...' Kyrkjebø glanced over at Mork before she continued. 'We know that he went to your school on the night of the murders.'

Presumably the whole of Fredheim knew that by now, so I don't know why my heart started to race.

'He was also in contact with her that evening.'

This was going from bad to worse.

'Or rather, he tried to contact her,' Mork said. 'But her phone was broken, so she didn't answer him.'

Broken, I thought. Shit, was *that* why she hadn't answered me?

'What...' The words stuck in my throat. 'What did he want?' I asked.

They didn't reply. I looked at Imo. He seemed to be as surprised as I was. The more I thought about it, the worse things looked for Tobias.

'Do you have any idea where your brother might be?' Kyrkjebø asked.

'No.'

'Do you have any recent photographs of Tobias we could use?'

I was so lost in my own thoughts, at first I didn't realise she'd asked the question.

'Yes...' I said, after a pause. 'I'm sure I do.'

I went through my phone. Found a picture I'd taken of him when we were painting the house during the summer. He had a few paint smudges on his chin. I showed them the picture, then sent it to Mork.

'Thanks,' he said. Then turned to Imo. 'We have a search warrant for the house.'

'A what?'

'A search warrant. We need you both to leave the premises so we can go through it.'

'But why?' I asked.

Mork looked straight at me. He didn't need to explain. I understood perfectly. They believed my brother was involved in the murders.

55

Yngve couldn't help but admire the Tollefsens' house. Although it was somewhat run down, it had to be worth a fortune, he thought, even in a small place like Fredheim. It had so much potential, with its steep roof, its old wooden floorboards and a kitchen that was bigger than his living room. The house was so huge it could easily accommodate at least two families. On the upper floor there were bedrooms and cupboards everywhere. It was a perfect place to hide things.

Åse would have loved this place, he thought.

He found himself standing in front of the large mirror in the hall, when Therese came over.

'I just spoke to Weedon', she said. 'Tobias's phone has either been turned off or it has run out of juice. We only have its last position.' She pointed to the floor they were standing on. 'Here.'

'So he turned off his phone before he left,' Yngve said.

'Maybe,' Therese said. 'We have to get hold of his phone records. See who he was in contact with last night.'

Yngve was looking at Tobias's picture, the one Even had sent him. Tobias looked like any other teenager – unkempt, pimply, his forehead kind of greasy. He wore a cap on his head and stared at the camera with an almost offended expression. He'd had the same look on his face when Yngve had been here and talked to him on the night of Børre Halvorsen's murder.

Could killers be that detached? Yngve wondered. Of course they could, he answered himself. There were sociopaths everywhere. Even kids of fifteen.

'Mork?' came a voice from upstairs.

'Yes?'

'You need to take a look at this.'

Yngve looked at Therese for a second, then rushed up the stairs. They entered Tobias's room to find a technician standing by the desk, holding a key chain in his hands.

'I found this in one of the drawers,' he said.

The chain had three keys on them. Yngve heard Frode Lindgren's voice in his head: *The key chain has a blue-and-white string on it.* This fit the description perfectly.

Yngve looked at Therese. She seemed to be lost in thought for a moment.

'What is it?' he said.

'I just don't get it,' she said. 'Isn't it incredibly stupid to keep something that might connect you to the murders in your own bedroom?'

'Maybe he *is* stupid,' Yngve said.

'I don't understand what he's up to. Why not take the keys with him, or at least hide them carefully? Why leave them here for us to find? Surely he would have known that we would come looking for evidence?'

'He's only fifteen,' Yngve said. 'Maybe he just didn't think that far.'

Therese disagreed. 'What really sticks out in this case, in my opinion, is how quickly and smartly the killer acted. The way he left the school that night, for instance. Away from the CCTV cameras, onto the roof. In all probability he left with the microphone case, too, which we still haven't found. If Tobias did all that ... if he really is our killer ... why would he be so thick-headed as to keep a victim's keys?'

Yngve gave that some thought.

'It's a good question,' he said. 'Let's find him and ask.'

56

As I left the house, a terrifying thought occurred to me. What if my brother had disappeared because somebody wanted to get rid of him?

There was a killer on the loose in Fredheim. Maybe Tobias had needed to take a walk or something after our fight last night – he often went out to get a chocolate bar or a can of drink or something. What if he met someone who wanted to hurt him or maybe even kill him?

I went back to Tobias's school, in the hope that he'd shown up later that morning. I knew I was clutching at straws, but I managed to see Tobias's head teacher, a woman named Sara Anvik. At first she appeared cautious about talking to me. I guess she too had heard the rumours. When I told her we didn't know where my brother was at the moment, her hesitation turned to worry. I didn't tell her the police were involved.

'He does spend a lot of time on his own, your brother. I've tried to get him to join in on a couple of things, but he doesn't want to or say much.'

'He's not being bullied, is he?'

'I don't think so. He's just very quiet.'

On my way out, I was stopped by Tom Hulsker, the teacher I had spoken to earlier that morning.

'Hello again.' I could hear the concern in his voice. 'Have you found your brother yet?' I shook my head. I was about to walk past him, when I thought of something else. 'Mr Hulsker, this morning you said you knew my dad quite well.'

He nodded. I caught a whiff of cigarette smoke from his clothes.

'My girlfriend, the girl who was murdered, was writing a piece about my dad and me for the school paper. She didn't come to see you, by any chance, for some background information?'

'Me? Mari Lindgren?'

I nodded. He had a sudden bewildered look on his face.

'No, she didn't.'

I explained to him the kind of story Mari was researching.

Tom Hulsker checked his wristwatch, looked at me and said: 'Let's go outside. I don't have a class at the moment, and I want a cigarette.'

Before I had a chance to protest, he was already on his way outside. I followed him to the school fence, where he produced a cigarette and offered me one as well.

'No thanks, I don't smoke.'

'Good choice,' he said. 'These things will kill you.'

He smiled. I smiled back. He lit his cigarette and inhaled deeply.

'God, you look a lot like your father when you smile. I bet you've heard that all your life, right?'

I hadn't, but I just said yes. Hulsker took another drag of his cigarette then slowly let the smoke out.

'Your father was a very good man. We went to teacher-training college together,' Hulsker said. He shook his head, as though memories were popping into it, one by one. 'Man, those were the days.'

I waited for him to continue.

'Jimmy was an excellent teacher. Highly respected. He was a magnet for the ladies, too.' He smiled and shook his head again. 'But all that changed when he met your mother.'

I tried to imagine the man I had seen on the photographs at home, chatting to the girls, flirting, making witty comments. I couldn't – he just wasn't alive to me.

'How *is* your mother, by the way?'

I could have said all sorts about Mum, but now was not the time. 'Fine,' was all I said.

'I heard you'd moved back,' Hulsker said. 'I've thought about giving her a ring, but ... I just haven't got round to it.'

The usual excuse. You didn't have the time, or you didn't take the time to do what you should. It was like Mum said: some friends were only there for a certain part of your life.

'Did you have a lot to do with him around the time he died?' I asked.

Hulsker didn't answer straightaway. 'No, not as much. We'd both got families by then, and that takes up most of your time. But there was the occasional get-together, of course.'

He took another drag of the cigarette.

'If you'd been Mari, and you wanted to find out as much as you could about my father ... who would you go see, besides my mother?'

'She didn't talk to your mother?'

'Not that I know of.'

Hulsker seemed to gaze at something in the distance for a moment, before turning to me again. 'If I were Mari, I would have talked to my own mother about it.'

'You mean she should have spoken to Cecilie?'

'Yes. Jimmy and Cecilie were good friends back in the day. Colleagues, too.'

I thought about that for a second.

'OK. Thanks. I have to run.'

'Good luck finding your brother!'

57
NOW

I search for my mother's face again, trying to make eye contact. Her chin has sunk to her chest. She gives me an almost imperceptible shake of the head.

'What did you do after that?' Ms Håkonsen asks.

My mother's face sinks down, and she raises her shoulders almost all the way up to her ears. It's as if she's trying to make herself smaller. As if she wants to disappear into her shell, like a turtle. I feel sorry for her.

She knows what's coming.

58
THEN

After I had talked to Hulsker, I wanted to check in on Mum. Knut lived in a complex that had been built behind the old dairy factory a few years before. It was a grey building, full of small, almost identical flats.

I pressed the buzzer and Knut quickly let me in. He was waiting for me in the hall, which smelt of dust and spices from somewhere remote.

'Your mother is asleep,' he said.

'Oh,' I said. 'Good.'

We stood there looking at each other for a moment. He showed me inside, and offered me a cup of tea.

'No thanks,' I said. 'I'm good. I was wondering if I could ask you a question, though. Did you and Mum ever talk about ... well, my dad?'

Knut cocked his head. 'About Jimmy? Not really. Why are you asking?'

'Just curious,' I said. 'Did you know him?'

Knut didn't answer straightaway. 'I was a few years younger than your father,' he finally said.

'What did people in town say about the accident?'

Knut took a step back and looked at me. 'What's all this about, Even? Why are you asking all these questions about Jimmy all of a sudden?'

'I'm just trying to find out about a few things,' I said, realising how vague I sounded. 'So, can you remember anything?'

'I only read what it said in the papers.'

I studied him for a few moments. 'Where is she?'

'In the bedroom?'

'Can I go in?'

'Yeah, sure.'

I didn't particularly enjoy the idea of going into Knut's bedroom, where he and Mum no doubt did God knows what, but I wanted to see how she was, even if she was asleep. It was a small room, so narrow there was only room for one bedside table. And it was almost impossible to get past the large wardrobe that stood at the end of the bed.

Mum had pulled the duvet up under her chin. She was sound asleep, like a child. I wondered what was going on underneath that damp forehead of hers. She must have kept a lot to herself over the years. She didn't have a lot of friends in Solstad, and the ones from the old days in Fredheim hadn't reached out to her when she'd come back.

I don't know how old I was when I first realised my mother was unhappy. I remember coming home from school one day, to find her crying in the kitchen. I don't think she heard me come in. But I could instantly tell that she hadn't hurt herself. The reason for her tears came from some pain deep inside her. I asked her what was wrong and what had happened, but she didn't answer, she was far too proud for that. She probably thought I wasn't old enough to understand what would make an adult suffer like that. I guess she was right.

As I sat down on her bed and her eyes fluttered, I brushed some hair away from her eyebrows and nose and tucked it behind her ear.

'I'll wait in the kitchen,' I heard Knut say behind me.

I turned and nodded. Knut didn't shut the door.

'Hi,' I said in a whisper.

When Mum heard my voice, she blinked a few times, heavily at first, then faster. Then all of a sudden, she pushed herself up.

'Tobias,' she said. 'Has anything happened? Is he ... has he...?'

I looked at her for a moment, then shook my head.

'There's no news,' I said.

She sat up straight and pulled the duvet with her. Mum had a talent for bursting into tears. Within a second, with no warning. The day I opened the letter from Norway's Football Association, telling me that I had been selected for the under-seventeens friendlies against Malta and Italy, the tears had flowed. She was so proud. Now she was crying again.

I waited until she had calmed down a bit. She leaned over to Knut's bedside table for a box of tissues. She pulled one out and blew her nose. Kept it in her hand as she looked at me. Her eyes were still glazed. I wondered what kind of pills Knut had given her, and if I could talk to her properly. I decided I just had to go for it. There were too many questions gnawing at me.

'I ... I just talked to Tom Hulsker at Tobias's school,' I said.

She blinked. 'To Tom?'

'We started to talk about Dad,' I said, unsure how to go on.

'Why?' There was a more guarded tone to her voice now. She was fully awake.

'I don't know, it just happened,' I said, and wondered if my lie was shining like a light bulb in my eyes. 'You know that Mari was writing an article about me for the school paper, right?'

Mum nodded.

'One of the things we talked about was ... Dad – what it was like for me to come back to Fredheim and to go to a school where everyone knew who my Dad was. Stuff like that. We also talked about ... what happened to him.'

Mum squinted, as if she was trying to focus on me.

'Mari had been in contact with Tobias as well,' I said. 'Did he say anything about that to you?'

She shook her head.

'So he hasn't asked you any questions about Dad recently?'

'Tobias? No...' She paused, seemed to be thinking.

'Well...'

Another pause. 'He did ask if I knew what blood type Jimmy was.'

'Blood type?' I straightened up.

'Yes, I don't know why, but...' Mum shrugged.

'You didn't ask?'

'I guess I didn't.'

I thought about this for a moment. 'What actually happened that day?' I asked.

'What day?'

'The day Daddy died.'

Mum gave me a questioning look. 'Tell me you're not serious,' she said. 'You want to talk about that now? When Tobias is missing?'

'Yes,' I said, trying to sound firm.

'Why is that important *now*?'

'I just need to know,' I said.

Mum took a deep breath and sighed. 'We've gone through it all before,' she said.

'Not really.'

'I've got other things to think about.'

'Sure. But...'

She pushed the duvet to one side and put her feet on the floor. She was fully dressed.

'I'm starting to wonder if Mari maybe stumbled on something that got her killed.'

Mum turned around. Her look pierced me. 'Stumbled over what?'

'Something to do with Dad,' I said. 'And the accident.'

I didn't even have time to react. The palm of her hand hit me square on the left cheek, so hard that my head twisted to the side. She wasn't going to back down, either. She clearly didn't think I would retaliate. She just stood there, glaring at me.

Then she left the room with a mad look on her face. My cheek was still stinging.

59

My mother had never laid a hand on me before, certainly not as far as I could remember. And now, when I was almost an adult, she had slapped me. She had actually slapped me!

What the fuck was that all about?

OK, my timing hadn't been great, but did she need to slap me?

I was still bewildered when I snuck out of the bedroom and put my shoes on. Mostly I was furious. I didn't look at Knut when I heard him coming out into the hall – I didn't want him to see the red mark that felt like a warm cloth on my cheek. I left without saying a word.

It took me a while to calm down. I cycled around for a while, without any plan, but my cheek didn't stop burning. I knew that my dad's death had been difficult for her, but to slap me? Why?

I went through what I knew about the accident. Dad had blacked out and witnesses had seen the car zigzagging across the road for a few hundred metres, at high speed. Then it had careered off the road, straight into some trees.

I stopped and pulled out my phone. I wanted to find out why and how people lost consciousness all of a sudden, like my father had done. The most common cause, according to my Google search, was a sudden decrease in blood flow to the brain – often resulting from some kind of glitch in the nervous system. People could faint when they felt strong emotions, couldn't get enough air, when they'd seen an unpleasant sight, like blood, or had stood up suddenly.

Mum had never actually told me what had happened before my Dad had passed out, and I also realised that I didn't know where they were going that day – whether they were visiting someone or just driving around. I didn't even know where the accident had happened, other than on a narrow road with trees on both sides.

God, what an idiot I'd been.

I rang Imo. He was on his way to Solstad, our old town, to see if Tobias somehow had turned up there. I told him about my argument with Mum, and what she'd done.

When I was finished, Imo said: 'My God. I knew your mother had a temper on her, but...' A short silence followed.

'Do *you* know why your brother passed out that day?' I asked. 'I mean, you knew him better than anyone. I just wondered why something like that would happen to him.'

'Maybe he was stressed at work or something,' Imo said. 'It's a long time ago, Even. I don't really remember. Have you heard anything from the police?'

'No,' I said. 'But I have a feeling there might be bad news soon.'

Imo took a deep breath. 'We'll find him, champ. Try not to worry too much.'

'OK,' I said. 'Talk later.'

I cycled back to the house, half hoping that Tobias had come home in the meantime – that I'd find him sitting in his room. In all likelihood he wouldn't even have bothered to move the broken-down door. He would just be sitting there staring at the mess, like nothing had happened.

But he wasn't there.

There were even more cars outside the house this time. Yngve Mork was standing by the fence, talking on his phone. He ended the conversation when he saw me, and gave me a feeble smile.

'Hi Even.'

'Hey,' I said. 'Any news?'

Mork shook his head. I was about to ask him a question about the investigation, when my phone rang. It was Imo again.

'I've found him!' he shouted. 'I've found your brother.'

60
NOW

Miss Håkonsen takes another sip of water. This is one of the parts of the examination I've been dreading the most.

'Where did Imo find your brother?'

'In Solstad. At Ruben's. His best friend.'

'And what was he doing there?'

I glance quickly at Mum. 'Taking drugs.'

'Drugs?'

'Yes, he was doing drugs. Smoking weed or ... whatever it was.'

'Weed,' the prosecutor says, as though that's the important bit. 'And how had your brother got himself to Solstad?'

'After our argument the night before, he'd asked Ruben to come and pick him up.'

'In the middle of the night?'

'Yes. I don't know exactly what time it was. But I'm sure you have that in your notes somewhere.'

Ms Håkonsen clearly doesn't like my remark, but I'm too tired of all her questions to care. I'm wondering how much longer I need to be up here. A while, I reckon. We haven't even got to Ole Hoff yet.

'Your brother got Ruben to come and collect him, even though Ruben didn't have a driver's licence yet. He borrowed his father's car, didn't he? A man who works as a funeral agent.'

'Yes, that's right,' I say wearily.

'Then they drove back to Solstad.'

'Correct.'

I had smelled weed on Tobias's clothes from time to time, so it didn't come as a big surprise to me that he'd been smoking at Ruben's. What I didn't know, was that he'd been taking other substances as well. Pills, mostly. It was when Imo found my brother that I realised what he wanted extra money for. Why he'd stolen that iPad.

I wasn't angry about any of that, though. I was just happy he was alive and, for the time being, well.

'Did your uncle say anything about what state Tobias was in when he found him?'

'No. Just that he was tired – they'd been up all night.'

'So Imo's plan was to drive Tobias home.'

'Yes.'

'But Yngve Mork was standing beside you when you got that phone call, wasn't he?'

'Yes. And he asked if he could have a word with Imo.'

61
THEN

I handed the phone to Mork. He moved away from me, but I edged towards him, making sure I was close enough to hear what he said. My uncle was to drive Tobias straight to the police station, where my brother would be questioned.

Then something changed in Mork's eyes, in the expression on his face. It was as if something was going on at the other end, something that startled him.

'Imo, what's happening?' Mork said. He was looking straight ahead, eyes wide.

Whatever was going on, Mork's face told me that it wasn't good.

'Imo...'

My uncle obviously didn't answer, because Mork started shouting his name.

'What the hell is going on?' I yelled, but Mork just put a finger in his ear to block out the noise. Had they been in a car crash or something? Why wasn't Imo saying anything?

I thought of my dad, who had driven off the road. Maybe it was hereditary – maybe Imo had passed out too. I knew that he wasn't in perfect health with his back problems and all the medicines I'd seen in his bathroom cupboard. I wondered if history had repeated itself.

I don't know how long I stood there in front of Mork, waiting for an answer, but then, suddenly, it appeared as if Imo came back on the line. Mork asked what had happened. I watched as he listened, nodding. I could just about hear my uncle's voice. He was clearly agitated.

'OK,' Mork said. 'Is he stable?'

Stable?

Mork continued: 'Make sure he's in the recovery position. Keep him calm and I'll get the hold of the nearest ambulance. Where are you?'

Mork fired his instructions so fast I nearly didn't hear what he said.

'Akershus University Hospital is closest then,' he said. 'I'll call and give them your number.'

Then the inspector hung up and turned towards me. He looked at me for moment and took a deep breath.

'Even, your brother...' He paused while he handed me back my phone. Then he sighed and said: 'There's no easy way to say this, so I'll just be blunt and go ahead and say it. Your brother just tried to kill himself.'

⎘

I heard Mork call for an ambulance, giving them Imo's and Tobias's location. Then he gave the operator Imo's phone number. The last thing Mork said before hanging up, was 'hurry'.

Then he looked at me.

'Is he ... is he going to be alright?' I stammered.

'I...' Mork paused, then continued: 'I don't know.'

It was all too unreal. My throat was tight, but I didn't cry. Perhaps it was too early for tears. I had to find out what had happened first, and why.

'Did he do it while ... Imo was talking to you?' I asked.

'Seems like it,' Mork said.

'But ... how? How did he try to do it?'

The inspector put a hand on my shoulder. 'Imo said that he'd swallowed something, a pill or ... maybe lots of them – he wasn't sure. He just fell forward in his seat.' Mork took a deep breath. 'Imo put down his phone when it happened. From what I could hear, it sounded like he slammed on the brakes, ran over to the other side of the car and pulled your brother out onto the road. Then he stuck his fingers down his throat and got him to vomit. But...' Mork looked around '...Imo doesn't know if he'd got it all up.'

I tried to picture it. Imo must have reacted fast. We could only hope that he'd been fast enough.

'An ambulance will be there very soon,' Mork said. 'And then your brother will be in the best possible hands.'

It was cold comfort, though. I couldn't help feeling that this was partly my fault. I had half accused Tobias of being a murderer the night before. Maybe I'd pushed him over the edge.

'Would you like to go to the hospital yourself?'

'Yes,' I said. 'Yes, please.'

Mork took me to his police car and let me in.

'And what about your mother?' he asked.

'She's at Knut's. Should we go and collect her?'

He nodded and got in beside me.

I sat and stared at the road in silence as we drove to Knut's. Mork didn't say anything either; so I was left to my own thoughts: Was Tobias really in such a bad way? How much had he really suffered?

When Mum came out of the flat, her eyes were flooded with tears. She ran over and threw her arms around me, then sobbed against my neck. I let her do it; this was not the time to be angry because she'd slapped me.

⌗

It took us about thirty minutes to get to the hospital. We found Imo in a waiting room on the first floor. He got up as soon as he saw us.

Mum ran over and grabbed him, wanting to know how Tobias was.

'They're trying to ... to pump his stomach,' Imo said, holding her arm. 'He's got a tube down here...' He pointed at his throat. 'And they're ... flushing him out.'

'What does that mean?' Mum shouted.

'They're trying to get him to vomit as much as possible.'

I pulled a face.

'And then they'll give him activated charcoal. It binds itself to any poison that's left, so it doesn't enter his system. And then it will be discharged normally.'

Mum cried uncontrollably for a few more minutes. We all stood around, not knowing what to do.

Finally she pulled herself together enough to ask Imo to tell her exactly what had happened from the time he found Tobias to the moment he collapsed in the car. Even though Imo said everything slowly and clearly, I wasn't sure Mum was able to take much in. She just stood there, her face blank, shaking her head.

'Can I see him?' she asked, when Imo was finished.

'His body's had a bit of bashing, so I'm not sure that now's the right time to—'

'I just want to see him,' she begged.

'I spoke to the nurse just before you came. It's not possible. At least not yet. We have to give his body time to deal with this and then we might be able to talk to him later.'

Later, I thought. What would happen later?

Would my brother be sectioned? And how should we care for him if he wasn't? How could we make sure that he stayed away from drugs? Would we manage?

There was nothing we could do at the moment, other than wait.

The only thing I knew with one hundred percent certainty was that nothing would ever be the same again.

62

Yngve summoned everyone in the task force to a quick meeting in the town's arts centre. It took some time for everyone to get there, as they'd been scattered around Fredheim and local areas, looking for Tobias.

Yngve quickly brought them up to speed on the latest developments in the case.

'Wow,' Therese Kyrkjebø said.

'Wow?' Yngve raised his eyebrows. She looked pale, as if she was about to vomit.

'It's just that it's a huge surprise. If Tobias was already suicidal, why wait until Imo found him before trying anything? Why wait until they were headed back to Fredheim?'

'Two theories,' said Davidsen. He'd placed himself at the other end of the conference table from where Yngve was standing. 'One: Tobias had gone to Solstad to escape his dull Fredheim life. He despised the thought of going back so intensely that he decided he couldn't take it anymore. The means to do so were in his hands or his pocket or whatever.'

'Tobias did spend a lot of time by himself,' Yngve said. 'And a few people are saying that he's a bit socially inept, but that's not unusual in a teenager. Doesn't necessarily mean they hate their lives to the extent that they want to end it.'

'I agree with you on that,' Davidsen said. 'That was only my first theory. My second theory...' He waited a moment, to make sure he had everybody's attention. 'My second theory is that he knew he had questions to answer when he got back here. Why he was at the school play that night? What kind of relationship did he have with Mari? If it *was* Tobias who killed her and the other kids, a suicide could easily solve that problem. He wouldn't have to answer to anyone. He wouldn't have to go to prison. Wouldn't have to bear being labelled a killer for the rest of his life.'

Davidsen's second theory seemed to resonate better with the task force. The thought had occurred Yngve too.

'But it doesn't quite add up,' he said. 'In his chats with Mari, Tobias's tone was normal. Friendly. Nothing there to indicate he felt any anger towards her.'

'So what was he doing with her keys?' asked Vibeke Hanstveit.

'I don't know,' Yngve said.

None of them spoke for a few moments.

'How is he?' Therese asked.

'I don't know yet,' Yngve said.

Weedon, the tech analyst, entered the room. 'Sorry I'm late,' he said. 'I was in the middle of something.'

He found a seat, and from the expression on his face Yngve could tell that Weedon had something he wanted to share. Yngve nodded to him.

'I was just going through Tobias's computer,' Weedon said. 'I checked his chat log with this Ruben guy from Solstad. They did agree that Ruben was going to come and pick Tobias up last night, and yes, it appears that Tobias had managed to get hold of some drugs. Then I checked their messages going a bit further back. And I cross-referenced those messages with the time of Børre Halvorsen's murder.'

The room was dead quiet, hanging on Weedon's words.

'Tobias and Ruben were chatting non-stop between midnight and two a.m. that night,' Weedon continued. 'Børre Halvorsen's body was found under Fredheim Bridge at half past midnight.'

No one said anything for a long time.

'So Tobias didn't kill Børre,' Vibeke Hanstveit concluded with a heavy sigh. 'He couldn't have.'

'Not unless someone else was sitting there in Tobias's place, chatting to Ruben.'

Which is highly unlikely, Yngve thought.

'Maybe he was just depressed, then,' Therese said. 'Like Davidsen first suggested.'

Yngve could tell that a lot of energy had left the room. Åse was standing at the back, urging him to say something – something positive to motivate them all. He went over to the whiteboard where the names of the people most important to the case were written in capital letters, with a few keywords underneath each one.

'Let's first see if Tobias makes it through this,' Yngve said with a sigh. 'Meanwhile, we just have to work the other clues. Let's go through them all one more time, see if we come up with something fresh.'

His phone rang. Yngve pulled it from his back trouser pocket.

It was Reidar Lindgren. Mari's uncle.

'I have to take this,' he said to the room. 'Hi Reidar,' he said as he walked out into the corridor. 'What's going on? Have you managed to get hold of your brother?'

There were traffic noises in the background.

'No,' Reidar said. 'I still don't know where Frode is. But I've found something in his room that ... that worries me a bit.'

'What is it?' Yngve asked, suddenly excited.

It took a few seconds before Reidar Lindgren replied:

'A bloody T-shirt.'

63

Susanne was looking at a picture she had taken of Tobias with her phone a few weeks before. He had been caught unawares, and he'd become angry, demanding that she delete it straightaway.

She hadn't, though, simply because the photo had made her laugh. She needed something to laugh at from time to time. His half-closed eyes made him look drowsy. Maybe he was on drugs then. As soon as the thought entered her mind, she wanted to delete the picture immediately. She wondered if that's how he'd looked when Imo had found him.

On the picture Tobias had just a few hairs on his upper lip, but his face in general was covered in spots. Some red, some dark purple – almost blue. He always hid his face under caps or hoodies.

Susanne drew a heavy breath. She had tried to help him as best she could, hadn't she? It wasn't easy when hormones were running freely, when he didn't care about hygiene and when he didn't eat proper food. Susanne knew the food problem was mostly her fault, but Tobias didn't eat fish, he hated salad, and when she knew that he wasn't doing very well in any aspect of his life, she usually ended up cooking or buying all his favourites, just to make him a little bit happier. She *had* done her best, hadn't she? So how the hell could this happen?

She closed her eyes, glad she was sitting down. The words Imo had used to describe Tobias's state bounced back and forth inside her mind. She was trying to breathe and swallow, but it was hard to do both at the same time. Something was ringing in her ears as well – loud noises, high-pitched voices. And the light, switching from bright white to pitch-black. It made her head spin.

Tobias had seemed happy to get away from his school at Solstad and that stupid thing with that phony cry-baby, Amalie. But after they had settled in Fredheim once more, he'd only isolated himself more and more. Good friends were hard to come by. Susanne knew that only too well.

She opened her eyes and walked up and down a little, stopping again in front of a mirror, where she took a good, hard look at herself. The black, short hair. The dark pouches around the eyes. The wrinkles on either side of her mouth, like two parenthesis around her lips.

She saw a mother. A terrible, despicable mother.

A human being who deserved to be every bit as miserable as she was. She had had it coming, hadn't she, with the way she'd handled her life? The way she had acted, the choices she'd made. The way she'd allowed her children to fend for themselves. Because that was what she'd done, wasn't it? She wanted to punch the mirror, smash it into a thousand pieces. Just to punish that ugly face.

'When was the last time you had something to eat?'

She turned and looked at Even.

'Last night, maybe,' she replied finally.

'We better get you some food, then. There must be a canteen or something around here somewhere.'

'I'm not leaving Tobias.'

'You need to eat, Mum.'

'I don't want to eat. I don't feel like it.'

Even looked to Knut for assistance. 'Go on,' Knut said. 'Get yourself something to eat. You've got your phone. I'll call you if there's any change.'

Susanne didn't have the strength to fight the both of them. She also knew they were making sense. She'd only had a piece of bread last night with her glasses of red.

They took the elevator down to the first floor, where they found a canteen that offered soup and sandwiches. Susanne ordered a minestrone. Soup would be easy to eat. Even had a ham and cheese sandwich. He looked at it with a frown.

They took a seat at a round table covered with breadcrumbs and spots of old coffee. A small plant sat in the centre. There were some other people in the café area as well. People with grim-looking faces. They were all eating or drinking coffee almost in silence, eyes staring emptily ahead.

The soup was warm and surprisingly tasty. Susanne could feel her body responding to the sustenance it instantly gave her. She drank some water as well while watching Even try to eat his sandwich. It really didn't look tasty. White bread with a thick layer of butter. Ham more grey than pink.

They had been sitting there for a few minutes, when Susanne finally spoke.

'I'm sorry,' she said. She reached her hand across him, to touch his face. Laid it against his cheek, exactly where she'd hit him. 'I just...' She looked for the right words to explain – to defend what she'd done, only to realise that she couldn't find them. There was nothing to defend. She'd crossed a line. A big line, and there was no way to go back over it.

'It was just a bit too much for me at that moment.' She lowered her gaze. 'No child should ever be hit by their parents,' she added. 'I'm so sorry.'

Even looked at her. It took a while before he said: 'But I'm still wondering...' he took another bite of his sandwich '...why it's so hard for you to talk about this, even after so many years?'

Susanne put her spoon down. She took a deep breath before saying, with a heavy sigh: 'I guess you have a right to know.'

Susanne hadn't shared this with many people. Her mother knew, God bless her soul. Knut had asked a few times, but she hadn't really said anything. But people usually shied away from the topic of Jimmy, simply because they knew how traumatic it had been for her. How painful it still was.

She was certain, however, what people in town thought about her, what they said about her behind her back. That she'd never been able to cope with Jimmy's death. How she'd drowned her sorrows in alcohol like some kind of walking cliché. That she'd simply run away from Fredheim ten years before. She was sure some even thought she was responsible for Jimmy's death.

'I don't know how much you know about your father,' she started. 'But he was very well liked. Everyone loved him around town. Everyone.' She lifted her chin with a sad smile. 'Unfortunately Jimmy liked a lot of people, too. I mean, besides me. And I mean that in ... well, in *that* way.'

Even's jaw fell open.

Maybe, she thought, it was a bad thing to taint the memory of his father like this. But it was the truth. If Even didn't get it from her, he would get it from someone else later. He certainly didn't deserve *that*.

A part of her had always known that they somehow would end up here, back in the past. Back with all the ghosts and the demons of that horrible, horrible day.

'You know I used to sing in a choir?'

'Of course,' Even said. 'Imo was the conductor.'

'That's right.'

Susanne found herself thinking back with fondness. She really did love singing in that choir. Then the bad memories started flooding in again, and she had to take a deep breath before she was able to continue.

'One day I found some sheet music in the backseat of the car. We sang songs in several voices, and Imo always gave us our own sheet with our name at the top. So we'd know who was going to sing what.' Susanne looked at the tabletop. 'Well...' She stopped herself. It was as though the words had been buried deep inside her for so long that she was struggling to unearth them again.

She cleared her throat. 'I found a sheet of music with someone else's name on it. So ... I realised that your dad had had someone else in the car besides me. Someone who sang in the choir.' She sighed and tossed her head as if to shake something off. 'I also found some ... condoms,' she said. 'Or at least, wrappers. Under the seat.' She shook her head once more.

'Whose name was on the sheet of music?' Even asked.

Susanne paused before raising her head, looking directly into Even's eyes. 'Julia Hoff,' she finally said.

'What?'

'Oskar's mother,' she continued.

Once again Even's jaw fell open. She didn't want to tell him how she'd driven home to the Hoff's house that day. How she'd met Ole at the door and how she'd told him everything. Every suspicion. Every hard piece of evidence. How Ole hadn't said anything until she'd asked if Julia was in. According to Ole, she wasn't, though Susanne was one hundred percent sure that he was lying. That he was trying to protect Julia, afraid that Susanne might do something to her. Maybe even kill her. That cowardly bastard.

'I'm not proud of what I did that day,' she said. 'But I ... I'd had a few drinks after I found that sheet of music. I was just so upset. I went to your dad's school and got him out of there. Dragged him out with me, in the middle of his lunch break, with all his colleagues around.' She shook her head again.

'Cecilie tried to stop me,' she continued. 'Mari's mother. But I was so angry, so furious. Luckily your father just came along with me. He didn't want to make an even bigger scene.' She was crying now, reliving everything. 'Jimmy insisted on driving as I was...' She made a slightly flapping movement with her arms. 'I'm not clear on all the details of what happened that day, but Tobias was at nursery. I can't remember where *you* were.'

Even after so many years her voice trembled.

'Me neither,' Even said.

'Anyway, Jimmy didn't want us to go home until we'd talked things through. He didn't want us to argue in front of you and your brother. And I have to admit, I wasn't really arguing – I was just yelling most of the time. Screaming. Howling.'

She grabbed the salt cellar on the table. Turned it upside down, round and round. Then put it back.

'But he admitted to it?' Even asked. 'He admitted that you were right?'

Susanne didn't speak for a moment. Then she nodded and dried her tears. 'I don't know how far we'd driven, when he...'

Was she going to tell him everything? Was she really going to do that?

No, he would never talk to her again. Not ever.

She pushed back her shoulders. 'Then he went funny,' she said quickly. 'Just passed out, all of a sudden.'

She could see her son searching for answers in her eyes, but she wasn't going to give them to him. 'We drove off the road. You know the rest.'

Her hands were shaking as she put the glass to her lips. God, she needed something stronger. Something to take the pain away.

'Are you done?' she asked. 'I want to go back to Tobias.'

Even took a look at his sandwich, then said: 'I guess I am.'

Susanne pushed her chair back and got up. Then she walked out of the canteen with her chin held high. Tobias was waiting.

64

Reidar Lindgren lived in Schleppegrells gate in Oslo, right next to Dælenenga – the sports field that, over the years, had been used for bandy hockey, athletics, speed skating and speedway, but now was crawling with footballer players – children as well as grown-ups. When Yngve finally found a parking space close by and stepped out into the cold Oslo afternoon, he was struck by how many people were out, despite it being windy and no more than five degrees. They were coming in and out of Birkelunden, a small park in the centre of Grüner-løkka. Some were just on their way home from work, it seemed, arms full of groceries. Nearby, kids were playing in a school yard, dressed far too sparsely. What this part of the capital would look like on a hot summer's day, Yngve could only imagine.

Reidar Lindgren met Yngve in the doorway of his apartment building. He was a robust man in his late forties. He wore a thick grey sweater on top of dirty working clothes and his long hair was tied up in a ponytail.

'I could see you coming from the window', he said with a smile as he firmly shook Yngve's hand. 'The bell isn't working, you see.'

Yngve noticed his friendly ice-blue eyes.

'Come on in.'

Yngve followed him up the stairs. It smelled like wet dog fur. 'We don't have a lift,' Lindgren complained. 'And I live on the fifth floor. It's going to kill me one day'.

They were both breathing heavily when they finally reached the top. 'Come on in,' Lindgren repeated with a heavy exhale. 'Want a coffee or something?'

'I'm fine, thanks. Just show me to your brother's room.'

'You know, I wasn't sure if I should even say anything,' Lindgren said. 'Frode being my brother and everything. I don't know what he's got himself mixed up in, but I do know that he would never do anything to hurt his own daughter. Don't bother taking your shoes off.'

Lindgren took Yngve through a small hall and into a room with an exposed-brick wall. The curtains were pulled aside, giving the room some much needed light.

The bed was unmade. A sports bag was sitting open on the floor. A bloody T-shirt was lying beside it. Yngve bent down and using a pen from his jacket pocket, moved the T-shirt a little. It had blood stains all over it.

'You know when he wore this?' Yngve asked.

'No', Lindgren answered. 'I'm afraid not.'

Yngve noticed a couple of pairs of boxer shorts in the bag. Some trousers, a shirt, a few pair of socks. A mobile phone charger was plugged into a wall socket. A bottle of vodka was on the floor as well, almost empty. The room was pungent with the smell of stale alcohol.

'What has your brother been doing while he's been here?'

'Sleeping, mostly,' Lindgren said. 'At least when I've been around. He hasn't said much. I've never seen him like this before.'

Yngve stood up and turned to Lindgren. 'How do you mean?'

Lindgren seemed to think about his response. 'He's been so ... down, you know? At rock bottom. It was almost as if he was avoiding me when he was around.'

'Was he like that *before* his daughter was murdered, too?'

'Not in the same way, perhaps, but he certainly was in a dark place before that happened as well.'

'He must have said *something* to you about why he needed to sleep in your guest room – why he'd left home.'

'Not much, no,' Lindgren said. 'He made it clear from the start that he didn't want to talk about it.'

Yngve noticed some blood stains on the sheets as well.

'But I've been a bit worried about him,' Lindgren continued. 'Before I saw that, I mean.' He pointed at the T-shirt.

'What's been making you worry?'

He waited a beat before replying. 'Frode and me, we come from a family where problems aren't usually addressed. We don't *talk*. We don't share. Not personal stuff anyway. Which means everything builds up, you know, ready to burst.'

'So you're saying he's lost his temper before?'

'Oh, yes.'

Yngve took a step closer.

'My brother does have a temper on him, that's for sure. Got into some fights over the years, but mostly when he was younger.'

Yngve nodded, waiting for him to continue.

'Anyway, a couple of nights ago he came in late, made a hell of a racket when he did. Just threw his stuff about, tripped up, then kicked his shoes off. They hit my bedroom door.' He shook his head. 'He's been very upset, I guess is what I'm trying to say. There's been a lot of suppressed anger there, I reckon.'

'That finally burst out. He flipped his lid?'

Lindgren snapped his fingers and said yes at the same time.

'Do you know if he's had the use of a car while he's been here?'

'He has.'

'Do you know if he's driven it?'

'I don't, to be honest. Like I said, I haven't seen him much while he's been here. I've been at work. We're tearing down an apartment building over on Sagene. We're a bit behind schedule, so—'

'The night Mari died,' Yngve interrupted. 'Your brother had been to Fredheim High, for the school show. But he came back here after, is that correct?'

'He's slept here every night, yes, since Saturday.'

'Do you remember *when* he got here on Monday night?'

'It was late, I know that. I'd already gone to bed. I woke up when he came in, but I didn't think to check the time.'

Yngve made a final sweep of the room with his eyes. Couldn't see any other objects he could take for further testing. He placed the bloody T-shirt in an evidence bag.

'What are you going to do with that?' Lindgren asked.

'I'm going to check whose blood it is,' Yngve said. 'Thanks for telling me about it.' He headed for the front door.

'What's ... what's going to happen now?' Lindgren asked. There was distress in his voice.

'We'll have to find your brother first,' Yngve said. 'Then ... I guess we'll just have to see what happens.' He opened the door. 'Good luck with the demolition.'

65

Yngve had barely crossed the Oslo county border, on his way back to Fredheim, when the phone rang.

'It's DCI Bjarne Brogeland, Oslo police,' the voice on the other end said. 'You called about a Frode Lindgren?'

Yngve took his foot off the accelerator. 'Yes, have you found him already?'

'It wasn't difficult,' Brogeland said with a laugh. 'He's in a holding cell, sleeping it off. He was arrested this morning.'

'Why? How?'

'He was completely pissed, trying to pick fights – the usual. He didn't want to go home, either, or come with us voluntarily, so we had to bring him in on a public order offence. We've kept him here while he's sobering up. You're lucky – I was just about to let him go when you called.'

Yngve looked for the nearest exit off the motorway. 'Has he said anything?'

'He hasn't spoken much, but he's been very upset. He's been crying a lot.'

Yngve explained what had happened to Mari.

'Oh dear,' Brogeland said. 'I can see why he's so distraught.'

'Can I come and pick him up?'

'He's all yours.'

'Alright, thank you. I'll be there in twenty minutes.'

Half an hour later Yngve met Bjarne Brogeland outside Oslo police headquarters. Frode Lindgren was standing beside him, head down, his clothes dirty – as if he'd spent the night in a ditch. He looked pale and completely worn out.

Yngve knew of Brogeland's reputation. He'd been involved in a series of high-profile cases in Oslo over the last few years. He was in his mid-forties and was muscular – a tough guy. It was easy to understand why criminals respected and tried to stay clear of him.

'He's not in tip-top shape yet, but ...' Brogeland looked at Lindgren. 'At least he's sober.'

'Glad to hear it.'

'How's the investigation going?'

'We're moving in the right direction,' Yngve said with a sigh. He glanced around, almost expecting to see Åse standing nearby. Frode seemed preoccupied with something close to his feet.

'Need a place to question this guy?' Brogeland nodded towards the police headquarters.

'I think this guy needs a cup of coffee,' Yngve said, and took another close look at Frode. It looked like someone had stuck a needle into him and let all the air out. 'But thanks.'

Yngve drove them to Grünerløkka. He didn't ask Frode a single question on the way. Frode didn't offer anything either; he just sat there, staring out of the window, a distant look on his face.

'Let's talk in there,' Yngve said as he found a parking space outside the Nighthawk Diner in Seilduksgata. 'You hungry?'

'Very,' Frode said.

'Let's get something to eat, then.'

The Nighthawk Diner was exactly as its name suggested: a diner serving American foods in an American way. Most of the staff spoke English.

They both ordered a Nighthawk Combo – a hamburger with melted cheddar cheese and smoked bacon, some mayonnaise and salted potato chips.

'I've been trying to reach you,' Yngve said as he poured some water into their glasses.

'My phone's been dead the last twenty-four hours,' Frode said, examining a spot of grease on the table. 'Have you caught the bastard?'

'No'.

'Then what do you need me for?'

Yngve didn't answer straightaway. He just examined the broken man in front of him. 'Have you hurt yourself?' Yngve asked and pointed to Frode's hands – the red flakes of dried blood that flecked them.

'Got into a fight the other night,' Frode said.

'With who?'

'The wall.'

Yngve nodded, slowly. 'Looks like the wall won.'

'I don't know about that.'

Frode emptied his glass. Yngve filled it again.

'How did you treat your wounds?'

'I didn't,' Lindgren said. 'I just wiped the blood off on a T-shirt.'

'What colour?'

'Hm?'

'What colour was the T-shirt?'

Frode lifted his head. 'You've been to my brother's.'

'Like I said, I couldn't get hold of you.'

Frode nodded. 'It was a white one. All white, I hate those T-shirts with all kinds of letters and stuff on them.'

'Me, too.'

Their food arrived, and they just sat there for a while, eating.

'Do you know what I did the other night?' Frode asked, before emptying the glass of water again. 'I followed Even Tollefsen. In my car.' He shook his head. 'I was so angry. So...' He stopped himself. 'I know you've heard the rumours,' he continued. 'How everybody thinks he did it.'

'I don't think—'

'I wanted to run him over,' Frode interrupted. 'Really, Mork, I wanted to kill him. I almost did, too. I don't think he saw me, but ... maybe. I don't know.' He cut off a piece of his burger and shoved it into his mouth. 'I just felt that I had to do something, you know,' he said with his mouth full of food. 'Silly, right?'

'No,' Yngve said. 'It's not silly at all.'

A few moments of silence passed.

'Why have you been trying to reach me?'

'Well,' Yngve said, 'partly because you're here and not at home with your wife.'

Yngve didn't think it necessary to elaborate. Frode chewed a little more slowly, before swallowing and putting his cutlery down. Then he folded his hands.

'Cecilie and I, we...'

Yngve could see that Lindgren wasn't far away from crying again. He exhaled violently, as if he was tired of being in pain and was trying to push it away.

'We had our problems before our daughter was killed, too. Couples argue, for sure, but this time ... this time it was worse. That's why I went to my brother's. I needed time out from everything.' He put his hands on the table.

'Can I ask what happened?' Yngve asked.

Frode stared into the empty glass for a while. 'You can ask, but I'm not so sure I want to answer you,' he said. 'It's a private matter.'

'Not if it involves your daughter's murder,' Yngve said.

Frode stared at him. 'How do you mean?' he asked abruptly.

'We're looking for a good reason why anyone would want to kill Mari,' Yngve said.

'Well, you're not going to find it in our house,' Lindgren protested. 'No way.'

'Are you sure about that?'

'Of course I'm sure about that. The problems Cecilie and I are having are completely ... normal. It happens all the time, everywhere.'

'Mari didn't stay at home the last two days of her life,' Yngve said. 'She didn't want to talk to you at the school show, either.'

Deep lines formed on Frode's forehead. He swallowed a few times, then met Yngve's gaze.

'Cecilie had been cheating on me,' he said. 'For years. I found out, and ... well, we argued. Mari was caught in the middle of it. I think she was afraid our marriage would fall apart, and ... I guess she had every reason to be.'

Frode grabbed his knife and twirled it round and round in his hand before stabbing a potato chip and putting it in his mouth.

'Sorry,' he said. 'I didn't mean to get agitated. But our small family drama can't have anything to do with Mari's murder. Why would it?'

'What did you do after you tried to talk to Mari that night?'

'I ... left.'

'You didn't wait for her after the show?'

'No, I ... I knew that she had work to do, and she clearly didn't want to talk to me, so...'

'Why was she upset with *you*, if Cecilie was the one who had cheated on you?'

'I don't know,' Frode said. 'Maybe ... I was very angry that day,' he said. 'When we argued, I yelled a lot. Threw stuff at the wall and ... I think I might have scared Mari a little bit.'

'But still.'

'Yeah, I know. I didn't quite understand it. Maybe she just needed some space from it all. From us and our family.'

'You drove back to Oslo after the show?'

'Yes. And Mari and I never got to talk things through before...' He was unable to finish the sentence. He sighed. 'I've just been walking the streets feeling sorry for myself these last couple of days. I've been angry. I've been *so* angry, Mork, you have no idea. I've tried to find answers. I've tried to move the pain away from here...' he pointed to his chest '...to somewhere else.' He looked at his hands. 'But it still hurts like hell.'

Yngve knew how Frode felt.

Yngve's phone rang. It was Weedon.

'Sorry, I've got to take this,' Yngve said and lifted his phone to his ear.

'Hey, boss,' Weedon said. 'I went through the CCTV recordings one more time, looking for a way to identify our guy going in at ten forty-nine p.m.'

'Yes?'

'I think I may have found something. Where are you?'

'Oslo.'

'OK. I need to show you, it's easier that way. How quickly can you be here?'

'Pretty quick, if it's important.'

'I think it is.'

'Alright, stay put, I'll be there as soon as I can.'

Yngve hung up and looked at Frode. 'I've got to head back to Fredheim. You're going to be alright now, yes? You're not going to start another fight with the walls or the Somali congregation down on Grønland anytime soon?'

Frode smiled briefly. 'Don't worry,' he said. 'A day in a cell has a sobering effect.'

'Good. Go home to your brother. Charge your phone. I bet a lot of people have been trying to reach you.'

It didn't look as if Frode really wanted to speak to anyone.

'I'll call you as soon as I have any news about the case,' Yngve added.

'Thanks.'

🗗

Weedon was half asleep when Yngve entered his office.

'Oh, sorry,' Weedon said in a gravelly voice, sitting up straight.

'What did you want to show me?'

Weedon moved over to the bank of three computer monitors.

'I went through the images we have of our guy going in, frame by frame, trying to find something that could help us identify him. Look at this.'

He clicked his mouse. Zoomed in on a reflection in the window showing the man's jacket. Weedon enhanced the image, repeating the operation a few times, then waited a few seconds for the software to bring the picture back into focus.

'What does that look like to you?' Weedon asked and pointed to a yellowish colour on the screen, and something that looked like the picture of a car. Yngve leaned in closer and squinted. It was the letters of a logo.

It said TAXI.

He stood up suddenly.

'He's a cab driver.'

'Certainly looks like it.'

Yngve knew quite a few cab drivers in Fredheim, but right now there was just one that came to mind.

'Excellent work, Weedon,' Yngve said. 'Really. Top notch.'

'Thanks, boss.'

66

It was nine o'clock in the evening before a doctor came and told us that Tobias's treatment was successful – that he was going to be fine. A psychiatrist had been monitoring him for a few hours too, and they'd decided he would have to stay overnight, maybe even a couple of nights, for further observation. The most important thing was that he was alright and that there was no permanent damage to his brain or any of his other organs. Mum was so relieved that she sobbed and gasped all at once.

At first, Tobias didn't want to see us, but an hour later, after Mum had nagged and begged anyone in a uniform, we were allowed in to see him. We were under strict instructions not to pressure him to talk about what he'd done.

When we went into the room, he was half sitting, half lying in bed. He was as pale as I'd ever seen him. He fiddled with his covers, and he didn't want to meet our eyes. His room was small with white walls and a square mirror above a white porcelain sink. It was as unfriendly and harsh as it could possibly be.

At first Knut and I just stayed in the background. Mum needed to speak first.

She carefully walked up to the bed. 'Hi,' she said in a whisper.

Tobias kept his eyes trained on the cover. Mum leaned forwards and gave him a hug. He let her kiss him on the cheek, on the forehead, on his hair, before pulling away, irritated. Mum apologised and sat down on the bed. Put her hand to his cheek. Dried a tear from her own.

'How are you feeling?' she asked quietly.

Tobias shrugged. Still didn't want to look at her – or at Knut or me. She pushed the hair back from his forehead. The overhead lights made it gleam.

I could tell that Mum had a thousand questions for him, that she had to fight not to blurt them out all at once. Instead she produced a volley of inane comments, things that only got a yes or a no reply. She told him how GP was and then started on some silly story about one of her co-workers at the children's clothes shop.

When she finally ran out of stupid things to say, I asked if I could have two minutes alone with him. Mum was reluctant at first, but she agreed – as long as I promised to be gentle with him. I said yes of course I would be, not knowing if I'd be able to stay true to my word.

When I finally had my brother to myself, I said: 'I owe you a door.'

Tobias frowned at me. I explained what had happened. He didn't seem particularly interested.

'You owe me a Playstation controller, too.'

'I know,' I said. 'How are you feeling?'

'Like shit,' he said.

I nodded.

He seemed angry. With himself? Or with the doctors who'd treated him? Or me, just because I was there? Or maybe he was simply angry at the world. It wasn't easy to tell.

'Is there anything you need?' I asked. 'A glass of water or something?'

He shook his head.

There was a chair beside the bed, so I sat down. His hair was greasy, but the spots on his face seemed to have dried up a bit. I didn't know how to ask the questions I needed answers to, but I had to do it, some way or another.

'We've been in touch with the police,' I said. 'They won't come by today.'

Tobias looked down at the bedclothes again. I didn't know what he was looking at – his eyes were vacant.

'But I think you can expect some company tomorrow. One thing they want to know is why you wanted to talk to Mari on the night she was killed.'

I heard a man shouting somewhere in the hospital. Once, and then again.

'I know about the texts you sent her.'

Tobias put his hands together, started to pick at his nails.

'You know you have to answer, don't you?'

'So we're there again, eh?' Tobias said. His voice was calm, quiet. 'You playing detective?' He said it with contempt in his voice and without looking at me.

'Why is it so strange that I want to know?' I asked.

Tobias still didn't want to meet my eye. He just let out a big sigh. Then finally he said: 'I'd helped her find some pictures of you. For the story about you and Dad.'

He explained the context, and I nodded. I already knew Mari's motives for going behind my back like that.

'I met her a week ago, something like that. You were at football practice.'

'To give her the photos.'

'Yes.'

'And that's it?'

'What do you mean?'

'That's all you did? You gave her the photos, and then you left?'

'We talked for a little while, too.'

'What about.'

'You know, stuff.'

'What kind of stuff?'

'I don't know. School stuff. At some point there she starting talking about blood types.'

'Blood types?'

'Yeah.'

'Are you fucking kidding me? You were talking to *Mari* about blood types?'

'She'd been studying them in school.'

'I know that. But why did she talk to *you* about it?'

'She wanted to know if I knew our dad's.'

I looked at him. 'Really?'

'Yeah, really.'

'Why did she want to know that?'

'I don't know.'

'You didn't ask?'

'I just thought she needed it for her story.'

'Huh.'

I was missing something here. I just didn't know what.

'So you found out.'

'Yeah, I asked Mum.'

'And then you told her. You told Mari.'

'I did.'

'When was this?'

'Three or four days ago, maybe. Friday perhaps.'

I just looked at my brother for a few seconds. Once again I asked him what he'd been doing at the show that night and why he'd been in contact with Mari. It took a long time before he answered.

'Mum had discovered that some of her photos of you and Dad were missing. You know what Mum's like, how obsessed she can get. So I wanted to get them back before all hell broke loose at home.' Tobias paused. 'That's why I went to the show. To talk to Mari. I couldn't get hold of her, she wasn't answering my texts. So I went in and found her. She said the pictures were in that school newspaper room, but that she couldn't get them for me then, because she was working. She said I could just go in there and get them myself.' He paused for a beat. 'The room was locked, so I borrowed her keys. But I couldn't find those fucking pictures, so I thought I'd catch her again after the show. I went outside to wait for her. But she never came out. I stood there for ages, waiting.'

'So you...' I couldn't get my thoughts straight.

'I had her keys,' Tobias said. 'I'd forgotten I had them – I'd just put them in my pocket when I couldn't find the photographs. And then when she was dead, I...' He opened his hands. 'I fucking panicked,' he said. 'I knew how it would look.'

'So where are the keys now?'

'In a drawer in my room.'

'God, Tobias.'

The police must have found them, I thought. And they must have drawn their own conclusions.

I was relieved and angry at the same time. Relieved that there was an innocent explanation why Tobias had been at the school that night – why Børre Halvorsen had seen him in the window, and why Tobias had had Mari's keys. Angry because he hadn't told me before. It could have saved us a lot of worry and heartache.

I asked why he hadn't said anything. Again, it took some time before he answered. 'I liked Mari as well, Even. She talked to me in a proper way, not like...' He glanced to the side. 'I didn't want anyone to think that I had...' He stopped himself.

We sat there in silence for a short while. I thought about Mari. The last day had been all about finding Tobias, about getting answers. Now she filled my head again, and I realised how much I missed her. There was so much I wanted to ask her. Tell her.

'There's something else, though.'

Tobias licked his lips. He looked like he was steeling himself. I felt uneasy again.

'After I talked to Mari that night at your school, I went outside to wait for her.'

'You've told me that already.'

'I know, just hang on a minute. As I was standing there – it must have been quite a while after the show had ended – I ... I saw Knut drive in and park his car.' Tobias nodded at the door, as though I hadn't understood who he meant.

'What the hell was *he* doing there?'

'To begin with, I thought he was just waiting for a fare, thinking people might need one after the show. But he just sat there.'

'You didn't go over?'

Tobias scoffed. 'I barely speak to him at home,' he said. 'What would I ask him? How he was? How many fares he'd had that evening? I don't give a fuck about Knut, you know that. After a while, though, he went inside.'

I swallowed. 'What time was this?'

'I don't know. It was starting to get late, and most people had gone home. I'd been standing there waiting for so long, and it was starting to get cold, so I thought, to hell with the photographs, they can wait till tomorrow or another time. And then I went home.'

'What about the iPad you stole?'

He seemed to have forgotten that small detail for a moment, but then he nodded.

I tried to digest what my brother had just told me. 'So, you're saying that Knut went into the school building not long before Mari and Johannes were killed?'

Tobias took a deep breath. 'That's what I'm saying, yeah.'

67
NOW

'How well did you know your mother's boyfriend?'

Ms Håkonsen has sat down again. She is leaning forwards on the table, eyes seeking mine.

'I wouldn't say that I knew him at all, really. He was full of surprises – that's for sure.'

'How so?'

'That chill pill he gave my mother, for instance.'

'*Chill* pill?'

'I don't really know what kind of pill it was. I hadn't thought he was the kind of guy who had sedatives just lying about. I just thought he was someone who never said much, and basically did whatever my mother wanted him to. But maybe he was kind of secretive too.'

The prosecutor seems to give this some thought.

'When your brother told you that Knut had gone into your school that night, what did you think? Did you think Knut might have been the killer?'

'That was my first thought, yes. And my second and third thoughts as well, to be honest.'

'Why is that?'

'Well, it was the same day my mother had slapped me when I suggested that maybe Mari had been killed because of something she'd discovered about Dad's car accident. I wondered if Mum knew something about that, and if Knut did too, and wanted to protect my mother somehow.'

'So, you thought he'd killed Mari to stop her talking? To keep her from revealing whatever she'd discovered about the car accident, maybe even about your mother?'

'That's what I thought, yes. Apparently he'd been in love with Mum since high school.'

'And according to your own statement just now, you thought Knut would do whatever your mother wanted him to.'

'Yes.'

Ms Håkonsen waits a few seconds. Then: 'Did you think, at that time, that your mother might have put him up to it?'

'I didn't think that then, no. I was more worried about what was going to happen to *me*.'

'Why is that?'

'Because right after I'd spoken to Tobias at the hospital, Mum wanted Knut to drive me home.'

68
THEN

'It's school day tomorrow,' Mum said. 'You need to get some sleep.'

'Yeah, but...' I didn't know what to say.

'Of course I can drive him,' Knut said. 'But what about you?'

'I'll stay here,' Mum said. 'I'm not leaving Tobias.'

I looked at my brother. He wasn't exactly thrilled at the prospect of Mum staying, but, like me, his options were limited.

It was a strange feeling, to be standing in a room with three people who I, at some point during the past few days, had been or still was suspicious about, at least when it came to the murder of my ex-girlfriend. The weirdest part was that they were all family – or, in Knut's case, almost. I wasn't sure at all how I felt about any of them. Tobias's explanation did make sense, but there was something odd about it all the same. I couldn't understand why it was so important for him to get the photos back for Mum. He didn't really care about our mother. He didn't care much about anything. On the other hand, it had been a while since anything my brother did made much sense to me, so why should this be any different?

'OK,' I said carefully. Then to Tobias: 'You'll be alright?'

He nodded.

'Sure?'

'Yes.'

'Alright,' I said. 'See you.'

Then Knut and I left.

We didn't say a word to each other on the way out to his car. Just walking beside him made me uneasy. I wondered if he had Johannes Eklund's microphone case hidden away somewhere. Maybe even in his taxi.

I sat in the passenger seat and put on my seatbelt. Knut drove like a priest, religiously sticking to the speed limit.

We'd been driving for about ten minutes, when he said: 'I'm actually glad it's just you and me right now.'

I turned towards him.

'I thought maybe we could talk.'

With everything Tobias had said fresh in my mind, Knut's voice sounded colder. More calculating. As though he'd been waiting for this moment.

'About what?' I said and coughed into my palm. Knut wasn't big or strong, but I knew that he ran a lot, which meant he was fit. If he was angry enough – or thought he had enough reason – I had no doubt that he'd be able to kill someone.

'Your mother and I, we...' He paused, then carried on: 'You know we've been together for a while now.' He paused again before continuing. 'And we ... we've been thinking about moving in together.'

My jaw dropped.

'Or rather, that I move in. With you.'

I didn't know what to say.

Knut carried on: 'It's probably a bit unexpected, and I know you have other things on your mind right now, but, given what we talked about earlier today, I think it would be good for your mum. To get some help with ... whatever.'

We were out on the motorway now. Cars sped past us.

'Just ... think about it', he continued. 'And talk to your brother about it too, of course, when you get a chance. We won't do it if you think it's a bad idea.'

I wanted to ask what the hell he was doing at our school that night, but I just couldn't get myself to do it. I don't know if I was afraid of how he would answer, or if I was scared what Knut would do if I confronted him. I didn't really know anything about this man. Would his true self appear somehow?

Neither of us spoke the rest of the journey. Not until he pulled up in front of our house. Then something made him stop.

'What is it?' I said. Then I followed Knut's gaze, and saw it, too.

On our front door, in black spray paint, someone had written:

MURDERER

'Fuck,' I muttered and scrambled out of the car.

I wasn't sure which one of us the message was referring to – my brother or me. Or maybe even my mother.

Knut turned off the engine and got out as well. We walked to the front steps. I touched the letters on the door. The paint was dry.

Børre had been a tagger. Was this some kind of message from his friends?

'Do you have some paint?' Knut asked me.

'Yeah, I think there might be some left over from when we did the house this summer.'

'Go get it. Susanne can't see this.'

'You don't need to help me,' I said. 'I can do it myself.'

'I don't doubt that,' he said. 'But I'd like to help you all the same.'

It didn't take us long to give the door a fresh coat. I took a few steps back and looked at it. From a distance it was still possible to see the contours of the letters.

'Fucking bastards,' I muttered.

Knut wiped some paint off his hands with an old rag. 'You need to paint it again tomorrow.'

'I know,' I said.

He came over to me and stood by my side for a few moments. 'OK,' he said. 'I better get going.' He started to walk towards his car.

'Thanks,' I said. 'For...'

'Don't worry about it,' Knut said. 'Soon this will all be over. I'm sure the police have some solid leads they're working on.'

69

For a long time Fredheim had had its own dairy factory, but after years of running at a loss, the whole thing had been bulldozed and replaced with an apartment building that consisted of four almost identical flats, all grey and square, completely free of ornament. It was basically a box of rooms. Every apartment had a west-facing balcony, so the tenants could enjoy the afternoon sun. Whether Knut Anthon Meyer did that or not, Yngve had no idea, but he knew that Knut lived on the third floor, in apartment C301.

Yngve was sitting in his car in the parking lot, where he could watch Knut's apartment while keeping an eye on whoever entered and left the building. It was a little after one in the morning, and the lights were still on in Knut's apartment – a flicker that changed in intensity and colour. Knut, it seemed, was watching TV.

Åse used to call them wallflowers – people who never spoke unless spoken to, who always preferred to stay in the background, so that no one would notice them or engage them in conversation. Knut, Yngve thought, was a wallflower, a man it was hard to get close to, simply because he never volunteered a 'hi' or a 'how-are-you', or did anything whatsoever to make your acquaintance. Even in his own taxi, Knut never engaged in small talk. He was the kind of guy who'd let you go first in a queue, even if it wasn't your turn.

Knut had lived in Fredheim all his life. He'd never been involved in any kind of trouble. No criminal record, no financial problems, nothing. As far as Yngve knew, Knut had never even had a girlfriend until he hooked up with Susanne Tollefsen a little over a year ago. How that could have happened in the first place, was a mystery for another day.

As the murders in Fredheim had occurred late at night, Yngve had decided, after conferring with Therese Kyrkjebø and Vibeke Hanstveit, that he should observe Knut's night-time behaviour – see what he got up to. Yngve didn't sleep much anyway, so it really was no bother. It was too late at night for them to get the right permissions to check Knut's whereabouts when Børre Halvorsen had been killed, but Ulf, the homeless man who'd discovered the body, did say that he had seen a taxi nearby right before. That didn't mean it was Knut's, but at this point in the investigation, Yngve really didn't want to take any chances on anything. There had been three murders in Fredheim on his watch. That was three too many.

He had brought a book, some slices of bread with brown cheese and enough coffee to sustain an entire regiment through the night. Every time he turned a page of the book, he lifted his gaze towards Knut's apartment and the entrance to the building.

No change.

He had put on lots of layers, as he didn't want to leave the car running. It had been a while since he'd staked someone out like this. He hadn't missed it. It didn't take long for his back to start aching. Good thing the book was brilliant. It was a story about the death of a young boy in the North of England, a mystery no one had been able to solve for fifteen years until a well-respected podcast reporter had taken it upon himself to get to the bottom of it all. Only as Yngve held it in his hands did he realise that it was the last book Åse had given him.

He was forty-three pages in when the door to the building opened. Knut came out. Yngve tossed the book aside and slid down in his seat. Susanne Tollefsen's boyfriend was wearing his taxi jacket. He got into his car, which was parked some fifty yards away from Yngve's.

As Knut drove past him, Yngve sat up, waited ten seconds then started his own engine. Knut hadn't lit up his sign, so he wasn't going to work.

Yngve followed him, keeping his distance. Knut was on his way to the town centre. He drove across the main street and over the bridge to the other side. He signalled, then turned into the petrol station, which was open twenty-four hours, but he didn't stop at any of the pumps. He just parked and went inside the shop.

Yngve drove on a few hundred yards before making a U-turn. When he got back to the petrol station, Knut was coming out with a half-eaten hot dog in one hand, and a bottle of Coca-Cola in the other. He got back in his car. Yngve waited for him at a bus stop, then followed him back the same way he had come.

Knut, as it seemed, had been hungry.

Yngve exhaled.

For a good ten minutes he'd actually thought he might be on the heels of a killer who was about to strike again. It took Yngve a while to regain his normal heart rhythm.

At 2.14 a.m. Knut turned off his lights. Yngve sat back to read again.

The chances of Knut moving again were slim, but Yngve stayed there till morning.

He was just about to close his eyes for moment, when he heard her voice from the backseat. She wanted to know how he was doing. His first instinct was to say 'terrible', because that's how he'd felt for so long, but it wasn't true. The fact was, he'd felt more alive in the last couple of days than he could remember. It made him feel guilty.

Don't be, she said.

'Well, I do anyway,' Yngve answered.

Now that she was there again, with him, he wanted her to tell him as much as possible about how things were where she was, if she met other people, or if it was all just quiet. He wanted to know whether it was warm or cold, dark or bright. If it was possible to feel anything at all – anger, joy, sorrow, pain. She didn't want to say anything, though. All he could see in the mirror were her tired, beautiful eyes and that shiny, hairless head of hers.

All of a sudden an intense wave of fatigue hit him. It was like he couldn't even sit up straight anymore. Like the muscles in his body suddenly just caved in.

Tomorrow you can rest, she said.

'What was that?' he asked.

She said that it would all be over tomorrow.

'How do you know?'

She couldn't tell him. She just knew.

70

That night I dreamt about Mari. I went into a room full of people, and there she was, listening to some authors blabbering about their books. She didn't see me at first. I just stood there watching her, until she lifted her head and our eyes suddenly locked.

Her whole face lit up. She seemed surprised to see me, but all the happier for it. She was seated in the middle of a row, so she couldn't get up to meet me. I could see that she wanted to, though. She blushed as she turned back to watch what was happening on stage, but I could tell she really wasn't paying attention.

As soon as the talk was over, she got up and came to meet me. We hugged briefly. For some reason we didn't want anyone to know we were a couple, so we didn't kiss. I did put her hand to my chest, though, because I wanted her to know how fast and hard my heart was beating. That made her hug me again – it was as if she couldn't help herself. It was a tighter hug this time, and it lasted longer than hugs normally do between friends.

I snuck a hand under her hair and cupped it round her neck, so I could feel her warmth. Through her soft skin I could just feel her pulse, a rhythm that was picking up pace. When I gently pushed her away from me, I noticed all of a sudden that she couldn't breathe. It was as if something was stuck in her throat. As I looked around for help, she became more and more desperate. She tried to say something, but no words came out.

That's when I woke up. I sat up straight and gasped for air myself for a few moments, still able to feel the rhythm of her heart in my body. Upstairs, the old wooden clock chimed seven times. It was time to get up and go to school.

I got dressed and went outside to see if the paint was dry and if the letters that formed the word *MURDERER* were still visible. They were, so I quickly gave the door another coat. It might even need a third, but at least the neighbours wouldn't see the letters unless they got up close.

The thought of going back to school, of actually sitting there, trying to learn something again, had been the furthest thing from my mind the last few days. But when I got there that morning, it was as if nothing had changed. People were standing in groups, talking, smoking, laughing. There wasn't even a photograph or a shrine or something on the staircase where Johannes had been killed. No flowers or messages. Everything was normal. Life went on, and so, apparently, did our classes.

In the first break, I got Oskar to come with me to the music room. 'Why do you want to go *there?*' he asked.

'I just need to see it,' I explained. It was silly, but I thought the room would speak to me somehow, that I would be able to feel Mari's presence, or maybe even hear her voice or something.

When we got to the door to the room, a sudden wave of uneasiness swept through my body. I had to steel myself as I grabbed hold of the handle and pushed the door open. Inside several desks and chairs were piled on top of each other. The piano stood against one of the walls. There were music stands. Drums, guitar cases. A double bass. There was a picture of Beethoven on the wall as well. A shiver went down my spine. This was where my Mari had drawn her last breath. This was where someone had killed her.

I looked around and wondered where, precisely, she had died. Where she and Johannes had sat when she'd interviewed him. If he'd tried to flirt with her, and if she'd let him. If anyone saw. But no, I couldn't get her to speak to me. It really had been a silly thought.

I left the room and made my way to the school newspaper room, Oskar following behind. When we got there, we found a man sitting at one of the desks.

'Can I help you?' he said.

I didn't know what to say at first. Then I explained who I was.

'Ah yes.'

He pointed to the whiteboard. *4/16* was written at the top, with lots of keywords underneath. My name was up there. I assumed I was looking at the contents of the paper's next edition.

'You're the football player.'

'Sometimes, yeah.'

There were only four desks in the room, pushed together in the centre, with low screens between them.

'I'm the editor of the school newspaper,' he said. 'Kjell-Ola Trulsen.'

He stood up and put out his hand. I shook it. He looked like he'd been desperately saving up for a beard, but could only afford a few tufts of hair. He was wearing a red-and-white checked shirt that looked as if it hadn't been washed in a decade or two. He reeked of smoke and old coffee.

'What can I do for you?'

'Do you know if Mari had delivered the text of the article she was writing about me?' I asked.

Kjell-Ola shook his head. 'I'm not an editor *per se,*' he said. 'They only needed someone to take charge during the meetings and unlock the doors and stuff.'

I nodded.

'But there are going to be some changes now,' Kjell-Ola said and pointed to the board again. 'To the next edition, I mean.' He seemed genuinely upset. 'I'm not looking forward to writing the editorial, I can tell you that much. It'll be more of an obituary. I've never done one of those before.'

I went over to the window at the far end of the room. The one the killer was supposed to have climbed through to get out onto the roof. I opened it and stuck my head out, feeling a cold breeze on my face. It made me realise how warm I was. I looked down at the entrance to the school. I wondered where Børre Halvorsen had been standing when he saw Tobias – if he just happened to be passing, or if he had planned to graffiti a wall or two in the school grounds.

I turned to Oskar. 'When you talked to Børre that evening, was his friend with him? The guy with the red hair?'

'He was, yes.'

'Do you know him?'

'No, but I know who he is. Everybody just calls him Vic, but I think his real name is Victor. Ramsfjell, I think, is his surname. Why do you ask?'

I looked out of the window again. Børre's murder was as much of a mystery as Mari's and Johannes'. But if Børre was killed because he knew something, maybe his friend did too?

71
NOW

'This sounds like the moment you decided to try and find Victor Ramsfjell.'

'Yes,' I say, nodding.

'How did you go about doing that?'

'I knew he was my brother's age, so I figured they went to the same school. So I just went there at the end of the day and looked for him.'

'That would be Fredly Junior High, is that correct?'

'That's correct, yes.'

'And did you find him?'

'I did, yes. I managed to get hold of him just as he was about to leave.'

'How did he react when he learned that you wanted to talk to him?'

'At first I think he was scared.'

'Scared?'

'Well, yes. At that point most people still believed I'd killed his best friend. But he agreed to talk to me, but he didn't want to do it there, in front of everyone, so I just cycled along beside him.'

'And what did he tell you?'

'Nothing new, really. Certainly not then. He hadn't been with Børre the evening Mari and Johannes were killed. He said he didn't know anything about what went on.'

'But he did? He did know something, didn't he?' Ms Håkonsen discreetly dabs at the corners of her mouth.

'Yes,' I say. 'He knew something important. He just wasn't aware of it at the time.'

72
THEN

'Thanks for coming in.'

Yngve extended his hand for Knut to shake. The taxi driver was wearing his uniform – a white, unironed shirt under a dark-blue jacket. His trousers were dark blue too. His hair was brown, but short and unkempt – as if he'd been sitting with his head out the car window all the way to the precinct.

'What's this about, officer?' It was the same question he'd nervously asked when Yngve had called him and asked him to come to the station.

'We just want to clarify a few things. Please come with me.' Yngve showed Knut into his office. 'How's Tobias today?'

'He's alright, I guess,' Knut said. 'I'm seeing them later.'

He offered Knut a seat, then said: 'At ten forty-nine p.m. on Monday night you entered the school by the main door, but you didn't come out the same way. What happened?'

Yngve hadn't known for sure that Knut was the one they'd been looking for, but as he sat down and looked back at him with a guilty frown on his face, all of Yngve's doubts were gone.

'I...'

Knut seemed to be searching for the right words. 'I ... was looking for someone.'

'Who were you looking for, Knut?'

He looked at the desk in front of him for a while, seemingly worried about the direction the conversation was headed. When he spoke, his voice was like a whisper. 'Mari.'

'What was that?'

'I was looking for Mari.'

Yngve stared at Knut for a few moments, at first in disbelief.

Knut continued, his voice a bit more firm. 'She'd booked a fare with the company. I responded to the call.' Knut didn't look at Yngve as he spoke. 'At first I was just waiting for her outside, but the meter was running, and she didn't come out. She hadn't left a number either, so I went inside to see if I could find her.'

'Her phone wasn't working,' Yngve said, trying to gather his thoughts at the same time. 'So how could she even book a fare?'

'You can do that online these days as well,' Knut explained. 'Just leave your name and allow the computer to share its location with the application, and you're all set. You have to put in your credit card details on your profile, though, before you book anything, so we don't—'

'Alright, OK,' Yngve interrupted. 'I get it. So you went inside to look for her, but you didn't come out the same way. Why was that, Knut?'

'I couldn't find her.'

'Really.'

'Yes, really. And I knew the clock was ticking; it was getting closer to eleven, when the doors would be closing – I even heard that ding-dong thing as soon as I went in too, so I just did a quick search around for her. When I got to the other side of the school, I just went out that way. Alone.'

'And where on the other side would that be, precisely?'

'I was quite lucky, actually. I didn't think Tic-Tac's door would be open. But it was, so I just used it. I'm glad I could, because otherwise I think I might have triggered the alarm.'

'How come you knew about Tic-Tac's door?'

Knut snorted. 'Doesn't everybody? The door was there when I went to Fredheim High as well, twenty years ago. It's probably been there since the whole thing was constructed.'

Yngve nodded and made a note on the pad before him.

'When you did your quick search for Mari, did you look for her on the second floor?'

'I went up there, yes. Briefly. I couldn't see her, so I went back down again and decided to see if I could find her in another section of the school.'

'Did you see anyone else while you were doing that?'

Knut shook his head.

'What did you do after you left the school?'

'I hurried back to my car and waited a little while. Then I left.'

Yngve cursed under his lips. The CCTV cameras were only facing the school entrance, not the surrounding areas.

'How long is "a little while"?' he asked.

'A good ten minutes or so. I figured Mari had got a ride home with someone else without cancelling my call. I didn't want her to have to pay for it, so I just deleted the booking.'

Yngve sighed heavily. Therese had spoken to the taxi company before they'd brought Knut in. They could confirm that Knut had been on duty on the night of the school murders, but they didn't have any records of him completing any fares between 11.00 and 12.16. Now they knew why.

'What I'm dying to know, Knut, is why the hell you didn't come forward with this information before I dragged you in here. You were on the school premises literally minutes before two teenagers were murdered. You didn't think we'd need to talk to you?'

A line of sweat had formed on Knut's upper lip. 'I was only there for a couple of minutes,' he said tentatively. 'Five maybe. I didn't see anything. Didn't hear anything, either. I figured you wouldn't be bothered with my statement.'

'You figured wrong.'

'Well, I'm sorry,' he said. 'I thought it would be a waste of your time.'

'You could have *saved* us a lot of time. And trouble.'

Yngve thought about his sleepless night in the car and wanted to swear at the man in front of him, but he managed to hold back. 'God knows how many hours we've been working trying to figure out who that person was on the surveillance tapes.'

'Again, I apologise.'

Yngve rubbed his eyes.

'After you'd come out of the school, and while you were waiting in your car, did you see anyone then?'

'No, it was raining quite heavily. Which was why I didn't want to waste any more time just sitting there.'

'It was quite service-minded of you,' Yngve said, 'to go in and look for Mari like that. Would you have done that for any other customer?'

Knut seemed to give that some thought before answering. 'I don't know. I think I would. But I knew she was Even's girlfriend, and I thought I could score some points with her, and with him, if I went in and got her. God knows it's not easy coming into a family like Susanne's the way that I have, late in the boys' lives and all.'

Knut had been working when Børre Halvorsen was murdered as well, but he'd been on a trip to Lillestrøm at the time. The taxi company had a copy of the receipt he'd collected afterwards. He'd been paid at exactly thirteen minutes past midnight. There was no way Knut could have made it back to Fredheim in time to kill Børre.

Yngve asked him a few more questions, then sent him on his way, sweating profusely and apologising once again for not coming forward. Afterwards Yngve went to see Therese.

'Someone's lying to us in this town,' he said. 'I can't see any other explanation.'

'Yeah,' she said. 'I think you may be right. I've just heard from the doctors at Akershus University Hospital. They have given us the go-ahead to interview Tobias.'

'Let's go then.'

73

I said goodbye to Victor Ramsfjell and checked my phone. Ole Hoff had called. I suspected he'd heard about Tobias and wanted an update. But after what my mum had told me about Julia, his wife, I really didn't want to talk to him. Besides, our family drama was nobody else's business – especially not the media's.

I was wondering what to do. I didn't want to go home to the big empty house and sit there with my own thoughts, waiting for updates on Tobias. As I was standing on the pavement, my bike leaning against my stomach, I tried to go through everything I knew about the case, step by step. I thought about Mari and what she'd done the last few days of her life – besides breaking up with me. I remembered how she'd stayed away from school and spent the last two nights of her life at Ida Hammer's, apparently because of some argument with her parents.

A new plan formed in my mind, but I wasn't sure if I should go through with it. My previous encounter with Cecilie Lindgren hadn't gone well, and if it really was Frode who had been following me in his car that night, going to see them now might not be a good idea. But I needed answers.

When I got to their house, I could see that Frode's car wasn't there. I leaned my bike against the fence and tried to muster up some courage, before walking slowly to the front door and ringing the bell. I heard footsteps inside, a slow shuffling that made my heart beat faster. The door opened and Cecilie Lindgren looked at me. She didn't appear to be angry or upset. She just stared squarely at me, waiting for me to speak.

'Please,' I said, holding up my hands. 'Don't ... chase me off. Please, just ... I need to talk to you.'

It was as if the person in front of me didn't have the energy to even speak. She just held on to the door handle and looked at me with empty eyes. It looked like she hadn't showered or slept for days. She was thin and feeble, a bit like Mum.

'Why do you want to talk to me?' she asked finally, in a flat voice.

'I just ... want to try and understand a few things,' I said.

'Sorry,' Cecilie said – she sounded utterly exhausted. 'I don't know if I can bear to talk to you, Even.'

'Please,' I begged. 'I've been through a lot in the past few days too. It might do us both some good if we talk.'

I was afraid that my psycho-babble might upset her again, but instead of sending me on my way, her shoulders dropped and she let out a heavy sigh.

'Do you drink coffee, Even?' she asked me.

'Not often,' I said with a small smile. 'And not a lot. But I'll be happy to have some now.'

As soon as I entered the house, my eyes searched for Mari's things. Her shoes. Her jacket. A hairband lying on a dresser. A glass she had used. But I saw nothing. I wondered if Cecilie had cleared out all her daughter's belongings already. Whether that was how she'd managed to get through the past few days.

Cecilie indicated the living room and pointed to the sofa, and I went in and sat down. Shortly after, she came in with a coffee pot and two cups. She poured a cup for me, but only helped herself to a few drops.

'Put plenty of sugar in,' she said. 'It helps.'

We sat there for a little while, just feeling the silence between us. I'd always felt a bit awkward around Cecilie. Like she really didn't like me. There had always been a certain distance or a coldness in her gaze. Like she was suspicious of me or something. I had even asked Mari about it, but she had just dismissed it. 'You'll win her over,' she'd said. 'Just act normally, and she will love you just as much as I do.'

'It's strange, isn't it,' Cecilie said. 'It's at times like these you discover who your true friends really are.' She poured a bit of milk into her cup and stirred. 'At first everyone wants to pay their respects. We've received flowers, cards, messages of support and love from God knows where. It's when things start to calm down a bit you really need people. When the emptiness fully hits you. That's when you need something – some*one* – to help get you through the days.'

I thought about my mother, who had recently said something similar. She'd also been angry at the woman sitting in front of me.

As though she'd read my mind, Cecilie said: 'I wasn't a very good friend to your mother after your dad died. It was a very difficult time for me too. Your father was a good friend of mine. A good colleague.'

I remembered what Tom Hulsker had said about them.

Cecilie looked away. 'The accident had a deep impact on me. My grief ... it was hard for me to explain or control.'

She looked up at me. Old grief mixed with new.

'I think your mother was disappointed with me,' she said. 'The fact that I wasn't there for her when she needed me most. But I just couldn't, not when...' Again she turned her head away.

I wasn't sure I knew what she meant.

She looked at me again and smiled. 'You're very much like your father,' she said. 'You've got the same chin. The same eyes. Your hair's a bit longer, though.'

She smiled again.

'Mari seemed to be really interested in my dad just before she...'

Cecilie's smile vanished in an instant. Then she stood up and went over to the table in the corner. It was where we'd had dinner together. She grabbed the back of a chair and just stood there, holding on to it. She was crying, even though she didn't make a sound.

'Did she ever tell you why she split up with me?' I asked.

It took a while before Cecilie nodded. Then she shook her head. 'She couldn't be with you, Even,' she said, suddenly overcome with tears. It sounded like an echo of the message Mari had sent me the day she dumped me. That I was the best guy, but that she just couldn't be with me any longer.

I got up and slowly moved closer to Cecilie. 'Why?' I asked.

She sniffed. 'Have you really not guessed it yet, Even?'

I shook my head. 'Guessed what?'

Cecilie took a deep breath, lifted her shoulders, then dropped them again. 'Your father and I, we ... we were *more* than just good friends,' she said, with a sob. Then she gave me a piercing look.

And that was when I understood the tears. The sobbing. The questions Mari had asked my brother, about blood types. I finally understood why Mari and I couldn't be together. It was because we had the same father.

74

While he was driving towards Akershus University Hospital, Yngve asked Therese to re-examine their timeline thoroughly and repeat it to him. She started with Jimmy Tollefsen's car accident, then continued with Even and Mari's relationship ten years later. Mari then broke up with Even, just as Frode and Cecilie Lindgren's marriage was falling apart. The murders on the night of the school show premiere took place next, and then Børre Halvorsen was killed. After that she went through all the people they'd interviewed, most importantly the ones closest to Mari Lindgren, discussing all the possible motives anyone could have for being the murderer.

'We just can't find any motive that sticks,' she said.

Yngve glanced over at her. She was pale again. She leaned forwards slightly, touching her belly.

'Are you OK?' Yngve asked.

'Not really,' she said. 'I puked like crazy this morning.'

'Want me to take you home?'

'Now?' she asked. 'We're halfway to the hospital. I'll be fine. I may ask you to pull over in a little bit, though.' She feigned a puking motion with her mouth.

'Just say the word,' Yngve said.

They drove on for a few miles. Neither of them spoke, both deep in thought.

'Wait a minute,' Yngve said, more to himself than to Therese.

'What is it?' she asked.

'Just hang on for a second.'

He thought of Tic-Tac's door again.

'What?' Therese was getting impatient.

Yngve grabbed his mobile phone and dialled a number.

'Who are you calling?' Therese asked.

'Knut,' Yngve said.

The taxi driver answered quickly. 'I just have a few more questions for you,' Yngve said. 'When you left the school that night, it must have been somewhere between ten fifty and eleven, correct?'

'Yes, I assume that's—'

'Did you see any cars parked outside the entrance at the back of the school at that time?'

Knut appeared to be thinking. 'Yes,' he said tentatively. 'I think I did. Yes,' he confirmed, more sure of himself. 'Yes I did.'

'Was it more than one car?'

There was a moment's pause. Yngve could feel Therese's eyes upon him.

'There was just one,' Knut said. 'Right outside.'

'On the janitor's parking spot?'

'Yes. I don't think there's room for more than one car there. Why – is it important?'

Yngve looked at Therese for a second. 'It might be. Did you see whose car it was?

'I did,' Knut said, another hint of pride in his voice. 'I'm good with cars. And this car is kind of special, too, so it was easy.'

'OK,' Yngve said impatiently. 'So whose was it?'

75

Mari was my half-sister.

Cecilie had got pregnant by my dad while she was married to another man and he was married to another woman. Her best friend.

I couldn't believe it. I really couldn't.

Especially after what Mum had told me about Julia, Ole Hoff's wife. Man, my Dad had really been a player.

'I wasn't even sure of it myself,' Cecilie sniffed. 'But Mari had just studied blood types at school, and she realised that *her* blood group couldn't have come from me and my husband's. It's easy enough to find out, and I'm not sure, really, why I didn't...' She stopped herself, needing a few more moments before she could continue. 'Mari had been working on that article she was going to write – the one about you and your father. She'd talked to a number of people, who no doubt said good things about him. He was so well liked, your father. She asked me about him, too. But then she ... dug a bit deeper. I told her that he was a good friend of mine. A good colleague.' She looked away. 'I don't know if it was the way I said it or if she could see the truth on my face. I've never been a good liar. And I guess deep down I always knew that Jimmy was Mari's biological father. Which is why it was so difficult for me when ... Mari and you got together. I couldn't really deny her the right to be with you, could I? That, surely, would have raised some questions that would have been hard for me to answer. Anyway.' She shook her head. 'Somehow she'd found out what kind of blood type Jimmy had. She was cross-questioning me about it when Frode came in the room. He'd heard the questions, too, and ... I ... well, I was basically cornered by the two of them. So ... I decided I'd better tell them the truth.'

My phone vibrated – a text – but I didn't want to check who it was from. Cecilie was too distraught. I took a breath, then went over and put my arms around her. We stood like that for a while, then she pulled herself free and said sorry for being so emotional.

'I understand completely,' I said with a low voice. 'Don't apologise.'

It was easy now to understand why Mari had been avoiding me. How could she explain this to me? And where would it lead? What would I have done with that information? How would Mum...?

I thought about how my mother hated gossip, the way a story like this would be the talk of the town for months on end. Not only would the truth destroy her. So would the chatter.

I couldn't digest the fact that Mari was my half-sister. The things I had felt for her. The things we'd done...

'I guess I should go on home,' I said after a while. I had barely touched my coffee. Cecilie nodded and followed me to the front door.

'You were right,' she said. 'It *was* good to talk to you about this. I think I needed to. And deep down I know you couldn't have hurt Mari, Even. I know that you love ... that you liked her.'

I tried to smile.

'How *is* your mother?' Cecilie asked.

I took a deep breath and wondered what I should say. 'Not so good,' I said. 'My brother's a little out of sorts these days, too, so ... we're struggling a bit – all of us, to be honest. But ... we'll get there eventually. One day at a time.' I looked at her. 'And don't worry,' I said. 'I'm not going to tell her what you just told me.'

Cecilie gave me a thankful smile. We hugged again.

As we embraced, I wondered what the next few days and months would be like for her. If anything, or anyone, could help her fill the void somehow, if she would be able to get back on her feet again, to get back to teaching. If there would ever come a time when she could burst out laughing at something without feeling guilty. I somehow doubted it.

⌐

The text I'd got was from Ole Hoff. I opened it before getting on my bike. It said:

Call me. Important.

I rang him back, but the call went straight to voicemail. I sent him a text too, telling him that I could speak now, if it was urgent. Maybe he'd discovered something, I thought. Ole was a good journalist. He knew a lot of people in this town.

As I cycled towards the centre of Fredheim, I once more tried to fit the pieces of the puzzle together. I couldn't see how Mum could have had anything to do with the murders. If she had found out about Cecilie and Jimmy, it would have had an enormous impact on her. She would have fallen apart completely. She would have cried and cried and made life a living hell for everyone. But she wouldn't have held it against Mari. Not to the point where she killed her. And if *she* didn't have a real motive to kill Mari, then I guess neither did Knut.

The tone in Ole's text got me worried, though. So I cycled to his office in the centre of Fredheim, to see if he was there. I put my head through the door, and one of the women sitting closest to the entrance, told me he was out.

'Do you know where he is?' I asked.

'I only know that he was going to Solstad earlier today. I don't know if he's still there now.'

'Solstad,' I muttered and thought about my brother. Our old neighbourhood. 'Did he say about what?'

'No, sorry,' the woman said.

'OK. Thanks.'

I had just got back out onto the road again when my phone rang. I guessed it would be Ole calling me back, but it wasn't. It was Imo.

'Even,' he said. I could hear that his breathing was shallow. 'I need some help. Can you come over?'

Something was up. But maybe it was simply that he'd done his back in again or something.

'Yes, of course,' I said, with the tiniest hesitation. 'To your house? What's going on? Is something wrong?'

'I'll explain when you get here.'

76

'So what if Imo's car was still parked there?' Therese said. 'It doesn't have to mean anything. We know he stayed behind after the show.'

'Yes, but he also told me that he left school somewhere between ten-thirty and ten-forty, and that there were about fifteen to twenty people still left inside the school when he did. According to Knut, there was practically no one there when he went inside to look for Mari, and that was closer to eleven. We now know that Imo's car was still there. Which means that *he* was still there.'

'Fuck.'

'He could have got the time wrong, of course,' Yngve continued. 'But we can, for sure, place him at the school quite close to eleven.'

'Unless he went home some other way that night.'

'Why lie to me about that, then?' Yngve said. 'I don't think he did. He told me he drove home all by himself. He was tired. It had been hectic the week before the opening night. Lots of rehearsals, blah-blah.'

Therese seemed to be thinking.

'We haven't got a single witness account of the person leaving the school via the roof,' Yngve continued eagerly. 'Tic-Tac's parking space is a short stone's throw away from the fire ladder. Imo could have made it to his car from there without being seen.'

'So there would be blood in his car, then?'

'For sure.'

'We need to check that.'

'He probably cleaned it as soon as he got home.'

'There might be some traces left.'

'Which is why we need to search it immediately. We need to get back to Fredheim, too. As soon as possible. Tobias can wait.'

Yngve found an exit from the road. 'Just think about it,' he went on. 'Imo's leather gloves, which *happened* to go missing on the night of the school show. He was quick to let us know, wasn't he? So we would rule him out. And when I woke Even on the night Børre Halvorsen had been killed, Imo was still up. He hadn't gone to sleep.'

'He was working, wasn't he?'

'That's what he said. And Even had passed out from drinking.'

'Doesn't Imo usually stay up all night working in his studio?' Therese argued. 'I think I read a piece about him in the *Fredheim Chronicle* a few months ago. "The Man and His Music" or whatever it was called.'

'I guess that's part of his routine, yes.'

'So he could, in theory, have been working.'

'He could, in theory, have killed Børre Halvorsen, too.' Yngve was clinging on to the steering wheel.

'But if he knew that the door on the first floor was open, why didn't he use it? Why go through the trouble of climbing onto the roof and all that? It's not an easy climb for anyone, especially in the rain.'

'He was being smart,' Yngve said. 'Tic-Tac was the only other person who knew about the door being open. By using it he would have pointed the finger at himself. And he would have had blood on him, too, after killing Johannes, so he probably would have had a hard time not smudging the door or the doorframe or whatever. Keep in mind how he left marks all over the place on the second floor. By going out over the roof he kept the suspicions away from himself.'

Therese winced a little, holding her belly. 'We still don't have a motive for any of this,' she said.

'I know,' Yngve said and floored the accelator. 'We'll get to that.'

77

It had begun to get dark by the time I got to Imo's house. The unsurfaced road leading to the farm and the house itself was surrounded by forest, which made it even darker. The noise of the traffic on the main road faded behind me.

Imo's Mercedes was parked outside the house, as usual, but there was another car there too. I was pretty sure it belonged to Ole. I was right: I looked through one of the windows and spotted an umbrella with the *Fredheim Chronicle* logo on it.

I leaned my bike against the house wall and asked myself why Ole couldn't have helped Imo with whatever task he needed me for. Or maybe he'd arrived after Imo called me.

The door was closed, and there was no light on in the kitchen. But it was on in the studio, and I heard music coming out from the open door. It was Imo playing the guitar. I could tell. I recognised the song, too. It was Johannes' solo – the song Imo had written for the school show. The show-stopper. I called my uncle's name.

'Come on in, champ,' he yelled back.

I stuck my head round the door. Imo was sitting in a leather chair. 'Come on in,' he repeated, as he continued to play. 'It's a great song, isn't it?'

'It is.'

Imo was singing the lyrics very quietly – almost to himself. 'I wrote it a long time ago,' he said. 'Before you were born, in fact.'

I was a little taken aback.

'Where's Ole?' I asked.

Imo didn't answer, he just closed his eyes, as though he was enjoying his own music. His fingers danced back and forth, up and down the strings.

'What do you need my help for?' I asked.

'Your mum's choir sang this back in the day.' Imo still had his eyes shut – as though he hadn't even heard my question.

I looked out of the window to see if there were any signs of Ole. 'Imo, where's—?'

'Shhh,' he interrupted. 'This is the best part.' Then he started on the chorus. His voice was a bit louder.

When the chorus was finished, he stopped and opened his eyes. 'Your mother had a great voice,' he said. 'I don't know if you remember. Don't think she's sung much in recent years.'

Imo looked at me. For a long time. He seemed ... tired. Sad, even. I had never seen my uncle like this before. It worried me.

'You know all this will be yours one day, right?' He threw his arms wide.

'Mine?' I asked. 'How do you mean?'

'The studio, the house, the farm. Your brother's not really the type to look after pigs. Or a house, for that matter. Who knows what will become of that kid.'

I didn't know what to say. It certainly wasn't like Imo to be talking like this. Was he dying or something?

He stood up and put down his guitar. 'I wrote that song for your mother,' he said. 'Not long before she met your dad.'

I stared at him. 'You wrote it for Mum?'

He nodded.

'But...' My thoughts went off in all kinds of directions. The lyrics of the song were bouncing back and forth in my head. Everyone had thought the song was a declaration of love for Fredheim.

Imo took a step closer. I thought of the talk we'd had a couple of days before, when I'd asked him if there had ever been a special someone in his life.

Of course there has.

So what happened?

Nothing. That was the problem. She didn't want me, so...

It was *Mum* who'd been Imo's great love. I couldn't believe it.

'She didn't want you after Dad died either?' I asked with a wobble in my voice. I couldn't breathe properly.

Imo didn't answer immediately. Then he shook his head.

'Did you ever tell her?'

'Oh yes,' he said. 'Several times. Maybe not straight to her face, but ... I'm sure she knew.'

I didn't know what to make of all this. It was too much in one day.

'Jimmy wasn't particularly nice to your mother, Even.'

'No, I know that now,' I said. 'I've...'

I stopped. Should I say it? I had to. It was killing me to keep this secret to myself.

'I've just discovered that Mari was my half-sister.'

Imo shot a look at me. He seemed to be thinking for a quick moment, then said: 'So you've found out, too.' Imo shook his head, before saying: 'Ole Hoff had as well. Well, he would have anyway. Sooner or later.'

For a minute there, I had completely forgotten about Ole. The fact that his car was outside, but Ole himself was nowhere to be seen, worried me.

'For over ten years,' Imo continued, 'your mother and Ole thought it was Julia, Ole's wife, who'd had an affair with Jimmy. She didn't. It was Cecilie.'

'But...?'

'It's silly, really,' Imo continued. 'I had decided to switch lead singer on one of the songs we were doing. "Pie Jesu" by Andrew Lloyd Webber. Ever heard it?'

'No.'

'Ah, Even,' Imo said. 'It's one of the most beautiful songs you'll ever hear. Makes me cry every single time.'

'Imo, what's this got to do with—?'

'Susanne found those sheets of music with Julia's name on them in the backseat of her car. They weren't hers, though – because I'd switched the roles around. Instead of printing a new set of notes for Cecilie, I just gave her Julia's. And that started ten years of agony and heartache.'

I didn't know what to say.

'So Ole didn't know about Cecilie?' I asked.

'No.'

'He didn't think to ask his wife about it?'

'He did,' Imo said. 'Today. They had lunch together or something. He finally manned up.'

'But why didn't he do it before? Like, ten years ago?'

'He was afraid to. He was scared of the truth. Besides, Jimmy died that day, so he thought all his problems were solved. Whoosh – like that. They could go on with their lives as if nothing had happened. He thought he'd let sleeping dogs lie, so to speak, so he just decided to forget about it.'

'Until he couldn't any longer.'

'Yes. What's happened this week has brought it all back, I guess. Running into your mother again like he did.'

I was still struggling to see where this conversation was going.

'So Julia hadn't cheated on him?'

'No.'

'Jesus.'

'Ole wanted to see if I knew about any of this, so he called me.'

'He called you from Solstad?'

Imo looked at me quizzically. I explained how I knew Ole had been there.

'I don't know where he called me from. It's not important. We talked for a while, then agreed to meet up here to have a coffee and a chat – face to face is always better with things like that.'

I was getting more and more confused.

'He got here before. I think that's why he decided to have a little snoop.'

'A snoop?'

'A little look around. And that's when he discovered *that*.'

Imo nodded towards one of the walls in his studio. And there, on the floor, was Johannes' microphone case.

78

'Imo,' I said. 'What the fuck?'

'Mari would never have managed to keep it a secret,' Imo said. 'The fact that you were half-siblings. And if your mum found out that Jimmy had another child, too, who'd been conceived when they were married ... I don't think she would have dealt with that especially well. It would have destroyed her.'

He sat down and shook his head. 'I couldn't let that happen. I couldn't let your mother go through that, on top of everything else she'd already had to deal with. And I certainly can't let that happen now, after Tobias...' He stopped himself again.

I closed my eyes.

No, I said to myself. No, no, no.

'I want you to know, Even, that I never wanted any of this to happen. I tried to convince Mari to let it all lie, but then she split up with you – obviously, because she discovered you both had the same father. But she knew you would never just accept it without a decent explanation, so...'

'So it's *my* fault, is that what you're saying?' I shouted. There were tears in my eyes.

'No, no,' he said quickly, hands raised apologetically in front of him. 'Not at all. You're not to blame for any of this. You just fell in love with the wrong girl – you can't decide things like that. It's like me – I wish I had fallen in love with someone other than your mother. But the heart does what the heart wants.'

I balled up my fists, and before I knew what I was doing, I'd punched him in the face.

Imo staggered backwards, straight into the mixing desk. Blood started to trickle from his nose, but he didn't make a sound, just held on to the desk and tried to steady himself.

'Come on,' he said, and wiped some blood off his face. 'Get it all out. You can punch me as much as you like. I know I deserve it.'

I was just about to let loose, when something pulled me back. The thought of Ole Hoff being here somewhere, that Imo had the microphone case and that he had called me because he needed help with ... something.

'Tell me what happened,' I said, my voice shaking. 'Tell me everything.'

Imo wiped the blood from the corners of his mouth then rubbed his fingers on his jacket. 'I'd taken all the equipment out to the car, and, as usual, none of the others had bothered to take one of the drum sets to the music room after the show, so I had to do that as well.' He rolled his eyes slightly. 'Mari was just getting ready to go when I came in. She'd finished her interview with Johannes.' He shook his head. 'We talked about the show for a minute. The song. She said she'd never heard anything so beautiful.' The memory brought a smile to his face. 'But you weren't the only one who wondered why she'd split up with you,' he continued. 'I wanted to know, too. So I asked her.'

He paused before continuing. 'To begin with, she didn't want to say anything. I said she couldn't hide from you forever. I asked if she wanted *me* to tell you anything – something that might help explain what had happened. And ... it was like she gave up then and there. Like she couldn't bear to keep it inside any longer. She sighed and seemed to ... implode. Then she sat down. I did, too.'

Imo started talking faster now. 'She told me what she'd discovered about Jimmy and her mum. That she'd found out she was your half-sister. The very thought of it made her sick, but she knew that she would never be able to keep the truth from you. It would come out somehow, she said, and she was tired of trying to hide, tired of keeping secrets. She had decided to tell you the next day.'

I looked down and knitted my fingers together.

'I told Mari that she couldn't do that. For Susanne's sake – but also for everyone else's. For her own parents' sake too. And that's when she told me that they already knew about it, that their marriage was probably over as a result. But even though they were unlikely to tell their neighbours and the rest of Fredheim, Mari wouldn't be able to keep the truth from you. Not in the long run. So ... I...' Imo paused for a long time. And it's as if the world paused with him.

'I had to stop her.'

Imo paused again. I don't know how long for.

'I never intended for it to happen, Even. I just grabbed her as she got up to leave. She started to struggle with me, and before I knew what I was doing, I had my hands around her neck.' He lowered his head. 'And then ... she just collapsed in my arms.'

He let out a heavy sigh. 'I tried to resuscitate her, but of course, I couldn't. And that's when Johannes appeared in the doorway.'

I swallowed again.

Imo took a deep breath. 'He'd left his phone behind. He looked at me, and he looked at Mari. And then he ran. I had to make sure that he couldn't tell anyone what he'd seen. What choice did I have?'

'So you beat him to death with his own microphone case.'

Imo didn't reply, but then again he didn't need to.

I shook my head. I wanted to punch him again.

Imo seemed to read my thoughts. 'Come on then,' he said. 'I want you to get all your anger out, because you're going to have to make a decision soon. A big, important decision.'

My fists were still clenched, and there was blood on the knuckles of my right hand. I didn't feel any pain, any sting. Just anger.

'What are you talking about?' I snarled.

Imo straightened up. 'You can go to the police, and you can tell them everything I've just told you. And then it's over. But before you do that, Even, I want you to think carefully about the consequences. Do you think your mother will be able to live with the fact that she's one of the reasons for all this? I've been trying to protect her. That's all I've done.'

Before I could answer, he continued: 'She would never cope, Even. She would drink herself to death, I'm sure of it. And how do you think your brother would react? He's just tried to commit suicide. Without your mother, without me ... are *you* going to look after him for the rest of your life?'

He looked at me. 'Your family will be destroyed, Even. And if you decide to go to the police, it's *you* who will have to live with that. Or ... you can consider the alternative.'

He waited a beat before continuing.

'Ole is the only one who's seen the microphone case. He hasn't had the time to go to the police yet, so apart from you, he's the only one who can give me away.'

I put my hands to my face. Now I knew what he needed my help for. Why he had wanted me to come. Why he had told me all this.

He wanted me to help him get rid of Ole Hoff.

He wanted me to be his partner in crime.

He pointed at the microphone case. Only now did I see that a pair of gloves were sitting on the floor next to it. Of course. He hadn't lost them after all.

I was struggling to understand how the person in front of me – a man who'd been like a father to me for all these days, my friend all this time, too – could suddenly be so cold and calculating. Where did this instinct for murder come from? How did he know how to get away with it? It all seemed so cool and professional. I couldn't speak or move.

'So it was you who killed Børre as well?' I said at last.

He didn't answer.

'Why did you do it?'

'We haven't got time for that now,' he said.

'Yes, we do.'

'No,' Imo said, emphatically. 'We don't. I've got a singing lesson here shortly, and you and I have to have everything done by then. And afterwards we'll have to act as normally as possible.' He stopped for breath. 'In other words, it's time for you to choose, Even. What happens next is entirely up to you. If you choose to help me, you also choose your mother, your brother, your family. Or you can throw it all away. You need to ask yourself something, Even: what is most important to you?'

He put his hands on my shoulders. I didn't have the energy to push him away, even though I wanted to.

'All this will go away, if you just help me with this last little thing.'

He waited until I met his eyes.

'Ole will not be the one to tell the police,' he said.

It was impossible to hold back my tears. I couldn't believe that Imo was forcing me to make such an impossible choice. To make this decision at all.

'All this will go away,' he said. 'And I know that you're strong enough to deal with it. You're strong enough to see the bigger picture. To know what we have to do.'

'So you ... think I should just keep my mouth shut about what you've done for the rest of my life?' My tears were streaming now.

'That's exactly what I think, yes.'

I shook my head. 'I can't. I won't be able to do that.'

Imo felt the bruise on his cheek, looked at his red finger, then his eyes pierced right through mine.

'How do you think everyone will react when they find out that Jimmy was Mari's dad?'

I shook my head – I didn't understand.

'What if someone out there starts to think that your dad's accident wasn't an accident at all?' Imo continued.' That it was your mother who lost it in the car that day? What if *that* rumour starts to spread?'

I looked at him with big eyes.

'Jimmy was fit as a flea – he'd never fainted in his life. Don't you think that one of the gossipmongers around here might think it was just something your mum told the police so that they wouldn't suspect her?' He paused briefly. 'Forget about evidence,' he continued. 'The real judgement lies with your neighbours, your local community. People will get ideas; they'll think it was your mother who killed him, and you know as well as I do that your mum won't be able to deal with that.'

I couldn't get a word out. It was all too much at once.

'I spoke to Susanne on the phone that day,' Imo carried on. 'Before the accident. She wanted me to pick Tobias up from nursery. She sounded like a madwoman, Even. It wouldn't be hard to get people to believe that she went for your father in the car that day; she'd found out he was being unfaithful and no doubt tried to knock the truth out of him while he was driving. Maybe that was why the car veered off the road, because she was shouting at him, distracting him. Maybe she was hitting him. Maybe it was her fault, Even. Maybe it *was* your mother who killed him.'

Imo gripped my shoulders again. 'That's what people are going to think. You know it's true.'

I felt like I was struggling to breathe. As if I was drowning.

I didn't want to believe what he was saying, but deep down I knew he was right.

'And one more thing,' he said. 'If I end up in jail, I'll never get out of there alive. You know that. Prisoners don't take kindly to someone who has killed children or teenagers.'

Another thing he wanted me to have on my conscience.

Yet another life.

My head ached.

'There's just one thing left,' Imo said. 'Just one more thing we have to do and then we can put this all behind us. And we'll never talk about it again.'

I couldn't stop weeping. No matter what I did, everything would turn to shit – with my mum, Imo, Tobias, me.

Could I carry on living after this?

Could I allow the murders of Mari and Johannes, Børre and Ole to remain one of those unsolved mysteries the newspapers would write about every now and then? Could anything ever be normal again?

I had to make a choice.

My family.

Or...

I thought long and hard before I dried my tears and looked at Imo. Then I nodded and said: 'So where is he?'

79
NOW

'So you decided to do what your uncle wanted you to?'

The prosecutor has come right up to the witness stand again. I look at Mum. I look at Cecilie, at Oskar and my friends who are sitting in the courtroom, closely paying attention to every word I say.

I clear my throat and say: 'Yes.'

80
THEN

If Imo hadn't gone first, I wouldn't have been able to move. I just followed his footsteps, one by one, as though on autopilot. I felt like I would throw up any second.

'Where is he?' I asked again.

'In here,' Imo said, and pointed to the pig shed.

I looked at it. 'Imo, what have you...?'

'Just think about it,' Imo said over his shoulder. 'If we bury him or drop him in a lake somewhere, there's always a risk that someone will find him or that some animal will dig him up. If we take him somewhere else, there's a chance that someone might see us. We can't take any risks at this stage. It's too dangerous.'

My stomach felt like it was doing somersaults. I couldn't feel the ground under my feet. I hoped that he would stop and come to his senses, that he would turn around and say, no, we're not going to do this after all – it was just a terrible, awful dream. But there was nothing to indicate that Imo would change his mind. He kept moving towards the pig shed, his face set hard, determined.

Fucking bastard, I thought. How could he do this to me? He'd said we would never talk about it, but how did he think we could live normally after this? Did he imagine that we'd just have a shot or two of tequila whenever things got too hard to handle?

No fucking way.

I wasn't going to have anything to do with him, ever again.

Inside the pig shed, Ole was lying on the floor, curled up. His eyes were open. He was blinking furiously, breathing in through his nose. His mouth was gagged and his hands were tied behind his back.

I sighed in relief. He wasn't dead.

At least not yet.

The pigs started to grunt as soon as they saw Imo. His appearance meant food.

Today, that food was Ole Hoff. My best friend's father.

I just stood there with my mouth open, trying to breathe. Ole was trying to say something, but the sounds coming out of his mouth were muffled.

'He texted me before,' I stammered. 'He called me, too. What if he's tried to contact someone else? What if he told someone he was coming here?'

'That's a risk we'll just have to take,' Imo said.

He started to walk towards the pen. I closed my eyes. And when I opened them again, Ole was looking at me. I could tell he was begging me not to go through with this.

The pigs were making a racket now. 'Can you get him up?' Imo yelled over the noise.

'Me?'

'I did my back in when I carried him in here,' he said. 'He'll struggle now that he's awake.'

I looked down at Ole again. 'We can't throw him in there alive!' I said. 'That's just ... sick.'

'Pigs aren't predators,' Imo shouted through the racket. 'We would have needed to starve them first, at least. No, we'll have to chop him up.'

Chop him up.

Jesus.

The biggest thing I'd ever killed was a wasp. And even that made me feel queasy.

Everyone can be a killer. That's what I had said to my mates. Now I had to become one myself.

And that's when I knew.

I was never going to do it.

I couldn't. I just couldn't.

Which is why I shook my head and said no. Imo turned and looked at me. 'What did you say?' The pigs were still grunting.

'I can't do this, Imo.'

He just stood there staring at me.

'I can't kill Ole. And I'm not going to chop him to pieces so the pigs can eat him. No fucking way.'

Imo said nothing to begin with, just stared at me. 'Even, we have no choice.'

'Yes, we do,' I said. 'This is wrong, and you know it. You're not crazy.'

'No, but can you tell me any other way out of this?'

I thought.

Hard.

And I couldn't.

'You have to help me,' Imo begged. I could see the plea in his eyes.

I wished there was something I could do to make this all go away. Tears welled up in my eyes again.

Imo walked quickly towards me. For a brief moment I was afraid that he was going to hit me or drag Ole into the pen himself. Instead he walked straight past me and out of the pig shed.

Where the hell was he going?

I stared at Ole, uncertain of what to do – scared of what might happen in the next few minutes if I didn't do *something*. I bent down and removed the gag from his mouth. Immediately he gasped for air.

'You have to call the police, Even,' he wheezed, 'Quickly, before he comes back.'

I needed a few seconds to pull myself together. I thought about what might happen today – or perhaps next month or next year – if we went ahead and got rid of Ole. How could Imo trust me to keep my mouth shut?

He couldn't. So maybe he'd kill me too. To remove any doubt. To protect him, to protect Mum, the love of his life.

I fumbled for my phone in my pocket. My hands were shaking violently as I tried to tap in the three numbers for the police. I could barely hold the phone.

Ole gasped, just as I noticed a movement in the doorway.

Imo was standing there, looking at us. He had a gun in his hand. And he was pointing it at me.

81

'Put it down, Even,' Imo said, nodding at the phone. His hand was trembling again. 'Right now.'

I looked at Ole. His eyes were shut tight. Sweat was forming along his hairline.

Imo came towards me, still holding the gun. I put the phone back in my pocket.

'So you were really going to turn me in?' Imo licked his lips and shook his head.

'Please,' I said, 'I'm sure we can find another way out of this.'

Imo came closer, his hand still shaking. Was he just nervous? I'd seen his hand tremble like this before, so maybe not.

'We can,' he said. 'We can call the police and I can tell them that it was *you* who asked me to kill Mari. That you were mad because she'd split up with you, and you were jealous of Johannes.'

I was dumbfounded.

'And you can deny it all you like, but it will be your word against mine.' Imo ran a hand over his sweating brow.

'You wouldn't do that to me,' I said. 'You wouldn't do that to Mum. Not if what you say is true – that you've done all this to protect her.'

He lowered the gun for a few moments, apparently thinking about what I'd just said. His hand was still shaking, as though the gun was too heavy to hold.

'Last chance, Even. Get him to his feet.'

I said no.

'Come on!' he said again. 'We don't have much time.'

I stood stock-still on the concrete floor and stared at him in silence.

'Fine,' he said with a sigh as he tucked the gun into the back of his trousers. 'I'll just do it by myself then.'

He grabbed Ole by the arms, but he tried to fight Imo's every move. My uncle was as strong as a bull, though. I had seen him toss pigs and fodder bags around as if they weighed nothing. No matter how hard Ole kicked or struggled, Imo kept a firm grip under his armpits and dragged him across the floor.

It was as if I was glued to the floor. Everything was happening so fast. As soon as Imo opened the pen gate, the pigs' grunting became deafening. It was then that I realised why Imo hadn't simply shot Ole already – there was no floor cover out here so it would be hard to wash the blood off the concrete. In the pen, the pigs scuffled about on hard, wrinkly plastic.

Imo suddenly jerked up straight and yelled out in pain. It must have been his back.

'Even, do something!' Ole shouted, then managed to twist himself free.

He started to crawl towards me, but Imo was over him in a shot. This time he hunkered down, then picked Ole up in a fireman's lift, screaming with the effort. But the seventy-something kilos he had over his shoulder wouldn't lie still. He staggered a bit, but he kept moving towards the pen, puffing and panting. He kicked the gate wide open with his foot. Then he threw Ole down on the floor.

Ole hit his head as he landed, but he didn't lose consciousness. Some of the pigs retreated to the back of the pen. Ole's eyes were full of tears.

Imo was holding a hand to his back.

Then he pulled out his gun.

This was it. He was going to shoot Oskar's dad. He was going to do it now. Then later he'd chop him up. He took a step towards Ole and lifted the gun. Again the pain in his lower back made him grimace. His knees seemed to give a bit.

In a split second, I knew what I had to do.

At the beginning of August, Imo had had surgery on his back. Every morning and evening for three weeks I had looked after the pigs for him.

Now, he leaned over in an effort to relieve the pain, and his open shirt revealed the five-centimetre scar at the bottom of his back. I grabbed a spade and went into the pen behind him. Raised it and aimed it at the point I knew would hurt the most.

And then I whacked him as hard as I could.

Imo screamed in pain and immediately fell to his knees. But he was still holding the gun. I tried to knock it out of his hands, but I missed and hit his wrist instead. That made him scream even more. And he let go of the weapon.

I stood over him, panting, ready to bring the spade down on him again, right in his face this time. I kicked the gun away from his reach. It disappeared in among the pigs.

Imo was lying on his side now, writhing with pain. He tried to push himself up with his good hand.

'What the hell are you doing?' he roared.

Keeping an eye on Imo, I went to help Ole up. He staggered to his feet, and I only just managed to keep him upright on the slippery, wet, filthy floor.

We lurched and slid towards the gate of the pen. I kept a grip of the spade, in case Imo came after us. As we struggled out of the pen, I looked around to see Imo still lying in the mud, his breathing laboured as he tried to get up onto all fours. Now he was feeling around for the gun, and when he couldn't find it, he began to crawl slowly towards the pigs. He would soon have his hand on the weapon.

'Your keys,' I said to Ole, as we hurried out of the pig shed. Ole stopped and held up his arms for me to search his pockets.

I found nothing.

'Imo must have taken them,' Ole said, frightened. I turned towards the pig shed, half expecting to see Imo's muddied face and shaking hand, the gun pointing at us.

Instead there was a bang.

From inside the pig shed.

The sound was so loud that I jumped, but it wasn't hard to guess what it was.

Ole and I looked at each other for a moment that seemed to last a lifetime.

It took forever for my mind to start working again. I just stood there, paralysed, staring straight ahead.

Imo.

My substitute father.

My friend.

I felt numb. I couldn't even cry.

Then I started to walk back towards the pig shed.

I heard Ole talking to me, but I didn't hear what he said – all I could think about was Imo and his pigs. They were probably not hungry enough yet, but if there was even the tiniest chance, I wanted to stop them before they got a chance to ... I didn't let myself imagine it.

Luckily it was so muddy around him that the blood and brains I knew must have been blown out of his head were not easily visible. I focused on his legs and used them to pull him behind me, out of the pen. Then I secured the gate.

I left him there and went back out to find Ole.

He had sat down on the wet grass, his back leaning against the car. He had a distant look on his face, like he was still in shock.

I think I was, too. I just couldn't believe what Imo had done – to Mari, Johannes and Børre, and what he wanted me to take part in. What I had prevented with maybe only a second or two to spare.

It took me a while to call the police. When I did, Yngve Mork told me they were already on their way. I didn't understand how, but it wasn't important. All I knew was that it was over.

Ole and I just sat there, listening to the sounds of the forest. The birds, the trees, the branches moving in the wind. Cones falling to the ground. Aeroplanes circling the skies above us, waiting to land at Oslo Gardermoen Airport.

Before there had been a storm inside me.

Now everything was quiet.

82
NOW

'Would you like to take a break?'

Ms Håkonsen's hand is on the box in front of me. It feels like my shirt is stuck to my body. My tie is too tight. I think about loosening it a little.

'No ... I don't think so.'

I just want it to be over. I can tell that this is getting to my mother as well. Her eyes are glazed, and she's staring straight ahead. My brother is not doing so well either. His eyes look vacant, as they have done throughout my testimony.

We haven't talked about Imo in our house since he killed himself. Not a single time – not on that terrible day, or on any of the days after. Mum started to cry when she heard, but then she controlled herself – it was like she'd flicked a switch. After that it was all about taking care of Tobias, doing everything so that he wouldn't get upset. The path of least resistance.

I, on the other hand, thought a lot about my uncle in the days that followed his death. Bang, and it was over. Bang, and he was gone. He didn't have to go to prison. He didn't have to look my mother or anyone else in the eye. Didn't have to live with what he'd done and what he'd tried to get me to do.

Ms Håkonsen waits until I turn my head towards her before asking her next question.

'Understandably, the police weren't able to get a confession directly from your uncle, but they had the microphone case and they had your uncle's leather gloves, which matched the piece they'd found under Fredheim Bridge after Børre Halvorsen's murder. And they had witness statements from both yourself and from Ole Hoff. So it was then possible for the inhabitants of Fredheim, and the people in the rest of Norway, to draw a line and put the murders behind them.'

She takes a small pause in the build up to her question. 'At what point did you realise something wasn't right?'

I seek out Ole Hoff in the audience. I spot him two rows behind Yngve Mork. I hunch my shoulders then let them drop again.

Then I say: 'It was after the funeral.'

83
THEN

Mari was buried on a Thursday.

It was a cold, damp day. Light snow had fallen over night. It looked like someone had sprinkled the dark hole in the ground and the fresh sand beside it with icing sugar.

By the time we had got to her funeral, both Børre and Johannes had already been laid to rest. I was glad, because the services for them had numbed me a little. I had heard the sad songs. I had listened to the priest's voice and what he'd had to say about God and worship and what we needed to do in times of despair. So as we all stood there grieving for my ex-girlfriend, my half-sister, I tuned out a little bit. Maybe it was a way for me to deal with the finality of her death and everything that had happened since.

Frode, Mari's father, sat next to his wife throughout the funeral. I noticed how they looked at each other from time to time, how she leaned her head against his shoulder. In the graveyard he pulled her closer, too. When Mari was finally lowered into the ground, and we all gathered around the family to pay our respects, he gave me a hug and squeezed me tightly. He didn't say anything, but I could see all I needed to in his eyes. He was sorry. For a lot of things.

Afterwards Cecilie asked if I wanted to join the wake at their home, but I respectfully refused. I didn't want to talk to anyone, especially people I didn't know who were only going to ask me questions about Imo or what actually happened in the pig shed that day. I was done with all that. At least, that's what I thought.

As I walked away from the graveyard, Ole Hoff came over to me.

'Even,' he said. 'Can I talk to you for a minute?'

'Yes, of course.'

He took me a few steps away from the rest of the mourners. We stopped by his car.

'What is it?' I asked – I could see that something was bothering him.

'It...' He waved to a man in a suit. I didn't recognise him at first, then I realised it was Tic-Tac. I'd never seen him in a suit before.

Ole turned back to me and said: 'Something's not right here.'

I looked at him and said, with a slight tremor in my voice, 'What do you mean?'

'How much do you really know about what actually happened that night?'

'Which night?'

'The night Mari was killed.'

I thought about it for a second. 'I only know what Imo told me. That he put his hands around Mari's throat, and before he knew it, he'd strangled her.'

'He didn't say that he'd hit her first?'

'Hit her? No,' I said, getting anxious. 'He didn't say anything about that.'

He nodded. 'Apparently Mari was hit before she was strangled. Before someone tried to resuscitate her. I read the autopsy report.'

I tried to think.

'You knew your uncle best,' he said. 'Is he the sort of man who would punch a girl that young in the face?'

I thought about my encounter with Ida Hammer that night in her bathroom. What Imo told me afterwards about how a real man should treat women.

There are three things you must never do to a girl, Even. One, you don't spread false rumours about her. That's mean. Two, you stick to one girl at a time. And three... you don't hit them. Not under any circumstance. A guy picks a fight with you, sure, you stand your ground. Not with a girl. Not ever.

Ole looked at me. 'So, what are you saying?' I asked, my voice shaking.

'What I'm saying,' Ole said, 'is that I don't think your uncle killed her.'

84

There are things in life that suddenly turn everything upside down. A comma in the wrong place, a plus or a minus that changes the whole equation.

A lot of the evidence pointed to Imo being the killer. The fact that he had confessed was one piece. The fact that Johannes' microphone case was found in his home was another. The story he'd told me about sitting down with Mari and talking about my dad and her own mother – he knew all the details.

So what was it that didn't fit?

I could tell that Ole had discovered something, that he was struggling with how to present it to me. 'Did you know that Imo was ill?' he asked.

I cocked my head. 'Ill? What do you mean?'

'He had Parkinson's,' Ole said. 'Still early-stage though. You know what Parkinson's is, don't you?'

I knew that it was a disease that made it difficult to control your limbs. Which explained Imo's shaking hands and all the medicine in his bathroom cabinet. I had just assumed they were pills he needed for his back problems.

'Parkinson's is a terrible disease to live with,' Ole said. 'Basically, it's just a very slow death.'

'So you think ... that he ... that Imo took the blame for what happened, because he wasn't going to live for a long time anyway?'

I was cold after standing in the churchyard, but that was not why I was now shaking.

'It's a possibility, yes,' Ole said. 'And while I don't think your uncle killed Mari, I am pretty sure he killed Johannes Eklund and Børre Halvorsen.'

I felt my eyes growing wider and wider. I had no idea what he was talking about, and he didn't explain, either.

But then the penny dropped and I found the mistake in my own equation – the plus that should have been a minus.

I understood what Ole meant.

I buried my face in my hands. 'Oh no,' I said. 'God no.'

85
NOW

'What did you do then?'

'First I had to pull myself together a bit – I was in shock. Then I called Victor Ramsfjell. Børre Halvorsen's best friend.'

'Why did you do that?'

'I ... needed to ask him about something. A detail that would confirm Ole's suspicions.'

'And which detail was that?'

I take another look at my Mum. She is crying. Uncontrollably.

86
THEN

After he buried Åse, Yngve had wondered what it would be like to set his foot inside a church again. He wondered how he would respond to seeing other people grieving for their lost ones, how he'd react to the sombre mood that always seemed to reside inside God's house. The hushed conversations. The slow, melancholic music. People wearing dark clothes. Men and women taking careful steps between tombstones afterwards, as though afraid of disturbing the dead.

It wasn't as bad as he'd thought it would be – not even at the first funeral. Yes, she'd been on his mind the whole time. He'd even seen her, right next to the altar, paying her respects to Johannes Eklund's family, but he hadn't spoken to her. Not even when he stopped by her grave after the ceremony. He didn't need to. Didn't need her to say anything, either. He was fine.

After Mari Lindgren had been put to rest, Yngve was sitting in his office, looking through some interview records, when the receptionist notified him that Ole Hoff and Even Tollefsen needed to see him.

'Send them in,' Yngve said and put the paperwork away inside a manilla folder. He met them at the front door to the main office. Yngve could see that something had happened.

'What is it?' he asked.

Ole looked around to see if anyone was listening. Therese Kyrkjebø was sitting at her workstation, looking up, her face slightly ashen, but clearly intrigued by their sudden presence. Yngve also caught Vibeke Hanstveit's inquisitive eyes looking out from behind the glass wall of her office.

Soon all five of them were standing inside her office. Even and Ole presented their story, what they had discovered. And Yngve had to admit, what they said did sound plausible, however shocking it was. The question was, how were they going to prove it?

'I think I know how to get a confession,' Even said.

'Really?' Hanstveit was sceptical.

'Yes, really.'

Yngve looked at the boy's clenched fists. The muscles in his chin, tight as a knot.

'We need an admissible one,' Hanstveit protested.

'I'm sure you can get that afterwards,' Even said. 'When you know.'

Then he explained his plan.

Yngve had to admit it was a good one. And Even seemed to be full of courage and determination – desperation maybe. There was also a generous helping of anger in there too. It was like he needed to do this, for his own sake. His father had been dead for ten years. Imo was gone now as well, having shocked the whole of Norway. Mari, Even's ex-girlfriend and half-sister, had also been murdered. And less than a week ago, Tobias, Even's brother, had tried to commit suicide.

'I'm not very comfortable about sending you in there like this,' Yngve said, before looking at Even. 'It might be dangerous.'

'I can handle it.'

Yngve could tell that Hanstveit didn't like this either, but she didn't voice any further concerns.

'Alright, then,' Yngve concluded. 'Let's do it.'

'One thing,' Even said.
'What is it?'
'Can I have dinner with them first?'

87

The dinner in our house that day consisted of Swedish meatballs, pasta and a tomato sauce with a heavy taste of basil. Knut was there, too. As usual he didn't say much.

Afterwards I asked Tobias if he wanted to play Call of Duty with me. It was ages since we'd done anything like that together. The psychiatrist at the hospital had concluded that my brother no longer was suicidal, but that he needed steady routines – no sudden surprises, no upset, only harmony. He'd seemed a lot happier the last few days. Lighter somehow, as though he'd managed to put the past behind him.

'I spoke to Victor Ramsfjell a little while ago,' I said somewhere in the middle of the first game.

'Hm?' My brother's hands didn't stop moving. He seemed to be focusing on what he was doing.

'Victor,' I said. 'Børre Halvorsen's mate. The one with the red hair, you know? He's the same age as you.'

Tobias didn't say anything at first. Then: 'Why did you talk to *him*?'
'I wanted to check something.'

Tobias carried on playing, but I could tell that he'd lost a bit of concentration.

'Victor wasn't at the school the night Mari and Johannes were killed. But Børre was his best friend, and they talked all the time. One of the things they talked about was when Børre saw you in the window of the school newspaper room that night.'

Tobias's hands slowed down.

'You told me you waited for Mari *outside* the school, Tobias, but that's not true. Børre saw you in that window *after* the show was over. A good while after it was over, too.'

Tobias stopped playing, but he didn't look at me.

I thought about my brother's suicide attempt. At first I had believed he was tired of his life somehow, which may have played a part in it, but mostly, I think he was just afraid of getting caught. That when Yngve Mork got him into an interrogation room, he would break down.

'Was that why Børre had to die?' I asked him. 'So he wouldn't tell the police *when* he'd seen you?'

My brother didn't answer.

'That would have branded you a liar,' I continued. 'Børre could have got you arrested. And then *you* might tell on Imo. And Imo couldn't take that risk.'

I thought about Ole Hoff and what Imo had tried to make me do. If we had gone through with it – if we'd killed Ole – Imo had said we would never talk about it again. Neither of us would have wanted to. We would have been intent on forgetting. If any alarm bells had rung in my head, I would have ignored them – as it would only have caused me problems. And with everything pointing in Imo's direction, there was no reason to doubt his confession or any of the evidence that seemed to support it. So there was no reason to ask Tobias any more questions.

But I had never understood why Børre had to die in the first place. He knew nothing about Dad and Cecilie and the fact that Mari was their child.

My brother's avatar died on the screen in front of us. He blinked. It looked like his eyelids were moving in slow motion. He inhaled deeply and looked at the ceiling for a few seconds. Leaned back in his chair.

'I just wanted to talk to her,' he said with a quiet voice. 'After Imo had. I wanted to talk to her, because … I didn't understand … she contacted me first, and she was all nice and friendly on the phone. Grateful when I gave her the stupid pictures of you and Dad and told her what stupid blood type he had.' Tobias picked at a loose thread in his jeans. 'And then she split up with *you,* and I thought … I thought that maybe … maybe…'

He ground to a halt for a moment.

'I didn't think she'd be like the other girls,' he finally said. 'I didn't think she'd be like that Amalie bitch in Solstad.'

After the funeral, Ole had told me that, before Imo attacked him, he'd driven to Solstad. He'd spoken to Ruben's father – the idiot who'd come to Fredheim to get Tobias in the middle of the night. I wasn't aware of just how serious the incident with Amalie, the girl who was in love with me, had been, but according to Ruben's father, Tobias had flown into a rage that day and put his hands around her neck. Thankfully someone had managed to stop him before it was too late. Amalie had been petrified.

Ole had tried to call me from Solstad. He had wanted to know what I knew about the incident. When I didn't answer, he turned to Imo. Ole went to his house, because he wanted to ask Imo some questions about Jimmy and Cecilie as well, having discovered the truth about his wife earlier in the day. And that's when he discovered Johannes' microphone case. Imo realised that Ole could put both Tobias and him in a lot of trouble, so he decided to put Oskar's father completely out of the equation. And by bringing *me* into the frame as well, he thought he'd covered all his bases. That it would all go away.

'I thought she liked me,' Tobias said with a soft sob. 'For real. But she didn't answer my texts and she didn't want to talk to me after the show, either, when I went to see her in that room. She was like a wall. Didn't even want to look me in the eye. That's when I realised she'd only been *acting* nice to get what she wanted. She was just like all the others.'

Tobias turned towards me with an angry, sad look on his face. I wondered if I should tell him about Mari's phone, that she hadn't answered his texts because it was broken, not necessarily because she didn't want to.

'And then I got so angry that I...'

'...hit her.' I finished the sentence for him. 'You hit her first, and then you strangled her.'

Tobias looked away. Then he nodded and took a sharp breath. 'It all happened so fast I ... didn't realise that...' His head sank down. 'I didn't mean to,' he said. 'It was just something that happened.'

I couldn't move. Not a single muscle.

'Then Imo came back in and saw what had happened.' Tobias took another jagged breath. 'At first he was...' Tobias shook his head. 'He tried to bring her back. Did everything he could. He pumped and pumped at her heart and blew into her mouth like a madman. And then Johannes came and...' Tobias stopped.

For a while I'd thought that Mari had been murdered because she'd discovered something about Dad's accident, proof that Mum's version wasn't true. Perhaps it wasn't. I still needed to question my Mum about that. But I had realised that what Mari really wanted was to find out as much as possible about her biological father. She may have just wanted to know how he'd died.

'So what happened after that? After you had both become killers.'

'Imo ... he paced around for a while, thinking. We had to get out of there, but we couldn't leave through the doors on the first floor. I told him about the newspaper room being open. We went in there and ... climbed up onto the roof through the window.'

'You both did?'

'Yes. We had no other choice. Imo had his car on the other side. He dropped me off not far from our house and told me to go home. Lay low. Go to school the next day and act as if nothing had happened. Wait for instructions.'

I thought about Børre's Facebook post that day, the one about me lying. That he'd seen me. I had shown it to Imo before we went to his house to eat and drink. If I hadn't done that, then maybe Børre would still have been alive.

'So what happened on the way back to Fredheim,' I asked. 'When Imo came to get you from Solstad?'

'He told me what I had to say to the police,' Tobias said. 'In order to save us both. Told me to tell them that I just wanted to get the pictures back so Mum wouldn't go all crazy on us. It was the only thing he could think of that would make any sense.'

I had been surprised that Tobias cared enough about Mum's feelings that he had sought Mari out on opening night to get the pictures back.

It just hadn't seemed like something he would do. It was easy, though, to imagine the journey back from Solstad to Fredheim. Imo going over the details with my brother, how they should proceed in order not to get caught. I could understand why Tobias had finally snapped and tried to end his own life. To put himself out of his misery.

I thought about my tequila evening with Imo. My uncle had been texting Tobias. *Just checking that everything is alright.* In other words: checking that Tobias was sticking to their plan and that he hadn't said anything about what they'd done. Perhaps that had been Imo's plan all along – to make sure that Tobias was alone and that I was so drunk that I passed out. So he could go out and kill Børre.

'How well did you know Børre?' I asked Tobias.

'Not very well, but I knew he used to hang out under the bridge from time to time.'

'And you told Imo?'

Tobias nodded.

And Imo had acted on my brother's information. He had found Børre and ended his life against the bridge wall that night.

'The other day, you told me that Knut went into the school that night. Why did you do that? You knew he hadn't done anything.'

Tobias paused for a moment, then said: 'You were on to me. You'd told Imo about your suspicions, about our fight. I was scared you might say something to the cops as well, so they would put even more pressure on me. I wanted you to focus on someone else.'

'So I wouldn't suspect *you*?'

My brother nodded.

'*You* thought of that? Not Imo?'

'It was my idea, yes.'

And it worked. For a while, at least.

I had thought I would be angrier with Tobias, but a small part of me actually felt sorry for him. He'd always had a difficult relationship with girls, and he'd struggled to find his place both in Solstad and in Fredheim. And he'd never had a lot of friends. Certainly not good ones. He didn't have football, like I did.

Maybe our mother's years of neglect and blatant drinking had had more of an impact on him than on me. He was, after all, two years younger. And maybe, just maybe, the apple indeed doesn't fall too far from the tree. Maybe he became a murderer because my mother was one. And maybe his rages, like our mother's, were impossible to control because they were just a part of who he was.

I would never be able to forgive him, though. And I wouldn't want to have anything to do with him ever again. He'd killed Mari. Our half-sister. If he hadn't done that, Imo wouldn't have killed Johannes. And Børre. Imo himself would not have been dead right now.

Before I gave the signal to Mork, who'd been listening to everything Tobias and I had said via a microphone that was taped to my chest, I wanted to give my brother a few more minutes of normality, a moment or two of youth before his life would change forever.

I picked up my controller. With a nod to the screen I asked him if we should play another game. He looked at me for a long time. As his eyes started to flood with tears, he nodded.

88
NOW

Tobias stares at the surface of the table in front of him. He seems far too small for his suit. He has lost a lot of weight since Yngve Mork arrested him last autumn. He hasn't bothered to shave his stubble. Even in a suit he manages to look unkempt.

Tobias never said he was sorry. Not to me, or anyone else. He never tried to express remorse to Mari's parents, either, and he's made no effort to catch my eye when the judge excused me and told me I could leave the courtroom. My brother has never even confessed formally, which was why all of us were called as witnesses.

But I am done with him now. I am done with the case.

I am ready to move on, although I'm sure the events in Fredheim last October will stay with me till the day I die. Everybody knows who I am now. Whenever people hear my name, whenever the people of Fredheim see me, they think of the crazy members of my family and what happened in our small community during the course of a few wet and cold autumn days.

I wonder if Mum, too, will become a pariah after all this. I've told all of Norway how she slapped me, how I'd suspected her of killing my father. Maybe she will hate me for the rest of her life, disown me and drink herself to death, like Imo suggested she would. Or maybe she will want us to move again, perhaps to a bigger city where it's easier to disappear and forget. I don't know. I don't even want to think about that right now.

Maybe the good people of Norway will think that I have it in me, too – the ability and the natural instinct to kill someone if my buttons are pushed hard enough. That it somehow runs in the family, and that you really can't escape it, no matter how hard you try. I don't know about that either. Right now I don't even care. I just want to leave the courtroom and go home.

EPILOGUE

A few weeks after the trial was over, Yngve had another talk with God. It was during one of the many nights when sleep was hard to find.

He didn't ask Him if Åse was fine now, because he knew she was at peace, that she wasn't angry with him anymore for not assisting her when she had desperately wanted it all to end. He didn't have to ask if he could see her again, either, because he still did, on and off, at random hours and in random places.

Instead Yngve asked whether God put any stock in Manchester United's new manager. If He couldn't provide them all with a mild winter for a change. He wanted the Big Man to keep a watchful eye over Fredheim the next few years, too, so Yngve could retire and not be alerted too often by the sound of sirens, the sound of misery and heartache.

He hadn't got any answers this time around, either.

It was Sunday, and he was enjoying his newspaper. He was having a cup of coffee as well, his third one of the day. The radio was on. He was listening to a geography quiz, 'Around the World in Eighty Seconds', and he rejoiced whenever he managed to answer before the contestants.

He took another sip and turned the page.

Could you put the kettle on, please, Yngve?

He got up and went to the cupboard above the stove. He opened it and stopped. Looked at the yellow package, still in its plastic wrapping.

He took it out and gave it a gentle squeeze, lifted it to his nose, astonished that he could still smell the tea through the plastic.

The phone rang.

It was Therese Kyrkjebø.

Yngve put the tea down. He was on call again, and he always feared the worst when one of his co-workers rang. He answered and heard a quiet sob at the other end. For a brief moment he was afraid that something terrible had struck the lovely town of Fredheim once again.

'He's here,' Therese said with a sniff. 'He came last night. It's a boy!'

Yngve exhaled with a smile. At first he couldn't get a word out, because he was thinking about God again.

'How wonderful,' Yngve said as the tears emerged from his eyes. 'I'm so happy for you, Therese. My warmest congratulations.'

ACKNOWLEDGMENTS

God, I don't even know where to begin.

But I guess Even Tollefsen's story, for me, began back in 2015 when lightning struck me – in the form of my wife. Yes, she can do that from time to time, and no, it's not a euphemism. We were in the kitchen, preparing dinner for the pack of wolves in the house, when I decided to run an idea by her. I probably had a glass of wine in my hand when I said, 'So basically I have a story in mind about a teenage boy whose girlfriend is found dead inside his school early one morning. She broke up with him two days before, and she's been murdered before he's had a chance to ask her why. Everyone in the small town thinks he did it, because he was angry and potentially jealous. I don't know yet if this is a young-adult book, where we just follow the main character's trials and tribulations, or if it's a normal crime novel for a normal crime-fiction reading audience, where you focus on the investigative part and hunt down the killer.'

My wife thought about this for about four and a half seconds, then looked at me with a slight shrug and said: 'Why can't you do both?'

First, I didn't know what to say. Write two novels about the same story? Who the hell does that? The quick answer was, no one. No one had published two novels at the same time, one for the YA audience and one for adults. And thus my mind started to contemplate and process the idea of doing exactly that. And the more I thought about it, the more I liked the idea of writing two books that ended the same way, but where the roads travelled would differ considerably. Uncharted territory, right? I was picturing Oprah Winfrey's book club going crazy about giving one book to the parents and the other to the kids in the household, and then they could all talk about it afterwards.

I wrote the YA novel first. Had a lot of fun with it, too. But for some reason, I just couldn't find the perfect way to do the adult one. I got pretty close, but my Norwegian publisher thought I should move on and write something else. Which I did. You listen to your publisher, right? I had spent two years on the project, the dots and commas and endless rewrites making my hair evermore grey. In the meantime, the YA book, in Norwegian called *Killer Instinct*, had already been published.

Almost a year and a half later, my brilliant English publisher, Karen Sullivan, read Kari Dickson's translation of *Killer Instinct* and said, 'There is some untapped potential here. This story could really work as an adult/YA crossover. Would you mind adding some elements to this story, Thomas?'

My initial thought was: God, no. No way. I can't do that. Really, I can't. I was finished with that story. I had moved on. But Karen, being Karen, managed to persuade me. Whoever said that 'writing is rewriting' was one hundred percent right. So, I rolled up my sleeves and got cracking at it once again. A lot of the work had already been done, so it was just a matter of constructing the story slightly differently and basically rewriting the whole bloody thing. And because we were up against it timewise, I had to do it all in English as well. But hey, you listen to your publisher, right?

I guess sometimes things just happen for a reason. In this case, I think the story just wasn't supposed to be told to a wider audience until Karen got her hands on it. So thank you, Karen, for being so wonderfully brilliant in so many ways. You truly are an amazing woman, editor, publisher and friend.

A huge thank-you also to West Camel, who gave me invaluable advice and the thumbs-ups as I went ahead with the rewrite. You also took a great deal of care over the edited version and made my English sound a lot better than it normally does. I could not have done this without you.

And of course, the Team. With a capital T. Team Orenda. You know who you are. I love all of you. Even you, Antti.

The biggest thank-you, as always, goes to my wonderful family, who continue to support and to baffle me in all kinds of ways. To my wife: Thank you for the lightning strikes. (You listen to your wife, right?) You're brilliant.

—Thomas Enger, *Oslo, 8th January 2019*